Bayou Born

by

Linda Joyce

Fleur de Lis Series, Book One

This is a work of fiction. Names, characters, places, and incidents are either the product of the author's imagination or are used fictitiously, and any resemblance to actual persons living or dead, business establishments, events, or locales, is entirely coincidental.

Bayou Born

COPYRIGHT © 2013 by Linda Joyce Clements

Cover Art by *Kim Mendoza*

The Wild Rose Press, Inc.
PO Box 708
Adams Basin, NY 14410-0708
Visit us at www.thewildrosepress.com

Publishing History
First Champagne Rose Edition, 2013
Print ISBN 978-1-61217-820-2
Digital ISBN 978-1-61217-821-9

Fleur de Lis, Book One
Published in the United States of America

Branna closed her phone and turned to James. "I'm grateful for the help. You've got stuff to do, so please don't feel obligated to stay." In truth, she hated to see him leave. Being close to him, despite her injuries, made her pulse beat stronger. Faster. Harder. She could finally admit to herself, there was only one reason for that, even if she wasn't ready to speak the words aloud.

"I'll have some food delivered for you. I've a class this afternoon. I'll call you later this evening."

He surprised her when he moved close and cradled her face with his hands. His warm lips pressed firmly against hers. She leaned in and kissed him back, wishing she could melt into his arms and hold him tight forever. The accident had brought focus to her mind and clarity to her heart. Being near him heightened each of her senses. Her toes curled. In his arms, the connection to him ran deep.

He touched her as though he cherished her. Tender and light. She loved that about him. Her heart skipped several beats. Quivering sensations flooded her body.

This was love. The real thing.

James owned her heart.

Praise for *BAYOU BORN*

"A true southern experience, Cajun style!"
~Kathy L Wheeler, author of Color of Betrayal
~*~

"The bayou isn't the only thing hot and sultry in this sassy romance. Linda Joyce captures all your emotions and tantalizes your taste buds in this saucy southern tale."

~Claire Croxton, author of Santorini Sunset
~*~

"Family, a little scandal, two people risking their hearts in the name of love, all mixed with Southern charm—this story has it all."

~Kellie Kamryn, author of Pleasure Island

Dedication

This book is dedicated to the love of my life,
Donald S. Clements

Acknowledgments

Many people helped with the journey of Branna's story. If I've missed someone, my greatest apologies.

Thank you to Mailan Le and Laurie Fickle for enduring the 140,000-word rough draft. To Val, Linda, and Erin from Midwest Romance Writers—Thank you, WCW. Many thanks to M-L Kamberg, my first writing mentor.

My heartfelt thanks go to Jodi's Pioneers—Claire Croxton, Jan Morrill, Gina Popp, Kathy Wheeler, and Romney Nesbitt were especially helpful.

To Leslie Tentler for guidance in the Virginia Ellis Memorial Critique Workshop. Thank you, Jackie Rodriguez, for your encouragement and the gift of your friendship. It means so much.

To Ally Robertson, my editor, you are a blessing. I pitched *Bayou Bound*, my next novel that The Wild Rose Press will publish, to Ally at OWFI. When Ally offered me a contract on that book, I told her about *Bayou Born*. Several months later, I sent her the completely re-written manuscript. The rest, as they say, is history. I am honored that Ally sees something in my writing, and I sing her praises every day.

In memory of Clara Villaman, thank you for smiling on me.

Chapter 1

Branna Lind sighed and melted into the seat of the realtor's car. She sipped sweet tea; its refreshing coolness flowed and revived her sinking spirits. She offered silent prayers of gratitude. One for the drive-thru, two for the break from climbing in and out of the car as they house hunted, and three for her hair.

The car's air conditioning fluttered her new short style. Though it had shocked Momma, Branna was thankful she'd taken the risk. Given the sheen of perspiration that covered her skin, long hair in May's humidity would have made the day even more miserable.

She and Meredith were once again en route to tour yet another house in the small, north Florida town. Day three and into her eighth hour of house hunting in Lakeview, never had she imagined finding a place to live would top the total-drudgery list. The growing number of rejects doubled her despair. Would she find an acceptable house in a town this size? What kind of hole had she dug herself into this time?

A home had to be special. A place that called to her the moment she walked inside. A place that said she belonged. Like Fleur de Lis, her family's antebellum home in Mississippi.

"I've got one last place to show you today," Meredith said briskly. "I'm thinking this one might be what you're looking for."

Turning to face the window, Branna rolled her eyes. Before pulling up to each property they'd visited, Meredith had raised her hopes with that phrase, only to dash them every time.

"A ranch in a quiet neighborhood. Tree-lined streets. If you're interested, I'm pretty sure I can manage a lease-to-buy option, which might be the perfect scenario for you."

"Cozy," Branna said breathlessly. "That's all I want." It had been her mantra from the start of the hunt. Something had to materialize soon, otherwise room 203 at the mom-and-pop motel by the interstate would be her address of record. That wouldn't look good when she started her new teaching job at the community college.

"Even though you told me that, *cozy* means different things to different people. Each property we've looked at has a charm of its own. *You* bring *cozy* to it." Meredith grinned as though she'd cleverly discovered the answer to the problem.

"Yes, well, you may be right." Branna tried to keep defensiveness from her tone, certain that the places they'd seen so far fit Meredith's definition of cozy, but definitely not her own. But any display of rudeness would not accomplish her mission, and she *was* grateful for Meredith's time.

"This one isn't far from the center of town and only two blocks from the lovely trail around the lake that you like so much," Meredith told her.

Branna reflected on the worst offenders. The cold modern condo at the country club could only scream cozy to a felon who missed cinderblock walls. The country house had soaring ceilings. If it had mumbled *cozy* to her, she would've heard it echo, echo, echo, like in the Grand Canyon.

That old yellow Victorian...a truly odd experience. The house, barely a quarter the size of Fleur de Lis, came with the exact baggage she sought to escape— repairs. No doubt, it had potential to grow into something grand, however, her brain began immediately calculating a list of needed improvements and tracking the *ka-ching* it would take to make them.

And that was after viewing only the outside. Who knew the condition of the interior? She'd live in a popup camper before tackling a project like that.

Though, in fairness to Meredith, that showing had been an unscheduled stop. The battered white pickup in the driveway prompted the realtor to investigate. The property was one she owned.

While that detour from their planned list of houses was mostly a short pause in the schedule, that momentary hiatus had caused her to pause repeatedly since then. She rubbed her right hand, the one he'd touched. Why did the man with the battered pickup, a man with whom she'd only shared a casual handshake—a guy she wouldn't know in a lineup— keep popping up in her mind?

Would Mr. Rough-Around-the-Edges buy Meredith's place? If so, did he have a clue about living in chaos? Because that was his future if he bought that Victorian. It wouldn't take a French-Quarter sidewalk psychic to predict that living in a remodel was madness. There were enough reality shows on TV to prove her point. Calamity was the norm for the duration of any home-improvement project.

A spark of regret nipped her conscience. She'd been rude to him, but not intentionally. Her bad mood was the direct result of her mental comparisons of the Victorian to her family's old home, which she'd chosen to leave behind...because of a man.

Pickup-guy would never know that her behavior had nothing to do with him personally. Men were the enemy, and he was guilty by association. But still...he plagued her mind.

She sighed. She might not know him on sight, but she'd sure recognize his rust-bucket ride. That was one truck she could spot anywhere, more rust than paint on metal.

Out of politeness, she'd accepted his extended hand when Meredith made introductions, but she refused to make eye contact with the shaggy, good ol' boy, instead choosing to focus on his old, scuffed work boots.

She stopped short from jerking away when a too-warm sensation surged as their fingers met. He held her hand way too long to be polite, which made her even more uncomfortable, but her good manners had operated on autopilot. After that, she had refused a tour of the inside of the house and waited in the car. She wasn't interested in the house, or the man.

But for some reason, she couldn't seem to escape him. What would her therapist make of that?

"We're almost there, Branna." Meredith continued northbound on the four-lane, then stopped before making a left turn off the main road. As she crossed the two southbound lanes, a girl darted in front of the car.

"Watch out!" Branna cried.

Meredith slammed on the brakes.

Tires squealed.

An oncoming black car stopped only inches away, avoiding an impact to the passenger side of Meredith's car, but the terror of the vehicle headed straight at Branna caused her to squeeze her drink cup tightly. The top popped. Brown liquid sloshed and spattered the side of Meredith's white skirt. The girl in overalls who had put everything into motion raced away, her long brown braids beating against her back.

"Darn kid," Meredith complained, flicking an ice cube off her lap.

The driver in the black car blew the horn and waved at them to get out of the road.

"I'm so sorry. I'll have your skirt cleaned, or replace it if it's stained." Branna shoved napkins in Meredith's direction.

"Serves me right for wearing white before Memorial Day." Meredith sounded disgusted as she cleared the intersection and pulled the car to the side of the road.

Branna chuckled nervously. "It's not like breaking the rule is a bad omen or anything."

Except that in her world it was.

G.G. Marie—the G.G. was short for Great-Grandmother—would naturally agree with Meredith's conclusion. White before Memorial Day? Never! G.G. Marie was no different from other southern great-grandmothers who stuck to tradition.

However, Branna disagreed. With the first day of summer countable in weeks rather months, she would argue that temperatures outside were the deciding factor of when summer began, rather than a date on a calendar. Though she often disagreed with G.G. Marie, she always counted on the old woman's wisdom.

"I'm sure the skirt will be fine," Meredith said calmly as she started to drive again.

"I can understand if you want to change. We could look at this place tomorrow." Would Meredith take the hint? The shock of the almost-accident frayed her nerves more than she cared to admit.

"We're so close. And I've got a really *good* feeling about this one."

As much as she wanted to end the search, she had to find a place to live. Weary or not. Besides, good manners dictated that she follow Meredith's lead. "All right, let's go see."

They drove another block before Meredith pulled onto a wide concrete driveway. "Here we are."

Branna lifted her gaze. The cottage looked like something from a Thomas Kinkade painting with its sloping roofline, carved shutters, and arched front door. "Interesting."

The well-tended flower garden in the front and the window boxes with trailing greens and sprouting purple and white flowers provided attractive curb appeal. One word came to mind. *Charming.*

Meredith pulled a listing sheet from a folder. "One car garage converted from a carport. Spacious two bedrooms, two and a half baths. One could be an office-slash-guest room. Not tiny rooms with no closet space in this home, which is an usual footprint in a house of this age. Not a cookie-cutter when built, however, the spacious master bath is a recent add-on."

"It makes a nice first impression." Branna stepped out of the car slowly, captivated by the view. A gentle breeze ruffled her hair. She smoothed imaginary wrinkles from her sundress. "This one, I'm anxious to see inside."

Meredith turned the key in the lock, then swung the wooden door open wide. Branna walked through first. Once inside the foyer, she scanned the living room, a fireplace created a focal point. Natural light streamed through the large windows. She sighed deeply. Her body relaxed as though she'd been holding her breath all day. The house had definite possibilities.

She explored like a kid at *Toys R Us* for the first time. Details mattered. Crown molding. A master bedroom big enough to comfortably fit a queen-size bed, a dresser, a chaise, and a reading light. Granite countertops in the kitchen and bathrooms. Gas, stainless steel stove. A dining room with French doors that opened to a large screened porch, where she could curl up and read mosquito-free in evening's dappled sunlight.

"The patio is brick. There are raised beds for vegetables and flowers. Do you have a green thumb?" Meredith asked.

"No. Not so much. However, I'm determined to learn." At home, they had a full-time gardener to make the scenery perfect. A formal garden in the front and back required expert care. A well-manicured landscape had proved to be an important detail to brides when selecting Fleur de Lis for their wedding location.

"The garage—it's only one-car wide, but very deep—has a new opener," Meredith said "There's not a lot of grass to mow, because of the raised beds. You'll probably spend more time weeding than walking behind a mower."

"I want another look from the front."

Back outside, Branna walked down three brick steps to the sidewalk and scanned the tree-shaded neighborhood. Across the street, an older woman carrying a shopping bag with a crisp "LL" logo strolled by. In the distance, a scratchy bark from a little dog punctuated the quiet. A late-model black sedan with darkly tinted windows drove slowly past. Was it the one that stopped short of hitting them only minutes ago?

"Not much traffic on this street," Branna said.

"It's quiet. The price is right. What do you think?" Meredith asked.

"I'm not quite sure. Give me a few minutes to take it all in."

"I'll be in the backyard in the swing. Call when you have a decision."

Branna strode to the street and turned back to look at the yard and house. Her gut said, "This is the one." But signing on the dotted line? True commitment. Was she ready for that?

After six months of therapy to heal the gash in her self-esteem that Steven had carved, her confidence remained tenuous at best. Could she trust herself to make such a major decision? It wasn't like cutting her hair. That would grow back.

Half panicked, she dug through her purse for her cell phone. Her cousin, Biloxi, would provide the perfect "atta-girl" support. As her hand grasped the small weighted phone, it vibrated. She jumped. Her breath caught in the back of her throat. A text message flashed on the screen.

I will find you. Steven.

She bobbled the phone and almost dropped it. With trembling fingers, she flipped to her cousin's number and pressed the button.

"Hello?"

"Biloxi. Oh. My. God. Steven just texted me."

"What? No!"

"I don't know how he got my number."

"What did he say? Are you going to tell your parents? Aunt Macy and Uncle Charles will want to know."

As Branna considered the question, she looked down the street to the main road. The battered pickup, the one from the Victorian property, distracted her as it crossed her view. The odd sensation she'd experienced when she met the vehicle's owner quivered in her chest.

It had to be a mixture of exhaustion, heat, and humidity, right? This was Lakeview, not an episode of *Doctor Who*.

"Branna? Hello? Are you going to tell your mom?"

"Ah, sorry. Um, no." She used to confide in her mother, but the mess with Steven had changed that. "No," she said slowly. "Besides, I won't give that man the satisfaction of knowing he caused any ripple in my life. I'm not going to bring it up with Momma." She drew in a breath for fortification. "However, I am going to tell them that I bought a house."

"Oh, Branna. Damn it. The family's going to kill you for sure."

Chapter 2

Standing beside his truck in his parents' driveway after an afternoon in a hayfield, James Newbern clicked his cell phone closed. Dr. Brown had asked him to make time to show a new faculty member around. "Like a sponsor or a good-will ambassador. Miss Lind is close to your age. From Mississippi. I'm assigning a seasoned faculty member to each of the three new ones. Thanks for helping out."

Dr. Brown had asked, but the task was non-negotiable. James weighed his summer commitments. Buy a house. Repair it. Truck hay to south Florida with Bobby. Teach summer school. And, lest he forget, farming. He understood Dr. Brown's desire to smooth the way for new hires, and he didn't object to the added responsibility, but how to fit it all in? He already had too much on his plate. But never would he refuse a Dr. Brown request. Their association began back when he had enrolled as a freshman at the community college, and Dr. Brown appointed himself as mentor.

Crossing the threshold to his parents' farmhouse, he walked in to aromas of supper. Savory scents of roast beef made his hunger churn. Homemade creamed corn and zipper peas, his mother's prizewinning dishes, simmered on the stove. A large bowl of her signature carrot and raisin salad with sliced bananas, just like he liked it, waited for delivery to the dining room table. A feast only made for special occasions.

"I'm starving," he said.

"Son, when have you ever been anything but hungry?" his mother, Emmeline, teased. Standing on a stepstool, she pulled her fine china down from a tall kitchen cabinet. "Come over here and help your poor mother."

When she took a good look at him, she drew back and refused to hand over the plates. "You don't have clean hands. Don't touch." She gingerly climbed down from the stepstool with the plates, and then *clunked* them against granite on the kitchen island.

Granny, his mother's mother, sat at the other end of the counter and smiled up at him. He grinned as she added buttermilk into her big, wooden biscuit-making bowl. With practiced efficiency, her hands swirled flour, shortening, and buttermilk into dough. He never sat down to a meal at home when biscuits weren't on the table. He kissed her cheek. "You're my favorite girl."

"Oh, you go on, now," Granny said.

"Yes, you go on now. Look at you!" His mother scrunched her face as if he were trash too dirty for even the garbage man to pick up. "You've got five minutes to take a shower and get your *be-hind* at the dinner table. Now go!" She swatted at him playfully with a dishtowel, but it would never touch him. His mother never allowed dirt in her kitchen, ever.

Before leaving, he squeezed the tops of Granny's shoulders. "You're lookin' lovely tonight. I'd ask you to go dancing, but the Queen has spoken, so let me take my *be-hind* out of here, if I have any hope of eating. Do you think she'd torture me by starving me if I don't shower first?"

"You charmer. *Dancing*, really. Get washed for supper."

He saluted, then pushed on the swinging door that separated the kitchen from the formal dining room. When he entered the living room, the lively discussion between his father and grandfather stopped. The two men straightened in their seats like boys guilty of mischief. He glanced from side to side at each of them as he headed to the hall.

His father, Cedrick, seated in his worn favorite easy chair next to the fireplace, cleared his throat loudly. The sound alone begged attention from even the most clueless person. Something was up.

James winked at his grandfather. "How are things today, Papa? I offered to take your girl dancing, but she turned me down." Then, he turned to his father, "Hello, sir." Not waiting for a response, he continued the long walk across the wide living room.

"Seems you've had a busy day, son." The amusement in his father's voice snagged him. He stopped at the entrance to the hall.

"I'm busy most days, sir." He turned. The back of the easy chair greeted him; his father gazed out the window.

What now?

He glanced in Papa's direction. The old man pointed his gnarled finger repeatedly in the air as though thumping it at Cedrick's chest. "Just out with it!"

"Fine. Wade Addington called here look'n for you 'bout a house."

James frowned. His secret was out.

"You think you want to tackle something like that?" Papa asked. "It's a *big* undertaking." The old man's narrowed eyes disappeared into the wrinkles on his face. To Papa, hard work defined a man, no matter if he had money or not. Farming was all Papa knew, along with hunting to put food on the table. He'd complained more than once that he couldn't understand anyone who wanted to live in Lakeview, let alone move to a big city like Jacksonville or Tampa. Clearly, Papa understood Mr. Addington's call meant he would be moving to town. Would there be yet another argument discouraging him from changing addresses?

"Well, I think you're man enough to do it. Certainly old enough now. 'Bout time if you ask me." Papa nodded and crossed his arms over his chest, as if daring anyone to refute him.

James chuckled. He hadn't thought about it exactly in birthday terms, but as far as presents went, a house was a solid gift. And, he was old enough, staring at thirty-one. Most parents wanted their kids out of the house when teenage-itis struck, or when college time arrived, but not his. He'd been a good farmhand since he learned to gather eggs from the hens as a kid, though since college, he'd lived in a single-wide mobile home on his grandparents' farm.

"Son, I'm curious. How'd you find this house?" his father asked.

"A couple of weeks ago, I was out running errands and drove along the lake. A "For Sale" sign stopped me, and the owner happened to drive up while I was looking around. She showed me the inside of the house."

"I hear Meredith grew up to be a real looker." A

sly smile and a wink came from his grandfather.

Surprised that Papa knew of Meredith, he stood straighter and focused his attention on the conversation.

"Yes, I'm an old man, but I still know a lot of folks." His grandfather raised one eyebrow as if to caution James about challenging him, then grinned. "Back in the day, I sold meat to her grandmother. I've known Meredith since the day she was born."

"So were you think'n about do'n this all by yourself?" Cedrick asked.

"Well, sir, I don't know. Meredith wouldn't tell me her asking price. Turned the deal over to her cousin, Wade-the-attorney. We've been going back and forth. I won't know if the project is doable until I have a contractor's final inspection report...and the final asking price. I'm waiting on the report, though I did make a contingent offer. It was a low one."

"The two of you just *looked* at the house together?" his grandfather asked.

He hid a grin and ignored the jab. His grandfather had always been too nosey. "We did a walk-through. Meredith showed me around and gave me the history of the house. There was another woman along. Pretty, but very aloof. Couldn't discern if she was a prospective buyer or just along for the ride. She didn't tour the house with me."

But he hadn't forgotten the pulsing sensations when he held her hand in his. She might not have looked him in the eye, but he'd bet money she had experienced the pulsing, same as he. More than once, his thoughts had drifted to her. Maybe she wasn't ignoring him that day, maybe ignoring the attraction? It didn't matter really, she absolutely wasn't his type. She probably liked opera and belonged to the country club. Her perfectly manicured nails said a lot about what she didn't do in life. No sense in expending time and energy on something doomed from the start.

His father motioned him over to his easy chair, then held up a pad and pointed. Wade's name, a phone number, and a dollar amount scrawled neatly on the paper. He shook his head in confusion.

"This is her asking price," his father said. He circled the number with the pencil he pulled from behind his ear.

"What? You sure?" He looked hard at his father. "That can't be right." He looked again at the circled numbers. Two-hundred thousand.

"Seems she wants to be rid of the house pronto and you're the buyer for her. Wade muttered something about you and your family moving in as soon as possible. All you have to do is call and accept the offer. Your family? What did he mean by that?"

"Hot damn," James snorted.

From the dining room, Granny called, "Language becoming of a gentleman, please. We're almost ready to eat. Well, those of us whom are clean."

"The house is at least four thousand square feet. Sits on over an acre. I'm sure it will appraise for more than that amount, even in these real estate times. The family thing. Meredith says the house needs a family. I told her if I bought the house, someday I'd have that."

"Shower. Now." His mother's fists were planted firmly on her hips as she stood between the dining and living room.

"I'm going," he told her.

His father tapped him on the arm. "Son, she has

one condition. You and your family must have a housewarming party within a year and invite her."

"I can't believe that's what she wants for the house. It's below market value," James said, ignoring any mention of family while suspicion rubbed his conscience. Did the house need a lot of work, and she knew it? Did she think because he looked like a redneck that he couldn't afford the house at any price? And why hadn't Wade called his cell phone rather than calling the house and leaving this information? "I want the place, but it's still contingent on an inspection and an appraisal. Have to have due diligence." He'd been fooled once by a pretty face. Houses, like women, might look great on the outside, but dig a few inches and looks could be deceiving. His hard-earned cash wouldn't leave the bank a moment before he had a complete inspection and hard numbers for repairs.

"Son, Wade said it needs some minor work. Insisted that Meredith had a contractor look at it when she inherited it. They say the needed work is only cosmetic."

Papa rose slowly from his chair, hobbled over to him, and slapped him on the back. "I answered the phone and reminded Wade of our families' long-time connection. But I'm so hard of hearing, even with that darn speakerphone, I couldn't understand half of what he was saying. Had to get your dad involved."

"Dinner is ready," his mother called from the dining room.

James glanced in her direction. She stood behind her chair waiting as she always did whenever they had a formal meal. His father would pull out her chair and she would sit, then place the cloth napkin in her lap. Family traditions learned from his grandparents.

Not wanting to irritate his mother, he sprinted down the hall. By the time everyone had a beverage of their choice, he'd be done and ready to eat.

"Finally," his mother said when he returned. "Your grandmother was kind enough to get you sweet tea." She pointed to the glass next to his plate.

His mother ladled gravy over roast beef and handed the first plate to him. "James is this really necessary?" she asked.

"The house, you mean?" He knew she wasn't asking about the food, but he wanted to tease her. Had she made his favorite meal as a bribe to make him stay or as a farewell dinner?

"Yes, this house business." She sniffed. "How can you afford this? I don't think you should buy a house until you can afford it."

"She means that she's worried that once you move to town permanently, you'll get too busy to come see us," Granny said.

He took a bite of the meat and chewed. "This is great, Mom. With cooking like this, I'll come every time I'm invited." He hoped flattery might distract her, and then he could change the subject. One of his mother's...interesting...pastimes was gossiping after church on Sunday with the church's ladies' committee. Unfortunately, they viewed gossip as a sport or competition. He wanted his private life to remain off limits to the ears of those with loose lips. He'd learned a hard lesson very well when he and Caroline broke up. And old men gossiped just as much as old women.

"I'm glad you like the food. I made all your favorites." She smiled modestly. "But what about the house?"

"Now Emme, stop that," Granny said gently. "Leave the boy alone. If he says he wants to buy the house, then he must have a way to work it out."

Granny corrected his mother? In front of others? Usually, she played the gentle mediator, always finding something good to say about everything, smoothing over any potential conflict.

"Momma," his mother whined, "I don't know how he could possibly afford it with all of his education loans."

"Your son's a grown man with a doctorate degree. If he says he can afford it, then you should believe him." Papa's low tone carried a sharp threat. Emmeline squared her shoulders, lowered her eyes, and picked at the food on her plate.

Staying out of the fray, intent on enjoying the feast of his favorites, he kept his attention on his food, took a fork full of zipper peas, and savored the flavor. No matter what, his mother could cook.

He shrugged off the family debate. In truth, he could afford it. No one knew that except his grandfather, who had taught him the value of money at an early age. However, if it hadn't been for his father's heart attack five years ago, he would've bought a house in town when he first accepted the teaching job at the community college. A thirty mile, one-way commute every day, mostly traveling a two-lane blacktop, got old.

"Great biscuits, Granny." He smeared butter between two halves.

Granny beamed. "Emmeline, if the boy buys the house, maybe that's a signal that he's ready to find the right woman and settle down. Maybe this time, he'll do it—house, marriage, *then* baby."

His mother brightened. "Grandchildren?"

The ringing telephone interrupted the banter. Silence smothered all conversation. The house rule—no one answered the phone during a family meal. His father always enforced it. Especially after Caroline had started calling whenever his truck was parked in the driveway at his parents' house. At first, her calls had been pleading, she wanted him back, but when he ignored her, she turned to issuing threats never meant for his mother or grandmother's ears. It wasn't that he wanted to purposefully hurt her, he'd just been too hurt by her to care how she felt now. She was none of his business.

After five long rings, the phone went silent. Papa launched into a joke, a corny one that only an old man could pull off, and everyone laughed.

Caroline. James pushed the pain of the past from his mind. After dinner, Granny and Papa would stay "at the big house" with his parents for a while and listen to his mother play the piano. They'd sing hymns to practice for Sunday services at the Baptist Church. Meanwhile, he'd take Beau for a run down the sandy limestone road to Papa's and back. Beau needed a workout, and James needed the exercise to clear his head. It was bothersome that a woman he'd met only once had captured his fascination. And that irritated him. After all, a woman in pearls and jeans with high heels shouted pampered and spoiled. Branna had to be the "high-maintenance" type. She'd kept her eyes trained on his boots the whole time, as though he wasn't good enough somehow. He couldn't name the color of her eyes, but he expected they would be as hypnotic as she was seductive. Still, the pulsing sensation between them mystified him. He had to shake it off.

A run with Beau would do him good. Afterward, he'd join the family, listen to his mother play...and begin to plan his future.

One without Caroline or baby Katie.

Chapter 3

The phone rang in the kitchen.

Branna jiggled the key in the door lock, praying it would turn the first time. She shifted the grocery bags in her arms when the lock wouldn't open.

"I'm coming!" Lowering the bags on her right arm to the ground, she jiggled the key harder. The ringing continued.

"I said, I'm coming!"

When the lock finally turned, the door opened, and she tripped across the threshold, barely staying upright. Her sunglasses slid down her nose. She grabbed for the phone.

"Yes?" she said, then set the three bags hanging from her wrist on the counter and shook out the pain in her hand.

"You must come. I won't take no for an answer."

Why did Momma always think that being chipper when issuing a command would make everyone snap-to and do her bidding?

"Momma, I'm sorry. We talked about this already. I *can't* make it for Memorial weekend." She picked up the bag she'd left at the threshold and nudged the door closed with her foot. She hoped that WD-40 in the lock would fix the ingress problem. She pulled the can from the bag and set it on the counter.

"The mayor has agreed to speak. I hired that blues

band you used for that wedding on New Year's Eve. The mayor and I decided that the cover charge for the event is a minimum of five cans of food per person to replenish the food bank. However, I need your help."

"I know this is your first run at handling a charity Memorial Day picnic, and I'm here for moral support. You can bounce any new ideas off me. But this isn't your first outing, and I'm sure you've got it under control."

Every day, she'd been on the phone with Momma about one or another function scheduled at Fleur de Lis. Often it was more than once a day. Her mother had suddenly bumped the charity-hosting schedule from one big event a year—the Valentine Auction and Valentine's Day Dance—to three, with under a month before the date of the first new one,which meant flyers and invitations needed to be designed, printed, and then mailed. Local vendors needed contacting to secure their financial support.

Was Momma purposely trying to drive her crazy?

"You know the family's gathering schedule. It's *tradition* we count on." Momma sounded disappointed, but did she have to play the tradition card?

"I am the face of family tradition. I'm the one deeded the duty to keep all Fleur de Lis traditions alive—in the future. I can recite the schedule in my sleep, but I can't put aside my work responsibilities here." She wouldn't allow Momma's tone to sway her from her focus. She couldn't be running back and forth to Mississippi if she ever intended to have a life of her own, to learn that she was strong enough and truly worthy of the "Keeper" role. Birth order didn't guarantee she had the talent to protect the legacy.

"Branna Noël Lind, I can't believe my ears. Are you suggesting that blood isn't thicker than water? Being Keeper is an honor, not prison time. Do I need to remind you of the benefits you have reaped because you are the first great-grandchild?"

"I moved. I didn't lose my memory," she muttered. "I have a *job*, Momma." With the phone scrunched between her shoulder and ear, she put a milk carton in the fridge.

"Attitude? From you? I expect that from Camilla or one of your cousins, but you?"

The demure, compliant teenager Momma sent off to college years before had grown up. Unlike her siblings and cousins, she had never rebelled. Ever. She always did all that was expected of her. Including caving about going out-of-state for college. That scholarship she'd given up had been a huge source of pride. It was awarded because of her work, not because of her family name or due to family influence. But Momma had insisted that she keep with tradition and attend college in state.

In truth, the disappointment that shrouded her life came when she ended her engagement to Steven. She was still learning to live with embarrassment and humiliation. If she wanted to feel differently, only she had the ability to change her life. And that's what she was trying to do.

Yet, as far as her parents were concerned, her recent departure meant she'd said to hell with rules, and order, and decades of tradition. But that wasn't true. She took the role of Keeper seriously. She'd worked hard to fulfill everyone's expectations of an estate manager. But she wasn't her mother, and she didn't just *love* planning weddings. They were a necessary evil that brought in extra revenue to support the estate, which belonged to all of them, though the future care of it rested with her. Beneath her façade of self-confidence, she feared the weight of the entire family's future on her shoulders.

She feared failure.

After all, she'd chosen poorly when accepting a proposal of marriage. Ending the engagement brought embarrassment on everyone in her family. Though folks in Bayou Petite had touted her wedding as the event of the decade, that wasn't reason enough to marry misery. Wanting to spare her loved ones the pain of her humiliation, she had told no one, not Momma or even Biloxi, the reason she'd called it quits with Mr. Steven Sterling.

His betrayal had dumped chaos into her life and rocked the very core of her self-confidence. Would she ever trust herself to lead at Fleur de Lis? Would she ever trust a man again?

"Forgive me, Momma. My schedule is backwards from what the family's accustomed to. Is Camilla coming home?" She didn't wait for an answer. It didn't matter. She'd forgiven her sister, but wasn't ready for a face-to-face encounter. Camilla's lack of sisterly loyalty hurt more than she'd ever imagined. It went beyond words. Like a bell, Camilla's actions couldn't be unrung. "I'll be home for the Fourth of July and Christmas, but I can't make it for Memorial weekend, and unless a miracle happens, you can't count on me for Thanksgiving. Hopefully, next year will be different. Be that as it may, how may I help now?" She pulled food from the grocery bags, setting the items on the counter.

"Design the flyers. I'll get them printed here."

"I can do that."

"Two years, Branna. The clock is already ticking down."

There was an unmistakable hint of glee in her mother's voice. "We agreed on two years for your...sabbatical from home. Love you."

"Love you, too." She clicked the "end" button on the phone, but before she could put it down, it rang again. "What now?"

"Hmm. I'm guessing you've been talking with your mother?"

Branna sighed. "Biloxi, you and your ESP. She's trying the guilt-trip of the century. Are you going home for Memorial weekend?"

"No. These days, I'm lucky to make it to the big thing—Mardi Gras."

"So, what's up with you?"

"The wall of secrecy about your sister seems to be growing. Are you going to tell me what happened? Where is Camilla? I need to talk with her and can't locate her."

She paused. Though she usually confided in her cousin, she couldn't bring herself to utter the words.

"Hello?"

"Camilla is fine," she answered brightly.

"Don't give me that sing-songy-sales-person voice. I want the truth."

"Have *you* talked to Momma about this?"

"Aunt Macy's her own PR department with a spin on everything. She offers glibness in place of substance or truth. Always a smile and a perky mood. I know my

Aunt Macy, and she's covering up something. What gives? I want to talk to my other female Lind cousin."

"Momma received a postcard from Camilla just before I moved. She's in Cody, Wyoming working for the summer. I think at a diner."

"Camilla? A diner?" Biloxi laughed hard.

"Momma's got the address. Seems Camilla somehow lost her cell phone."

"But Branna, *why* is she in no-man's-land Cody, Wyoming?"

"I don't know. Maybe that's where she ran out of gas and money." Or maybe Camilla thought she was far enough away that she could hide from her conscience? She wouldn't know for sure until she'd actually talked with her younger sister about her latest disappearing act. For the last six months, Camilla hadn't answered her calls.

"Did something happen between the two of you?"

"We never had a fight." Thankfully, those words had the added benefit of being true. She might not tell her cousin everything, but she never lied either.

"God! Talkin' to you is like pulling hens' teeth. When I get this figured out, you'll fess up."

"Nothing to fess-up to. If Camilla's got a problem with me, you need to go to the source. That would be her. But you can tell her to call me if you find her. Any photo contracts that might take you up that way?"

"No. I'm headed to Tokyo, then Holland for photo shoots. Are all families as complicated as ours?"

That made Branna smile. "Darlin', we're not complicated. We're normal. I've got to run to work— Lord, I love saying that—so when you find my sister, tell her to come home and stop breaking Momma's heart."

She hung up and finished arranging the newly purchased items in the pantry. She'd never grocery shopped for just one before. They always fed an army at Fleur de Lis. Her first grocery run in Lakeview, and she'd bought the smallest size or quantity of flour, sugar, and other staples. The assembled items looked like accessories for a dollhouse, petite and cute.

A peek out the kitchen window brought her attention to the sun. Or lack of it. A few moments ago, the sun blazed. Shadows that once stretched across the lawn had disappeared.

Typical Florida afternoon. Sun. Rain. Sauna.

An hour later, after changing clothes and checking her makeup for the third time—no telling who she might meet at the bookstore—she headed for the college.

Gray clouds hung low in the sky, so low that in the distance, the clouds appeared to blanket the ground. Dust and debris twirled in gusts of thick moist air that buffeted against her car. She drove past flickering streetlights, thankfully wrapped in the comfort of her Volvo's air conditioning.

The sky continued to darken, and the bank of clouds followed her eastbound.

The wind suddenly stopped, as if to catch its breath, then whipped up again harder. A ragged flash of white light ripped across the sky.

Shuddering, she counted, "One. Two. Three. Four."

Four miles? The wall of darkening clouds seemed closer

A deep rumbling bass shook the Volvo's windows.

She jumped. Had thunder really rattled the fillings in her teeth?

Lightning's long skeletal fingers could strike from miles away. That's what she feared most. People died every year due to lightning strikes, and after all, Florida was the lightning capital of the United States. The college would be a safe harbor to ride out the storm—if she managed to make it to the door before it started to pour.

She stopped behind a car at the red light on Highway 90 and gripped the steering wheel. "Change. Change," she shouted over the music of her favorite classical Bach CD. "Change! Darn it!"

The signal light flickered to green. Immediately after the car ahead moved forward, she made a right turn. She watched the clouds lumber across the sky as she drove past tall loblolly pines swaying in the quickening wind. If one fell, it would block the road leading to the community college.

"Almost there." She readjusted her tight grip on the steering wheel and resisted the urge to floor the gas and fly along the straight-of-way. She'd been warned on her visits to campus that sometimes the local police set up radar traps to catch unsuspecting speeders—college students were the primary goal, but they didn't discriminate if they caught a faculty member or two every now and then. It had been suggested to her that since the police bulletin in Sunday's paper listed names of speeders, faculty members might want to avoid their names in print. Not the best impression for students.

She'd never been ticketed in her life, but with the storm bearing down, maybe it was worth the risk today.

On her right, only yards away, the town's airport

runway ended perpendicular to the road. The oversized airstrip allowed commercial jets, cargo carriers, and even military aircraft to land. She'd read that tidbit on the internet when doing research to familiarize herself with Lakeview. In contrast to the small number of only five thousand city residents, the runway was a behemoth. And it made her tense each time she drove past it on the exposed stretch of road.

Watching her speed carefully, she recalled her second visit to the college. A huge gray, military-cargo plane had rumbled down the tarmac. Black wheels turned with dizzying ferocity. The engine roared as the plane picked up speed. They were on a direct collision course.

Cargo plane verses Volvo—no contest.

She had slammed on her brakes. Just before she panicked completely, the gray hulk gained lift, clearing the road and trees like a prehistoric bird taking flight. She'd bet money the pilot had a good laugh. He probably saw fear in her eyes and thought she'd peed her pants. He'd be half-right.

Today, thankfully, no plane was in sight.

"Finally!"

Before her, the gates to the college stood open. A large, carved stone sign welcomed everyone to Lakeview Community College. The spotlights on the sign flickered on as she passed. Could she outrun the storm? With no one else on the road, she floored it. She had a better chance of talking herself out of a ticket with a college security officer than with the local police.

A deep rumble shook the earth. With her tires throwing gravel, she spun into the Student Union parking lot. She grabbed her stuff and hoped to beat the on-coming deluge.

Her purse and tote bounced against her back as she sprinted to the building. Halfway there, fat drops started to fall.

Splat. Splat. Splat.

Cold rain stung her bare arms. When she made it to the canopy covering the building's back door, her clothes were mostly wet.

"Nothing like a summer baptism," she grumbled as she rummaged through her tote looking for a package of tissues. No such luck.

She pushed wet hair behind her ears, and then slapped wetness from her arms. How had she forgotten to put an umbrella in her car?

When she opened the door to the Student Union, cold air hit her. Not only didn't she have an umbrella, she was sweater-less. The building was cold enough to refrigerate beef. Damp all over, she'd probably freeze.

She shivered from the cold, but excitement, too.

Her dream had turned to reality.

The first job she'd landed all on her own. The next step on her new journey waited down the long hall.

With a determined stride, she walked. Or was she floating? She had a right to be proud. After the last six months of hiding, trying to protect her family from scandal, and drowning in self-doubt, this was the opportunity she wanted to define herself, her life, with no influences from any of her family.

A smile tugged at her mouth. It was a gold-star day when President Westcott had called and offered her the job. If she hadn't met him, based on their phone call alone, she'd be worried that he was weird. After all, whoever said, *"On the horns of a dilemma?"*

She rolled her eyes remembering the strange exchange, but she was all too familiar with small-town dealings where business was done because somebody knew someone related to somebody else. This job was even more special because she'd done it all on her own.

Her destination waited down the hall. Fluorescent lights cast a greenish tint on the white cinder-block walls and speckled linoleum floor. Inside the bookstore, a strategically placed sign on a worn counter by the cash register announced, "Back in fifteen-minutes."

That gave her time to wander around with no one to intrude on the sacredness of the moment. Tingling excitement made her giddy. The same kind of giddiness as when she'd hooked her seatbelt for her first-ever roller-coaster ride on the *Scream Machine* at Six Flags over New Orleans.

She quickly located the section that housed the textbooks for her class. An identifying sign listed her name and the course number.

"I've done it. I've really done it," she whispered as she stroked the cover of the book. Textbooks for her first official job as a college instructor. She was a full-fledged faculty member. Savoring the success, she committed each detail to memory.

Voices drew her attention. Two people entered the bookstore. She leaned to look between the bookshelves. A young woman stood behind the counter, she guessed her to be a student—a colorful one. Blond hair tipped with pink and green made the young woman look like a flower blossom, even in the gray-on-gray camo shirt. On the other side of the counter, a man tapped a pen, re-enforcing a point in their conversation.

She couldn't help but overhear their chatter about their weekend plans. Hers—a party at Dub's on Saturday night before classes started on Monday. His—a date with a new massage therapist in town.

"Hello," Branna called. It was bad manners to eavesdrop. Making her presence known was the polite thing to do. "I'm looking for an umbrella."

"You're gonna need one in this weather." The man walked in her direction. His sneakers squeaked against the linoleum. "Though with wind, not even an umbrella will keep you dry."

"Maybe I need to buy a tarp?" she asked.

"Or just ride out the storm in here," he said. He stopped beside her and glanced at her name on the shelf.

"Branna Lind? Did I get that right?"

"Yes, that's me." She smiled and noticed his nametag. Brian Murphy. Bookstore Manager.

"Checkin' out the supply?"

Something about his tone made her feel like a school kid getting caught doing something naughty. Warmth flushed her face. She hated when she blushed. "I wanted to see the books on the shelves." She shrugged. Was she acting like a college freshman rather than a new faculty member?

"Are you comin' to the potluck Friday evening? Mrs. Westcott usually does a nice job of it. We're a friendly bunch."

"Yes. Looking forward to it." Her voice sounded far calmer than she felt. Meet the entire faculty at President Westcott's home? Nerves clamped down on her giddiness.

The. Entire. Faculty.

She waited when Brian stayed glued to the spot beside her as if he intended to say something more. When he didn't continue, she dropped her gaze to avoid his stare and observed his golf shirt with the college's logo.

"Well...is there...anything I need to know about, for the pot luck?" she finally asked.

"Oh, let's see. Lots of stuff. But I don't want to frighten you off. We're happy to have you join our ranks. You're not the only first-timer here..." his voice trailed off. She followed his gaze and caught a glimpse of Dr. Brown, the Vice President, walking through the door.

"The umbrellas are over there." He pointed to where one wall of tinted glass met another to form a corner.

"Excuse me, please?" Brian turned and went to greet Dr. Brown.

She made her way to the corner and watched the storm raging outside. Would it rain like this before the Westcott's party? If so, what would she wear? She feared meeting so many people in a short amount of time. Face after face with names she'd want to remember. It couldn't be worse than being a human mannequin at a shop on Canal Street in New Orleans, could it?

Would she finally meet the faculty member Dr. Brown assigned to mentor her? The evasive Dr. Newbern clearly had a busy schedule. He was a "no-show" at the luncheon. Would he consider his mentoring duties akin to babysitting?

She pictured an older man in a tweed jacket with suede patches on the elbows. Dr. Brown hadn't said much about her mentor, except that he was very qualified, a student favorite, and very trustworthy. With that recommendation, she vowed to keep any interaction with the man strictly professional and necessary. No wasting his time. She was a quick study when she enjoyed her work. Maybe one day, Dr. Brown would make similar glowing remarks about her.

Nearby, a rack of blue-denim shirts with the college's logo on the front pocket stood ready for the onslaught of students arriving on Monday. Maybe one of those shirts would work with black jeans. Picking one up, she laid it across her arm. Where did Brian say she would find umbrellas?

"Hi. Brian sent me over. Do you need help?"

The young woman's pink and green-tipped hair fascinated Branna. Self-expression had always been discouraged by her mother. "Respectable" was the family hallmark for the Keeper.

"Thanks, I'm good. I'll hunt around while I'm waiting for the storm to rain itself out."

"Cool. But the umbrellas are over here." The young woman pointed.

Branna walked to the spot and discovered the umbrellas tucked between two tall bookcases. The selection ranged in size from long golf ones in multiple colors to the black micro version, small enough to fit inside a backpack. That was just the size she wanted. "This one will do."

"I'll carry it up front, and it'll be waiting for you. Give me the shirt, too. Take your time. I don't have anything else to do. Happy to help."

"Thank you."

Branna paused by a shelf of folded cotton knit

jackets. She rubbed the fabric between her fingers. Softness. Setting her purse down, she unzipped the garment and tried it on.

Ah...warm.

Why hadn't she thought of it sooner? She would wear it home.

She picked up her purse and glanced outside at the Commons, the park-like area bordered by campus buildings. On the opposite end from the bookstore was the parking lot, though due to the darkness and deluge, it remained invisible. Safe and protected inside the store, she watched the ferocity of the storm. Streetlights around campus glowed eerily, though it was only afternoon.

Out of the corner of her eye, something white moved in the downpour. She stepped closer to the window. With condensation covering it, the view appeared like a wet-on-wet watercolor painting.

In the rain, a brave soul eased his way along the sidewalk in front of the bookstore under the building's eaves. The man appeared in no particular hurry. A small black umbrella protected him from the overflowing gutters.

A quick flash of light made her breath catch.

Danger! Her brain screamed.

Lightning zigzagged.

Thunder boomed, then echoed.

The windows rattled.

She flinched, scrunching her neck like a turtle retreating into its shell, and closed her eyes.

When the rumbling lessened, she opened one eye first, and remembered the man. Pressing closer to the window, she rubbed a spot in the condensation. Had he made it to safety?

Another slash of light brightened the sky. The hair on her neck stood up. She jumped back and shivered. As though in slow motion, a jagged flash of lightning struck a pine tree in the Commons. Sparks flew. The trunk exploded. Steam, a visible cloud in the rain, drifted over the remaining stump. Most of the toppled tree blocked the sidewalk between the Student Union and the Administration building.

Trembling, she looked again. Where was the man?

She spotted him off to the left, under the shelter of the deep doorway, the front entrance of the Student Union.

He moved to stand directly on the opposite side of the glass from her. Water splattered as he shook his umbrella.

Thunder rumbled again. A streak of jagged light raced across the sky. She hesitated to move closer to the window, yet, something about the man drew her. She stepped so close to the glass, her breath fogged a spot. Any sane person would have backed away, but fascination held her captive.

The rest of the world was dark and gray—he was in living color. His long sleeved, white shirt looked crisp as though laundered and starched, not just pulled from a dryer. His dark denim jeans looked new. He didn't appear wet, or even damp, although water still dripped from the tip of his umbrella and formed a small puddle near his pristine leather cowboy boots.

About a foot away, with only glass between them, he appeared to stare at the damaged pine tree. A stray lock of dark brown hair fell over his forehead. He pushed it aside, but stubbornly it fell again. Was he a student? He looked older than the usual twenty-something, but that didn't mean anything. She had students of all ages in the adult education class she'd taught before.

She pressed her palm flat against the window. Her fingers itched to move the stray lock of hair off his forehead. Feeling bold, she smiled and winked. She could flirt safely, hidden behind dark tinted glass.

He took a step closer.

Her breath hitched in her throat.

He smiled and winked. When his hand pressed on the outside of the glass in the same spot where hers pressed from the inside, they were palm to palm, but for the tinted glass between them. The man grinned wider.

Had she ever seen a sexier smile? Even his chocolate brown eyes danced with laughter. Something about his smile...she couldn't look away. Had they met before?

A streak of lightning flashed like a giant strobe. She covered her ears, anticipating the deafening boom. The next lightning strike sent her diving to the floor.

The lights in the bookstore popped off.

Everything rattled.

She covered her head, expecting the vibrating windows to shatter, certain lightning had struck the building.

Lying there, she waited for disaster. Echoing booms of thunder lessened like soldiers calling out a cadence while marching away. Backup lights flickered on. Slowly the world came back into focus.

"Branna, you okay?" Brian Murphy yelled.

"I think so," she said, afraid to rise. She blinked a few times, too shaky to stand.

A deep thrusting groan from the air conditioning system muted the music that started playing again over the sound system. Fluorescent lights hummed on.

Panicked, she pushed herself up from the floor. Where was the man in the window? For a second, time had frozen them. Linked them somehow. Only she and he existed in the storm.

Where had he gone?

Who was he?

How would she ever find out?

Chapter 4

The next day, standing on the driveway, Branna shielded her eyes from the bright noon sun. She waited with a furniture moving crew she'd hired from U-Haul to help her dad unload and set up furniture, all the things her parents insisted on bringing from Fleur de Lis. Shifting her weight from one side to the other, she looked at her watch again. Her parents were thirty minutes overdue. Her mother had assured her they had their GPS and would find her house. It wasn't *that* far off the interstate.

With her eyes trained down the street at the intersection of the main road, she spied a battered white pickup passing by. She'd know it anywhere. Her heart pounded. She couldn't contain a grin. How silly. Why would she feel a connection to the guy in the truck? It had to be more of a mental game, like "I Spy." Momma had made the family play it on their trips to the beach to keep them entertained.

Who is he? She hadn't wanted to know when Meredith made introductions, but now... Had her brain manufactured the quivering sensation from their brief touch? That had to be it.

A minute later, a U-Haul truck turned on to her tree-lined street. She waved both hands to get her father's attention. Her parents and her furniture had finally arrived.

With hand gestures of a traffic cop, she guided her father's backing of the U-Haul onto the driveway and kept him from backing too close to the house. When he cut the engine off, she patiently waited while her parents climbed out. She would never admit to them how happy she was to see them, nor how homesickness plagued her every night before she went to bed. She had framed the postcard she brought from home—the one they'd made from Biloxi's award-winning photograph and sold to tourists—and kept it by her bed. It was the last thing she saw at night and the first thing in the morning.

"Hey!" She rushed in and hugged them. "I'm so glad to see you. You had a good trip, right? Daddy, Tom's the guy in charge."

She introduced the furniture-moving foreman to her father. "Tom, this is my dad, Charles." The two men walked to the back of the truck talking unloading logistics.

"This is it?" her mother asked. Skepticism punctuated her words.

"Let me show you." She jogged to the front door and waited for her mother to catch up before opening the entryway to the 1940's bungalow, all the while trying not to hold her breath. It was her choice of homes, she was happy, but she wanted her mother's approval.

"It's not exactly what I expected from the photos you took," her mother said, appearing to scrutinize every nook and corner. An airport-security searcher couldn't have been more thorough.

"You know I lack Biloxi's talent with a camera, Momma."

"It's rather small, don't you think? I hope I don't have to take any furniture back. We thought we'd drop the truck here and rent a car to go home."

Charles poked his head inside the front door, "We're ready to bring in the dresser and night stands. When we're done unloading, let's have dinner out. I hope this town has other restaurants, more than the ones I saw at the interstate."

"You name it. I'll find it for you, Daddy."

"*Tsk. Tsk.*" Macy shook her head as she measured the living room space. "Fifteen by fifteen."

"It's cozy, Momma. It suits me fine. The kitchen is over here." She walked from the living room, through the dining room and made a right turn past the breakfast bar. Her sneakers squeaked against the terrazzo floor. "I get to do whatever I want with this place. No family council vote on what color to paint a room. I wouldn't have that freedom if I rented an apartment. This is fine. Perfect for me. I can do almost any work the house needs by myself. By necessity, I learned to be handy at Fleur de Lis."

"Yes, there is that."

"You don't like it, do you?"

"No. It's not that." Macy paused. "I'm just wondering why you bought a house when you promised to move back in two years and take over your duties."

Rather than go head-to-head with the old argument, Branna sighed and changed the subject.

"Where do you think the couch will work best, Momma?" She tried sounding chipper.

Who was she kidding? She was the next Keeper of Fleur de Lis. The title had ruled her life since the day she was born. Was it a pipe dream to think she could break free of a hundred-plus years of family tradition encoded in her DNA? Why did legacy trump logic in a place where sweet tea ran more freely than the Mississippi River? Had no one but her ever considered the fact that just maybe she wasn't the person in the family best suited for the job?

"Well, you know how much I dislike a room with furniture plastered against all the walls—Branna, if you wanted to change the furniture at home in your room, why didn't you say so? You didn't need to do all this to make a statement or get my attention. I *do* value your opinion."

Little had changed in a hundred years at Fleur de Lis. Not only in the bedrooms, all the rooms, including the office where she spent many waking hours. Afternoon sunlight still streamed through the floor-to-ceiling windows and cast a warm glow on the ivory Aubusson rug. Matching Hepplewhite wingback chairs still flanked the fireplace. The antique clock on the mantel chimed every hour. Only one change in the décor of that room suggested modern times—a LCD monitor. Her life, like the office, had been structured and well planned.

The teaching job offered a ticket to a whole new life. At least for a little while. And a breather from the humiliation Steven had caused.

"Momma, let's roll up our sleeves and get to work. We've only got a few hours before you and daddy head home."

Chapter 5

Friday morning, Branna glanced at the salad ingredients on the counter. "Potluck dinners," she mused. "Jello salads and mystery food."

Every potluck she had ever attended offered at least one mystery—a casserole with unidentifiable ingredients masked by a cap of toasted breadcrumbs. Maybe things in Lakeview were different from Bayou Petite, the little town closest to home. She could hope.

She'd eaten her share of mystery food at church dinners and other community events, but other eating-out opportunities rarely happened. Fast food chains hadn't invaded Bayou Petite until several years ago. Before, she had to travel twenty minutes to Picayune for a drive-through experience, which held little appeal after growing up with Greta's mouth-watering cooking. Any white-linen dining event was still a special treat.

With Tab Benoit belting out *Jambalaya* on the stereo, she sang along and tossed lettuce and spinach with toasted pecans. Next, she sprinkled crumbled gorgonzola cheese on top for color and flavor, which made her mouth water. The salad always tasted better than it looked in the bowl. She hoped others would enjoy it. First impressions counted, and she wanted to put her best foot forward at the faculty potluck.

She finished off the salad creation by layering thin slices of strawberries—courtesy of Lakeland, Florida, the strawberry capitol—then she covered the large wooden bowl with plastic wrap. At the party, she'd toss the mixture with her special balsamic vinaigrette. The vinegar had been barrel-aged for twenty years. On the rare occasions when Greta allowed her to cook, she used only the best ingredients, especially for guests and strangers.

After placing the salad and bottle of dressing into a sturdy cardboard box, she added wooden "claws" for serving, then nervously hurried to the bedroom for one last check in the cheval mirror, the one her parents brought from Fleur de Lis, and completed a final once-over of her reflection.

Was she appropriately dressed for a faculty potluck? Did designer jeans and a blouse say casual, but smart? Hopefully. She hated the annoying jitterbug in her stomach. This wasn't an audition. She already had a signed contract for the job. The intention of tonight's event was fun.

But she hadn't done *fun* very well for many months, maybe years. "Organize and execute" were easier. Second nature to her.

"This is a new life," she said gazing at her reflection.

She wanted a new path, right? That's what she'd signed up for when she moved to Lakeview. She'd put "respectable" and "tradition" in the back seat and let "adventure" ride shotgun.

Heck, "adventure" needed to drive!

She re-checked the buttons on her sleeveless blouse with the tuxedo ruffle down the front. All buttoned correctly. The ruffle added a feminine touch—just in case she saw *him*. The mystery man from the storm.

After all, that must have been a brilliant first impression she made, diving to the bookstore floor during the storm. He couldn't possibly *not* remember her.

The man was gone when she had finally gotten it together.

With a sideways glance in the mirror, she checked her reflection again. White blouse, dark blue jeans and Jimmy Choo shoes—her one big splurge for the summer. They boosted her confidence. She plucked a tissue from the box on her dresser and wiped a smudge of lipstick from the corner of her mouth.

"It'll have to do."

Bzzz. Bzzz. Bzzz.

She raced to the kitchen without falling off the four-inch heels. The number wasn't one she recognized. "Hello?"

"Bran—talk—home—" She recognized her sister's voice over the lousy connection.

"I can't make out what you're saying." Why was she shouting into the phone? That never made things better.

"Talk—See—You—"

Before she could respond, the connection clicked, and her sister was gone. She pushed redial, but only a rapid busy signal pulsed in her ear.

She waited a minute and tried again. This time the call went straight to voicemail.

"Call me back," she said after the beep, then hung up. "Crap," she muttered, scrolling through her contact list. She found the number she sought, then pushed the call button. "Momma, Camilla just called me," she said before her mother had a chance to say hello. "The connection was bad. I'm on my way to a work function.

45

If I give you the number, will you try to reach her?"

"Word for word, what did she say, exactly?" her mother asked.

"All I could make out was 'talk' and 'home' before the line went dead. If you reach her, and there's no emergency, like she's dying or something, tell her I'll call her back at that number tomorrow. If it is an emergency, please call me back."

"I'm just happy she called you." The relief in her mother's voice gave her pause. Momma always worried about each of them, but until now, Branna hadn't understood how deeply Momma worried over Camilla, who was like a cat with nine lives and always landed on her feet.

However, neither she nor Momma had handled Camilla's current disappearing act very well.

"Love you, Momma. Got to run. Here's the number."

She ended the call after her mother's final good-bye, then turned in a circle scanning the countertops for her car keys. She spied them beside the fruit bowl, grabbed them, and then hoisted the box with her dinner offering into her arms before heading out the door.

The sun blazed in the late afternoon sky. A few wispy white clouds scooted across blue. A breeze was like outdoor air conditioning and had swept away some of the day's humidity.

Starting the car, she turned the A/C setting to high and blasted it, happy that air cooled her neck as she backed down the driveway.

Following the printed map, she drove the 35 mph speed limit. She'd heard the Westcott's had a palatial-size home, however, given the size of the faculty, she guessed the gathering might be held outdoors. She glanced again at the directions as she neared the lake and navigated through the oldest part of town. It once had an Indian name, which translated meant "Alligator," but as the town grew, the name changed to Lakeview in honor of the large body of water. Though, she'd been cautioned about wandering around the shoreline alone. A few gators still made it their home.

The road meandered. Coming around a bend, she spotted the yellow Victorian. No white pickup in sight. Had farmer-guy bought the place? Maybe in a few months, if she got up enough nerve, she'd knock on the door and ask for a tour. Most folks with old houses liked to show them off, though she still didn't understand why Meredith had chosen to sell.

"Give up Fleur de Lis?" she said, shaking her head. "Not wanting to be the Keeper is one thing, selling the place to strangers, well, that just won't ever happen."

Generations of family had lived there. Currently, four generations moved in and out as needed; their home would always remain in the family. Linds, Covingtons, and Dutreys would ensure its succession forever.

Once past the yellow Victorian, she chuckled, remembering farmer-guy's stained straw hat. Charlie One Horse. Her brother had bought one in Gatlinburg, Tennessee during a family vacation, and then thought he had to have a swagger to go with the hat. She had laughed so hard she'd cried. He always managed to brighten her mood. He was one man she would remove from the "enemy male" list.

"Daddy, too." She contemplated the list of men she knew. Many had wonderful qualities. There was only one man she'd toss to the Devil.

"Steven," she hissed.

If they'd married, they'd be celebrating their sixth-month anniversary—maybe. Odds were that if she'd married the snake, they'd be on their way to a divorce anyway. As Granddaddy Lind always said, "A leopard doesn't change its spots."

Steven hadn't crossed her mind in a while. A welcomed relief from the agony and shame of learning that he was both a liar and a cheat. After breaking their engagement, she'd cried for days, but never confided the reason she refused to marry him. She couldn't bring herself to say she'd found him in bed, the bed they picked out together, with another woman. As if that wasn't bad enough, he had the unmitigated audacity to try to convince her that it wasn't what she thought. Later, he tried to blame her with legal mumbo-jumbo about her part in the problem because he couldn't keep his pants zipped!

He'd destroyed her trust.

But she hated herself for not reading the signs. Hindsight was always 20/20. Broken dates with lame excuses. Dragging his feet on wedding details. Her sister had even covered for him once. That made the pain of his betrayal cut deeper.

"All men don't cheat," she reminded herself. Could there be a world without men? She'd managed without one for six months, and it left her feeling wiser.

And now she was on her way to meet a man Dr. Brown had assigned to her. How would that work out?

She made a right turn and pulled through ornate, wrought iron gates that swung open from tall stone pillars. Impressive, if not intimidating, the gates of Dr.

Westcott's home.

Vehicles parked along the wide u-shaped drive, some two abreast. She pulled her Volvo into the next open space and hoped someone wouldn't block her in, in case she exited early.

"Hey, Branna Lind, glad you could make it!" Brian hollered.

He trotted in her direction as she stepped from her car. She waved to him, then spied the old beat-up white truck. Was farmer-guy there? It might be easier to make conversation with him, than with other faculty members. They could talk "house." She wanted to hear about the remodeling, assuming he bought it. Of course, she'd make the appropriate apology for her prior rudeness.

"Hi Brian." She smiled when he appeared beside her. She reached inside her trunk for the box with her salad.

"Here, let me," Brian said, setting down a bag and extracting the box from her arms.

His familiar face eased the anxiety of meeting an entire staff of people. She picked up Brian's bag. A couple of liters of soda.

"Guys," Brian said. "We don't cook."

"Right." She'd never had a guy cook for her. Most guys she knew were interested in wrangling a dinner invitation from her only to eat Greta's cooking.

"So this is where the great and powerful Westcott lives?" she joked.

"Yes, Mrs. Westcott is very powerful." Brian grinned. "She is a Littleton. They're into everything...automotive."

She cocked her head, urging him to continue.

"She's from an old family. They own the Lincoln and Cadillac dealership in town, a tow truck company, an auto parts store and a detailing shop. You know, one of those places that paint trucks to look like that." He motioned to a blood-red Ford truck with yellow and oranges flames painted behind the wheels.

"I see." She filed the information way, in case she needed the tidbit in the future. Like at a party during a trivia game about the college president. Or to have her Volvo painted.

"Yeah, the doctor married up when he married her," he said.

Brian didn't bother to ring the doorbell, just opened the front door and walked in as if he owned the place. She followed his lead.

"My mother and Claire, Mrs. Westcott that is, are second cousins on their mother's side," he whispered. They reached the dining room where desserts covered every surface, and a woman directed traffic.

"Brian, as if I don't see you enough."

"Cousin Claire, this is one of the new faculty members. Please meet Miss Branna Lind."

"Welcome. And I'll bet you're the one who brought the salad," Mrs. Westcott said, peering into the open box.

Brian gasped with mock surprise. "You *know* I can toss a salad."

Mrs. Westcott smiled sweetly at her, then turned to Brian. "You can toss a football, toss a basketball into a hoop, but toss a salad? You can't toss that one over on me."

They laughed. She liked Mrs. Westcott. Though she couldn't quite reconcile the middle-aged woman in a pressed linen dress, wearing sandals and pearls as the wife of the much-older Dr. Westcott. She wondered if Mrs. Westcott had ever been on *the horns of a dilemma.*

"If you wouldn't mind, Brian, please take the salad to the buffet table out back. The food is arranged under one of the tents. Ms. Lind, I look forward to visiting with you." Mrs. Westcott left them to greet other incoming guests.

"I like her," Branna said.

Brian grinned. "Yeah, she's great. Paddled my butt a time or two when I was kid and got out of line. She's always Cousin Claire to me."

She followed Brian out the back door to a wide expanse of yard. A wooden dance floor had been constructed a few feet in front of the opening of the long tents that formed a *U.* Another tent on the other side of the dance floor protected the band as they played on a raised stage. Large fans, like ones she'd seen on the sidelines at professional football games, cooled the crowd.

The two side tents were dedicated spaces for dining. Cloth-covered tables showed off flower centerpieces and chairs offered seating. Pots and serving dishes and casseroles lined the tables of the self-serve food tent. Given the setup of the tents and the crowd flow, it appeared Mrs. Westcott had organized this type of function before. It all looked effortless, but Branna had experience with event planning and understood the magic that happened behind the scenes.

"Miss Lind, welcome!" Dr. Westcott boomed. From the food tent, he motioned to her. She picked her way, careful of where she stepped. Darn Jimmy Choos. Her heels caught in the soft ground making her bobble like a doll.

"Salads on this end," Dr. Westcott told Brian, who placed her salad bowl on the table. "Adult beverages are over there." Dr. Westcott pointed to the far side of the tent where a bar stood with tubs of drinks surrounding it.

"Thank you, sir. I think I'll get a glass of wine," she said. "After I toss the salad."

"Enjoy yourselves." Dr. Westcott slapped Brian on the back.

"I'll catch up with you in a few minutes," Brian said when Dr. Westcott wandered away. "Save me a dance." Then, he, too, disappeared into the throng.

Alone, she scanned the crowd as she crossed the tent to the beverage bar. She recognized a few faces, folks she'd met during her interview, but didn't see the man who owned the beat up pickup. Nor her mystery man. Maybe her assumption was wrong. Maybe he wasn't a faculty member after all.

"Dr. Brown, nice to see you." She greeted the Vice President with a handshake.

"Nice to see you, Ms. Lind. I hope you'll enjoy yourself this evening. You remember Ms. Parker?"

"It's Vivian. Please, call me Vivian," the woman said with a lilting laugh.

The woman's grace, her perfect blond hair, perfect manicured nails, chic summer dress and not-too-high heels charmed Branna. Vivian reminded her of her mother—in only the best way, however, she doubted Miss Vivian would appreciate the comparison.

"I want to introduce you to the man you haven't met, *yet*. But I haven't seen him. I'll find you when I can tie him down," Dr. Brown said, looking around.

"Branna," a raspy voice called.

Riggs made a beeline in her direction. The short stocky man was the antithesis of what she expected whenever she thought of a basketball coach. If someone had said football or wrestling, she'd believe that, but Lakeview Community College didn't have a football or wrestling team. The squat man chewed on the end of a fat unlit cigar and hiked up his pants at the waist when he reached her.

"You're gonna have to come watch us play," he said out of one side of his mouth.

"Ah, sure. I can do that."

"We're gonna make the playoffs this year. Might go all the way in our division!"

Branna stared and nodded. Did Coach think she was hard of hearing? Must, given the way he was yelling at her.

"Hello, Coach. I need to borrow Ms. Lind." Bitsy Webster, Dr. Brown's secretary, stepped into the conversation. She linked her arm with Branna's. "I brought my famous spinach and artichoke dip. I know how much you love it."

Bitsy took another step away and pulled her along. "Later," she called over her shoulder, continuing the retreat.

Branna tried to stay upright while she walked mostly backwards. Bitsy still clutched her arm. The woman had to be close to Grandmother Lind's age. Even had the apple-round cheeks and warm smile of a perfect grandmother. Her shiny gray hair curled into a halo around her head, and a pair of reading glasses hung around her neck.

"Whew! Thank goodness the heat and humidity let

up." Bitsy turned and continued to march her across the yard. "Riggs can be one intense man."

They stopped by two empty chairs and Bitsy motioned for Branna to sit. "I've known Arty for years. He's not much to look at, but he's a winning coach."

"I see." She couldn't think of anything else to say.

"Oh, yeah, honey. He's really a marshmallow-moon pie."

"Good to know."

"Well, he can get excited, ya know—talking sports—I didn't want you to ruin your pretty white blouse. He has a tendency to spit." Bitsy's mouth curled into an apologetic grin.

"Spit?" Did she really want to know?

"Talking and chewing at the same time when he eats. Not a good thing."

"I see." It wasn't a pleasant picture.

"Grab a plate and get some food. Everyone's nice." Bitsy hurried off when the band started up an old country song.

Branna sat. She watched Dr. Brown move Vivian around the dance floor, and then when the band came to the end of the song, Dr. Brown folded Vivian backward into a dip. Even over the music, she heard Vivian's lilting laugh.

She heard love in the laughter. Sadness pinched her heart. She had never laughed like that with Steven. She never looked at Steven the way Vivian looked at Dr. Brown.

Vivian was a woman in love. Would she ever look at a man like that? Well, certainly not at her boss. As for Vivian and Dr. Brown, their relationship in or out of school wasn't her business, and she wouldn't pry. Yet, she envied the ease of company the two shared. Their love.

She came to Lakeview to work. She'd pour all of her energy into her students and take up a new hobby. Maybe pottery. Maybe she'd get a pet. A dog. The one pickup-guy had with him appeared impressively obedient. Yes, she'd investigate a dog.

"I'm back," Brian said. "How about that dance?" He offered his hand.

"Now?" she asked. Brian had no clue that dancing made her squeamish. She'd embarrassed herself in public more than once at the charity ball her mother hosted each year. Folks at home expected sub-par dance moves from her. Often, she was the free entertainment. That wasn't the impression she wanted her fellow faculty members to have of her. "Maybe later?" she pleaded sheepishly.

"No pressure. I'll find you before the night is over." Brian snagged a passing woman and with a tug, both were on the dance floor.

Wanting to be farther from the dancing, she rose and started in the direction she'd originally intended— to the beverage bar. Something in her hands would mask her awkwardness. Maybe Dr. Newbern would show, they would make polite, but brief conversation, and then she could thank her hosts and leave. After living all her life in a small community where everyone knew everyone else, or was related, she'd taken social events for granted. Here, she was a fish out of water.

The crowd had doubled in size since her arrival. As if walking a maze, she wove her way between people, smiling and nodding as she wandered. She finally made it to the bar. No server waited behind the counter as she'd seen before. On the ground, washtubs filled with ice held bottles of soda and water.

She bent to pluck a bottle of water from a tub when Cole Haan loafers, just like the ones she'd picked out for her bother, stepped up to the opposite side of the tub. A masculine hand grabbed the same bottle she reached for.

"May I get that for you?"

She straightened. "It's you!"

"From the bookstore." The man smiled. Her heart melted. He was sexier than she remembered. Before, she had viewed him through rain-drenched glass, now with nothing between them, he appeared in sharp focus, filling the breadth of her vision.

Her face warmed, and she offered her hand, hoping her face hadn't turned ten shades of red. "I'm Branna Lind."

The man grinned wider, yet instead of taking her hand, he held his up, as he'd done when glass separated them that afternoon. "Hello Branna Lind. Nice to meet you."

Her face heated more. Was he mocking her? Or teasing?

"That was silly of me...at the bookstore. I don't know what to say. The storm. Lightning. The exploding tree..." She was babbling. Embarrassment did that to her. Hadn't she had enough humiliation? "Nice to meet you..."

When he didn't offer his name, to cover her discomfort, she twisted on the top to open the bottle of water. Soaked in condensation, it slipped through her fingers. He caught it before it hit the ground, opened it, and handed back to her.

"How 'bout a dance? I saw you watching Dr. Brown and Ms. Parker."

His smile disarmed her. A true deer-in-the-headlights experience. A lock of hair fell across his forehead, same as it had that afternoon. Lacing her fingers around the bottle stopped her from reaching up and running them through his hair.

"Dance?" After the bookstore incident, she couldn't look any more foolish to him, right? She'd already ruined any opportunity for a great first impression. Did anyone ever make a good second one? A twirl around the floor might be a way to redeem her image, if only she could move both feet without looking at them.

"Yes? Dance?" he asked.

Her brain said, "No. No. No," but she heard her mouth answer, "Yes."

"Great." His eyes twinkled. An energy about him made her wish her dancing skills could outshine any other woman's at the party. She'd settle for a chance just to spend time with him. Even if it meant dancing. There was something so compelling about him, she couldn't put it into words. The intense pull of attraction baffled her, but heck—she was up for the adventure.

Besides, he still hadn't mentioned his name. She wouldn't leave the party without finding it out. "What about your job?" she asked.

"Job? Oh, the bar? Naw, I'm just helping out. It's Brian's job tonight. He'll be back in a moment. Besides, there are only adults here. If they can't make themselves a drink, then they can do without." He held out his hand, tilted his head toward the band and the dance floor, then raised his eyebrows, challenging her once more.

"Well...Okay." What better way to get to know him than to dance? Was it the Italians who said dancing was like making love? That made her want to fan the blush creeping into her face. "Am I allowed to know your name?"

"How about a dance first?"

Flustered, she didn't know how to refuse. She had no clue who he was, but guessed he had to be a faculty member, otherwise, why would he be there? She took a sip of water, recapped the bottle, then gently grasped his outstretched hand. The quivering sensation that raced through her when their fingers touched made her jerk back. She stared at him.

He looked nothing like redneck-guy from the Victorian.

Was there something in the air in Lakeview, or was it the water?

He reached for her hand and held tight. She couldn't ignore the thrill of touching him. Just his hand. The rapid pounding of her heart made her thankful the band played loudly, otherwise, she was certain everyone could hear the thudding in her chest. She would never admit to anyone that she bubbled with giddiness as she followed that man, a stranger, to the dance floor. A bold move. Different from the Branna Lind that everyone in Bayou Petite knew. The one that was expected to be totally proper at all times. Which meant never dancing with a stranger. No matter how hot he looked.

On the dance floor, he moved well. She was a poor partner for someone so accomplished. When she missed a step and landed with her heel on his toes, he grimaced, then swung her into another step, one where her heels missed his toes. With her lack of smooth moves, she wouldn't have thought dancing would be enjoyable, however, unless he faked things really well, the grin on his face said he was having fun, too. When was the last time she'd danced and enjoyed herself, completely unconcerned about appearances? And she had thought fun was overrated. Silly her.

However, *déjà vu* haunted her.

The sexy man in front of her, the Brooks Brothers, country-club type, with broad shoulders and muscled arms, bore no resemblance to the shaggy-haired, unshaven, pickup dude she'd met while house hunting.

Except...her palms heated with a quivering tingle whenever they met his.

What was up with that?

Chapter 6

James spun Branna again, then dipped her to the shimmer of the drummer's cymbals as the band wrapped up their set. While they had danced, the world became a cocoon, a world of only two with music. Rapid pulses raced through him each time he touched her. It puzzled him, but the delight could become a powerful addiction.

Did she feel it, too?

The drummer made a final *boom* on the bass drum. Everyone ended their dancing and applauded the band's performance, then wandered off the dance floor when the band left on a break. The tinny sounds of recorded music flowed through the sound system, a poor second to the live performance.

Flames from Tiki torches staked around the yard licked the night air. Was it his imagination, or did the flickering light add sensuality to the scene? In the west, beyond the torchlight, the last hints of sunlight reflected off scattered high clouds. The humidity had dialed back with the setting sun, and the breeze made the almost-summer evening perfect.

He followed Branna, watching her walk. Her hips swayed. Her jeans hugged the curves of her butt nicely. Her short hair bounced as she stepped in high heels, reminding him of a perky rabbit hopping down a path. A path that led to where? He didn't care, as long she was in view.

While they danced, her face had glowed, even when she wasn't smiling. Her strappy sandals, pretty fancy for a backyard party, put her at the right height, fitting her body perfectly to his when they danced close.

Her hazel eyes had remained locked on his while they moved together. His gaze kept wandering to the sweet fullness of her lips...it took all he had not to lower his mouth to hers. Thankfully, when the intensity of the pull almost got the best of him, she managed to step on his toes. Only once did a pointy heel strike a seriously damaging blow. He'd ice his toes later.

His attraction to her surprised him, but he wouldn't allow an investigation into the allure. He never played where he worked. Never. A rule that had served him well. Besides, her captivating charms, her "beautiful" vibe, pushed his caution meter into the red zone. He always heeded that warning. Caroline had made him discriminating about his female company. However, he could enjoy any view with Branna in it. *Look, but don't touch.* The voice in his head mocked him. "Yeah, right. Good luck with that."

"You're a good dancer," he said, catching up to her and resting his hand in the small of her back. The urge to touch her, to connect with the pulsing sensation, drew him uncontrollably.

"You're a good liar." She smiled.

"How about a bite to eat? I know a good place that serves food." When she gave him a puzzled expression, he pointed to the food tent.

"Sure." She nodded, but he suspected she had thought he was offering to take her somewhere else.

All evening he'd been waiting for her to remember.

Waiting for that moment of recognition.

Would she give him the cold shoulder then? So far, she hadn't let on that they'd met before. He'd bet good money that she hadn't put all the pieces together. She couldn't possibly be that schooled in politeness. If so, he'd never play poker with her. Usually he could sense a bluff. She showed no signs. The idea that she would laugh and dance with him now, but hadn't given him even a brief "hello" at their first encounter, made him chuckle.

How would she respond when she finally figured it out?

He, however, remembered her *very* well.

The electrical charge when they first touched...if he were a Christmas tree, he would've lit up for the whole town to see.

He should have put the puzzle pieces together sooner, though. After all, how many new Brannas could there be in town? He hadn't stopped long enough to consider that fact when Dr. Brown gave him the mentoring assignment. He hadn't asked for Miss Lind's first name.

Something about her drew him like a starving man to a feast. What if, just for tonight, he could put aside his no-fraternization rule? After all, this wasn't a date, but a faculty party. Technically, since she was new, their official capacity of mentor/mentee didn't begin until Monday. What if?

He joined her in the short line at the buffet. As she waited for people before them, she turned to him. "I'm hungry, Mr..."

"Here." He pointedly ignored her hint at introductions. Instead, he offered her a plate from the remaining stack. It appeared most folks had eaten while he and Branna had danced.

"Thanks, but you still haven't told me your name. I'm sure it's not, *Mr. Here*." She pinned him with a stare.

He winked. "How about we stick with the mystery for a little while longer. I promise, I'm harmless."

Did her shrug mean surrender? At least for the moment?

Tonight he'd connected the dots from the woman at the Victorian to the one in the bookstore. That woman, a watery image beyond the widow, had looked vulnerable and scared. The antithesis of the woman before him. Who would've guessed that when he first met Branna, that day with Meredith, that she'd turn out to be his mentoring assignment for the semester?

And the most attractive woman he'd met in a very long while.

Had Dr. Brown set him up?

"Are you one of those guys who doesn't eat anything green?" she asked. She dished salad from a wooden bowl onto her plate.

"No. I eat green. Why?"

"Then, try this." With odd wooden paddles, she scooped up a pile of salad and plopped it onto his plate. "I happen to have it on good authority that it tastes great."

"I'll be the judge of that," he told her skeptically.

As they navigated the rest of the food line, he couldn't stop sneaking glances in her direction. Was Newton's Third Law at play? "Force is a push or a pull that results from its interaction with another." Despite the strong magnetic pull from her that said "*come hither*," usually, her kind of woman made him want to run for cover. Caroline had taught him that. Her kind fished for a guy, held him on her line, and after playing the line for a while, dumped him cold. Catch and release. Only Caroline had caught, released, then tried to hook him again. He wasn't a slow study. One "Caroline" experience was enough to last any man a lifetime.

In Branna's case, the worst of it was, she had beauty and brains, too. That made her more dangerous than the average high-maintenance type. He had to admit, the woman had a lot going in her favor. He'd read her resume and credentials before Dr. Brown hired her, though he still wondered why she had worked as an event planner in some small hole-of-a-nothing town. In Mississippi no less. For the last several years. And, why teach adult education classes at night?

Not his problem. Who understood a woman's mind, anyway?

"Any idea what this is?" Branna asked. She peered into a chafing dish where something had been topped with toasted breadcrumbs.

"Nope," he said. "And I don't eat mystery food."

Her laugh reminded him of soft tinkling wind chimes.

"Hmm. I would've guessed quite the opposite...coming from a mystery man." She placed a dollop from the dish onto his plate. Rather than argue, it was his turn to shrug.

When they neared the end of the food line, their plates groaning, Bitsy made a beeline toward them. He frowned, and tried to wave her away without Branna noticing. It didn't work.

"I see you've met our most eligible bachelor," Bitsy said coyly to Branna. She tilted her head, motioning toward him as though he wasn't standing there with a loaded dinner plate.

"Yes. Yes, she has," he interrupted, hoping Bitsy wouldn't blow his cover.

"Branna, you're in good hands."

"And, whose hands would those be, exactly?" Branna smiled sweetly.

"Why—"

"Bitsy, I see Fred over there by the bar." He alerted the older woman. She always kept a watchful eye on her husband. Fred's prescription caused unpleasant side effects if combined with alcohol. When Bitsy took off in Fred's direction, he motioned for Branna to join him in the other tent. He set his plate in front of an empty chair and held the next one out for her.

"You're good. But you know, I'll find out your name sooner than later."

She sat, and then he seated himself beside her.

"Hey, this salad is really good." He hoped to distract her from the topic she appeared bent on pursuing. The mystery kept them on an even playing field. Once his identity was revealed, he'd be her mentor and her colleague, and flirting would be off the table. He wasn't ready for that yet.

What had Dr. Brown been thinking? The man had listed an inventory of Ms. Lind's accomplishments and noted her background, then suggested that James and Ms. Lind had a lot in common. School, career, and old southern families. He should have been suspicious when Dr. Brown hadn't segued into a lecture about finding the right woman and creating a whole, fulfilling life. Nothing like an old reformed bachelor trying his hand at matchmaking.

Had Dr. Brown created this mentor program to push Branna at him? Couldn't be. But, if so, Dr. Brown needed to stick to college matters, he wasn't qualified to play cupid. That arrow was bound to go astray, and someone could get seriously hurt. And while the woman in question oozed with charm that drew him irrationally like a fish to a shiny lure, that same charm could be a Pandora's box of trouble. Trouble he didn't want.

"I think this is green bean casserole," he said, tasting the mystery food on his plate, courtesy of Branna.

She grinned at him.

They finished their food, and a server came to clear their plates. When the young woman reached for his, he touched her hand, trying to make it look like an accident.

No tingle.

No shimmer.

No pulsing sensation.

Nothing.

What was the thing happening between him and Branna?

"It's getting late. I need to be going." Branna started to rise.

"One more dance?" He hooked his little finger with hers. The mere connection of a finger looped with a finger started a rhythmic pulsating beat. It made him want to run, but the attraction to stay was stronger. He needed to look up Newton's Laws to understand the phenomena. There had to be an explanation. Otherwise,

Monday could be a problem. A big one.

No. He would put aside his personal issues and conduct himself as a professional. Helping Branna learn the lay of the land, helping her understand about the college and her job, was something he could handle with politeness. Anything more—beyond another dance tonight—was out.

"Okay, one more dance. Are you a glutton for punishment or what?" Branna giggled. She glanced at his feet pityingly and shook her head, then maneuvered through the crowd.

He followed, admiring the view.

One dance turned into four.

And he never knew the power of a scowl until that night. It kept several people from blowing his cover, but his time was running out. He had to tell her. Soon.

"How 'bout a drink?" Branna asked, touching her fingers to her flushed cheeks.

He caught her around the waist for one last twirl. His feet could use a break; his toes would be black and blue tomorrow. Tonight it didn't matter.

"I know the bartender personally. He'll give us a free drink." Branna winked.

"Wine? Or hard liquor?" He gave her a once over, trying to guess her preference.

"Well, what do you think?"

He studied her intently. "I think...you're probably both. But it's not yet a tequila night. Wine," he finally decided.

She laughed. "Water will do me fine. No alcohol when I drive. I'm leaving in a bit."

"What? The night is young!"

"Ah, but this girl turns into a pumpkin at

midnight."

"Don't you have your fairytales mixed up? Cinderella fled. The coach turned into a pumpkin. I'm a guy, and I know that."

"I don't think Coach"—she nodded her head in Riggs' direction—"would appreciate knowing he might be a pumpkin at midnight."

"Cute. Cinderella, I'll want another dance before I put you in your coach. Wait right here. I'll get you that drink."

He wrangled his way through the crowd, grabbed two bottles of water, and returned to find Branna deep in conversation with Dr. Brown. As he approached, the glint in Branna's eye said his identity had been revealed.

"I see you found him, Ms. Lind. This is the guy I wanted you to meet. The one who's been dodging me," Dr. Brown said gruffly.

"Yes, it does appear that I've found the famous Dr. James Newbern." Branna's grin was forced.

"Busted," James said sheepishly, disappointed to have been found out. He had no excuse for being an ass. Except as long as she didn't know who he was, he hadn't broken his rule of no fraternization. He could get to know her freely without any expectations.

"I believe you'll benefit from Dr. Newbern's assistance. The goal is to ease the transition of our new instructors."

Dr. Brown shook his hand, leaned close, and whispered, "She's got a lot of potential. A great asset to the college. Do your best, but keep it professional."

With a wave, Dr. Brown and Vivian left them. Alone with Branna, James offered her the bottle of water. "You promised me one more dance."

Branna drank slowly, smiled, then replied, "*Really*, Dr. Newbern? You want *more*?" She didn't sound like she was into the dancing idea, but she held out her hand. He wouldn't let her glare stand in the way of holding her in his arms one last time. Maybe he could convince her he wasn't a total ass.

This time when they danced, she moved mechanically in his arms, keeping a distance between them. She gazed at some faraway spot over his shoulder, rather than look him in the eyes. She stepped on his toes multiple times. Payback, he assumed, for his deception. For once in his life, he could read a woman's mind. Hers flashed—anger.

The moment the band stopped playing, Branna dropped her grasp of his hand and left the dance floor.

"Well, thanks for the dance." Hoofing it to catch up to her, he was certain a different type of storm headed his way. Had a hurricane ever started as tropical storm Branna?

"So you are the famous Dr. Newbern." Her smile was saccharine-sweet, and her voice smacked with accusation.

"I don't know about famous."

"Dr. Brown said you've been dodging him for a couple of weeks."

"Not dodging. Attending to personal business," he corrected.

Her smile fell. "Oh. Well, that explains it. I guess I shouldn't take it personally. Dr. Newbern, would you mind walking me out? In case someone's blocked my car? You can use your disappearing powers to make it move out of the way."

"Sure."

He stood at the top of the steps as Branna thanked the Westcotts, then gathered a wooden salad bowl from the table. The crowd's laughter drifted on the breeze. The white tents glowed red, green, blue, and yellow from the hanging colored lanterns. The break in the weather had made the festivities enjoyable. Mrs. Westcott had probably ordered that, too. From where he stood, surveying the party below, it looked like a spread from a magazine. Mrs. Westcott had done it again.

"Thanks for waiting," Branna said. She climbed the back steps.

They walked in silence, making their way through the house out to the horseshoe drive.

"I'm being nosy," Branna said and pressed the key remote for her car. The trunk of an old Volvo popped open, and she placed her bowl inside. "Do you see that truck over there?" She pointed to an old white pickup as she closed the trunk.

"Yeah."

"Do you know the guy that owns that truck?" Her gaze remained on the vehicle. "Was he here tonight?"

Her thoughtful gaze made him wonder about her speculation regarding *that* guy, and her question solidly confirmed what he already knew. She hadn't put two and two together. "He was there."

"Is he a friend of the Westcotts? Does he work at the college?"

Was she fishing for something? "Yes, he's acquainted with the Westcotts. Why?"

The dimly lit driveway made it difficult to see her face, but he hadn't imagined her grimace.

"I met him once. I think he bought the Victorian by

the lake. I thought maybe..." her words drifted off, and then her face brightened. "Oh, I just wanted to say, hello. That's all."

"Well, I'll try to remember to introduce the two of you the next time you're both in the same place."

He closed her car door once she was inside. She waved good-bye before driving away.

The evening had surprised him. She had surprised him more. But what would she do when she learned he and *that guy* were one and the same?

Chapter 7

Unwelcomed hints of morning slipped between the slats of the plantation shutters in Branna's bedroom. She groaned. It was Saturday, and she wanted nothing better than to sleep in. At home, the day always started early because of a wedding or a ladies' tea. She'd escaped all of that by moving to Florida, but there was no escaping her internal clock. Years of conditioning could not be undone in mere weeks.

Bzzz. Bzzz. Bzzz.

She reached for her phone and checked caller ID.

"Momma?"

"Good morning, Sunshine. I knew you'd be up."

"Of course," she said brightly as she snuggled down into the covers.

"I spoke to your sister, finally."

"And?"

"She says she's fine. Loving the wild west. However, she wants to talk to you."

Branna rolled her eyes and sighed.

"I heard that. Branna, when are you going to tell me what's going on? You and Ste—"

"Don't say his name!"

"You're being silly. What did Steven do that was so horrendous? You know, his mother keeps asking me what happened with the two of you. I'm embarrassed to repeat each month at bridge that I don't know.

However, it seems Steven isn't talking either. Although, he's saying he still wants to patch things up."

"With me or Camilla?" she muttered.

"What does Camilla have to do with this?"

"She took his side." The words sounded childish even to her, but she couldn't begin to utter the ugly truth to her mother. If she had her way, Momma would never know the depths to which Camilla had taken their sibling-rivalry.

"You're the oldest, Branna. You—"

"—have to set the example," she said, finishing her mother's sentence. She hated those words.

"If you won't talk to me, will you at least call your sister back?"

She hesitated. Taking the high road was expected of her, but she was sick of family expectations weighing her down. If her mother only knew the truth….she'd refuse to play bridge with Steven's mother ever again. Though that would only add fuel to the gossip about the breakup. How dare he try to cause a permanent rift in her family.

After months of dealing with warring emotions, she'd given up battling her pain and forgiven Camilla. She worried about her being so far away, but hadn't taken any steps to close the chasm between them. However, moving completely past Steven's betrayal...she'd failed that emotional mission so far, the battle still raged, but with much less fury than before.

"Of course. I'll call her."

"Today," her mother prodded.

"Yes. I promise, today."

"Someday you'll understand. As a mother, I want my family together. If I can't have them all together in a physical location, I at least want to know we're connected by love. Love you."

"Love you, too," she grumbled. So much for beauty rest and Saturday morning freedom.

She padded to the kitchen for coffee. At home, Greta made sure it waited in the pot, and no one ever had caffeine withdrawal. How that happened, she'd never given it any thought. Until now.

Brewed coffee produced a deeply satisfying aroma. She carried a mug on a plate with two chocolate-covered biscotti and wished for beignets. Making a mental note, she planned to check at the grocery store. Maybe they carried Café du Monde's beignet mix.

Snuggled in the covers, she relaxed. The call to Camilla could wait. She intended to enjoy the serenity of her bedroom, which hadn't happened by accident. She'd scoured magazines and websites for just the right decorating ideas. Modern mixed with traditional, rather than only period antiques, the décor that marked every single room at Fleur de Lis. And here, she had managed it all on a sliver of a budget.

Restless, she sat up, adjusted the covers, then sipped her coffee. Waking up slow and unhurried was luxurious. Today, there'd be no household emergencies before any scheduled event. She could even go back to sleep.

She dunked biscotti in her coffee and pulled the plate beneath her chin to catch crumbs before biting into the biscuit. The flavors melted together in her mouth, and she savored the texture of the melting chocolate. After setting the plate back on her nightstand, she pulled the sheet over her shoulder, turned on her side, and hugged her pillow close.

For one summer, between her junior and senior year of high school, she experienced freedom when splitting time between her Lind relatives, who lived on the island south of Slidell, Louisiana, and the small beach house her parents owned in Biloxi, Mississippi. After that, college, and then Fleur de Lis always took priority.

But this was her new life.

She wiggled her toes, and then slowly pulled her hands from beneath the sheet to examine them. The quivering tingle every time she touched James was weird. Had the lightning strike at the bookstore somehow messed up her nervous system? She'd seen something on NAT GEO about a man and his oddities after lightning struck him. But she hadn't taken an actual hit. Plus, there was the same sensation with the other guy, the pickup one. There had to be a reasonable explanation, right?

She traced the lines in her palm with her right index finger. She'd had her palm read once by a woman in a caftan and turban outside St. Louis cathedral in New Orleans. The woman told her things, many of which she couldn't remember. However, though she wasn't a palmist, a fortune teller or a medium, pure physics told her that she and James channeled some sort of weird current. An energy. Only, it made her want to touch James more.

"Dr. Newbern," she corrected. They were only colleagues. She had to remember his interest in her was merely professional. His job was to mentor her, and he was only doing his job. Maybe the whole thing was a test? Maybe because this was her first, full-time teaching job, Dr. Newbern was assigned to ensure her success? Or what if her success, or lack thereof, reflected on him? That could be a problem. She had to do well at work, not only for herself, but to make sure she reflected well on him.

James. The man had danced her off her feet. She hadn't played coy with him. Nor made excuses about her dancing abilities. He had no way of knowing that it wasn't her forte and that she'd failed dancing lessons 101 with a big fat F. After that, her mother had finally let her take up piano instead. She should have warned him that her dancing partners usually wore steel-toed boots. Instead, she abandoned her inhibitions and let him lead her to the dance floor. For once, she enjoyed the delight of someone asking her to dance. That was part of the new and improved Branna Lind.

"James Newbern, *Doctor* James Newbern." She chuckled. "Are you what the doctored ordered?"

His chocolate brown eyes had glinted with humor and tried to mask pain each time she stepped on his toes. Steven would have criticized once, then endured the rest of the dance in silence, always the gentleman he was raised to be when in the public's eye. After that, he'd make excuses not to dance with her again. It became a running joke between them. Usually Camilla or Biloxi, if she happened to be around, kept him occupied on the dance floor. That man loved to dance.

James, on the other hand, had been patient while she swallowed her embarrassment. The most magical moment of the night—when they danced until the drummer shimmered the cymbals to close out a song. James had twirled her one last time as if she were a princess at the ball.

But the picture fixed in her mind based on Dr.

Brown's earlier glowing remarks, and the man last night, didn't exactly fit. She'd thought Dr. Newbern was older and conservative, the tweed-jacket type.

She'd know more in time. Meanwhile, she had the whole weekend to herself. A luxury extraordinaire.

Rolling over, pulling the sheet over her shoulder, she drifted off to sleep.

Bzzz. Bzzz. Bzzz.

She jumped. Wading through the fog of sleep, she grabbed for the phone.

"Hello?" she whispered.

"Good morning. If you change into a pumpkin at midnight, what time do you change back?"

"Uh? What?" she stammered. "Who's speaking?" She tried to kick her brain into gear.

"James Newbern."

She sat up and clutched the sheet to cover herself, then rolled her eyes. For Pete's sake, he couldn't *see* her.

"What time is it?" she asked dragging her fingers through her hair.

"About ten."

"I won't become human again until noon." She stuffed another pillow behind her and leaned back.

"Wonder if the *New Rag* would be interested in an exclusive on you."

"Huh?"

"Well, then again, maybe they'll think I'm the crazy one for talking with a pumpkin."

"Ahh, a man who jokes before noon. I knew you were too good to be true." She clamped a hand over her mouth. Had she actually said those words aloud?

"You thought of me, too."

Her eyes grew wide. Was he flirting with her? Couldn't be. They were colleagues. Crap! How did she reply to that?

"I'm calling to invite you for a meal."

"Any meal or one in particular?"

"I'm trying to be nice. Trying to live up to the hype Dr. Brown's been feeding you about me. If you aren't busy, I'll give you a tour of the town. After all, its small, it won't take long. Then, a quick run to the college."

She looked at the clock. She could shower, change, and meet him at noon. She could delay painting her home office until later that afternoon.

"It's all about southern hospitality." His drawl drug out every syllable of every word.

She snorted. "Are you mocking my accent?"

"Now, why would I do that? Why would I insult you after inviting you out? I'm trying to be professionally sociable."

"I've been here for almost month. Whenever I came to campus, you were never around. So much for your southern hospitality."

"Hold on. Let's rewind. My peace offering is food. I feel bad we didn't meet before, but I wasn't dodging you. It wasn't personal. I have a busy schedule. Very tight deadline. Let me make it up to you. Lunch?"

"Well, maybe one o'clock?" She couldn't refuse. After all, they had to work together. No need to get off on a bad foot, especially after she had mangled all of his toes last night.

"Do you like bar-b-que?" he asked.

"Not so much." Just what she needed—up to her elbows in sauce and wearing it on her shirt.

"Fried chicken?"

"Um, well, yes, but too many calories."

"Well, how about a good ol' fashioned, home-style meal at the Magnolia Café?"

She'd heard it was downtown on the square where old-timers hung out and rubbed elbows with the lawyers and judges in town. Reviews by foodies said the place had an authentic, old southern feel, like grandma's kitchen, and the food ranked high for flavor and freshness.

"Perfect suggestion. I'll meet you there at one fifteen." She hung up before he had a chance to change the time.

Chapter 8

James stood back and looked at the room. It turned out how he'd envisioned. The first of the bedrooms to be painted, he was inspired when he started, but the spark had waned, and he was glad to be done. The information he found at the paint store recommended sea-foam green for calm, but calm came only after paint covered all the walls.

He dropped the roller into the empty metal paint tray. The clatter woke Beauregard, who raised his head as if to question the need for noise.

"Sorry, boy. I'm done. Feel free to go back to sleep."

He tried to force thoughts of Katie aside. They hit him every time he entered this room. Meredith had said it had been her nursery when she was born, then transformed into a pink palace for a little girl. He'd painted it a neutral color. All elements of "girl" had been removed. Though much of his grief over Katie had settled into sweet memories, occasionally, a painful one floated to the top. It always surprised him when some little reminder of his daughter grabbed him and wrung another pain from his heart. She'd been born three years ago, and lived for only five months.

Quite possibly, the room would've been hers. Would she have loved it? Had she lived, he would have painted the room any color she wanted, and then filled it with books and toys. Caroline had dumped all of Katie's things at Goodwill after Katie died.

He peeled off the blue tape used to protect the baseboards and moldings from wet paint. Splotches of color smeared his hands as he rolled the tape into a ball. Katie's sweet smile danced in his mind.

The first year following her death, he'd visited her grave each month. She rested there with other Newberns in Pine Mount cemetery, behind the church his great-great-grandparents had started. The church baptized, married, and buried generations of Newberns. He had paid extra to have a teddy bear carved on the back of the headstone. To his knowledge, Caroline had never seen it. The second year, after his mother suggested he might consider grief counseling, he visited Katie's grave every other month. During the last year, guilt had lessened, and he only placed flowers there on special occasions.

Ching. Ching. The doorbell interrupted his thoughts. He tossed a wad of tape into the trashcan, then wiped his hands on his jeans as he ran downstairs.

"Delivery," a uniformed man said, as if James couldn't see the large crate the man had perched on a dolly on the porch.

"Sign here." The man handed over a tablet-sized pad with a stylus attached. As James signed, the man wiggled the dolly from underneath the crate, then took back his pad and started down the steps.

"Wait," James called. "I need help getting this inside."

"Sorry. That's not what we do. Delivery is only to the front door."

"Shit. How do I get this inside?"

The man shrugged and ran to his truck pulling the wheeled dolly behind him.

As if on cue, James' cell phone vibrated in his back pocket.

"Hey! Wanna go skiing?" Bobby Park, his best friend since childhood, could be counted on for a good time.

"Can't."

"Whatever it is, drop it. Let's go."

"Got to find a way to get my gun safe from the front porch to the study *inside* the house."

"A problem?"

"Well, it's not like I'm used to pushing four-hundred pounds around with no help."

"I'll come."

"Naw. It's too far. Besides, I've got other work to do. It's not like someone's going to steal the thing. If they try, good luck to them. I'll call someone in town to come help me."

"House work or work-work?"

He shook his head. If he said he had a lunch appointment with a colleague, Bobby would ask with whom. If he told him, Bobby would call it a date, not work-work. Then, that news would be all over two counties before he could blink, with everyone taking bets on whether or not he'd make it to the altar with Miss Lind. Why did everyone think he had to get married?

"Work-work. The new semester starts Monday."

"Have fun, Professor. Maybe we'll ski and cook a pig over Memorial weekend. I can swing by tomorrow and help you."

"Great." He closed his phone as Beauregard

bounded down the stairs. At a fast trot, the dog cleared the front porch in a single leap and headed for the bushes. James looked at his watch. Noon straight up. He needed a shower before heading out to play tour guide. It wouldn't look good if he was late for the meeting—a make-up for the one he'd missed when the department chair welcomed Miss Branna Lind to the English department.

He owed her professional courtesy, but wondered exactly which virtues Dr. Brown had extolled about him. The older man was blind to all but his better qualities. He wouldn't want to embarrass Dr. Brown by being less than advertised. Maybe he'd call to invite the good doctor to join them for lunch.

"Beauregard, let's go. Back inside, boy."

He waited for Beau to enter and climb the stairs. Following the dob up the stairs, he trudged with the phone to his ear.

"Dr. Brown," he said when the older man answered. "I'm taking Miss Lind to lunch, then for a tour of town. Would you and Vivian like to join us?"

"We're on the boat on the St. Johns. Maybe next time you'll join us? Now, take good care of Miss Lind today. We want her to stay for a long while."

"Got it. Meeting her at one fifteen."

Walking into the bathroom, he shed his work clothes. Steam rose from the shower as he stepped inside. With hot water sluicing over his body, he contemplated his colleague. That's how he had to think of her. Anything else was too dangerous.

What would it take to persuade him to move, as Branna had done? Away from home and family. What was she leaving behind and why? Was it to escape?

He dried and dressed quickly. Downstairs, he rubbed Beau behind the ear. "Hey, fella. You're on guard duty, but I don't want to find any evidence of tail brushing on the wet paint in the room upstairs. I'll leave the music on to keep you company."

Hitting the button on the stereo, it sent out strains of Keb 'Mo picking on a Dobro guitar. Last October, he'd traveled to Austin, Texas to hear the man play. The Dobro had a sound all of its own, at least in the hands a master like Mr. Moore. Locally, country music trumped the blues, but that didn't matter to him. He'd never been one to follow the pack, preferring a solitary path, yet another reason he never dated anyone from work.

But he'd enjoyed Branna's company last night.

Was spending more time with her tempting fate?

Chapter 9

Branna arrived early for lunch with James. She parked her car in the lot behind the café and followed a stone path between two brick buildings. Flowerbeds trimmed the buildings' edges. She pictured a fairy world amongst the lush growing plants. Fragrance from hyacinth blooms tickled her nose. Taking in a deep breath, she allowed the scents of spring to renew her. A gentle breeze ruffled the skirt of her sundress as her flats tapped against the stone. She slipped her hair behind her ears, then adjusted her sunglasses without dropping her clutch. A perfect almost-summer day. She welcomed the new sense of freedom.

Ahead, a large sign loomed on the corner. She paused to read about Main Street's closure. The city's re-urbanization project revived the old square by closing the road to vehicle traffic. Brick replaced asphalt, making the historic street a pedestrian mall with old-fashioned gaslights. Aged wooden barrels filled with pink flowers and trailing greenery lined the sidewalks, giving the place an old, country-town feel. The effect was charming.

"Ahh, sweetness." Aromas of frying dough lifted to her nose and triggered hunger pangs. Her stomach grumbled loudly. Two biscotti and coffee hadn't lasted very long, but she had fifteen minutes until the scheduled appointment with James. Maybe window-shopping would take her mind off of food.

Branna gazed down the street. Two-story brick buildings with second-floor wooden balconies covered and shaded the sidewalk below. It gave the town even more of a bygone-era feel, a familiarity after living in an antebellum home.

"Jewelry store. Children's Shop. Lovely Ladies dress shop." She recognized the L L logo. "Designer shoes. Bookstore. Donut shop. Bakery. The oldest Drug Store in town," she itemized aloud. The sign advertised an old-fashioned soda fountain with malts and shakes.

Her mouth watered as her stomach growled like an angry hound. She had no one to blame but herself. She alone was responsible for selecting the hour of their meeting.

A small milkshake would stay her stomach hound. It was a short walk to the drugstore. She peered inside like she had done as a child whenever her mother took her to town, only now she didn't cup her hands to shade her eyes and push her nose to the glass. An empty counter with evenly spaced stools, bright red seats against shiny chrome, stretched the full length of the long sidewall. A man stood behind an antique cash register wearing an old-fashioned paper hat, a throwback to black and white photographs she'd seen of soda jerks from the fifties.

Across from the counter, three rows of long shelves held twenty-first century sundries. The theme of the store might be vintage, but the items for sale were contemporary. In one of the aisles, a teenaged girl stood in front of a nail polish display with her hands folded in prayer. The earnestness on the young face touched Branna with an aching tenderness. She removed her sunglasses for a better look. Then, looked again.

It was the girl who had run out in front of Meredith. There couldn't be two girls in town with the thick long braids that bumped their butts, could there? She looked maybe thirteen, fawn-colored hair, peaches and cream complexion, and a pink cupid's-bow mouth. The girl would grow into a beauty. Her flowered T-shirt hung over an ankle-length faded denim skirt that looked like hand-me-downs from the sixties. Maybe a thrift-store find. Either her parents were old hippies or she wanted to stand out in a crowd. An unusual trait when teenagers usually tried painfully hard to fit in.

The girl unfolded her hands, then glanced around skittishly. She turned and positioned her body with her back to the cash register.

Curious, Branna watched. The girl opened a bottle of blood-red polish, painted a swath on her pinky finger, and then capped the bottle quickly. She reached her hand away to admire her single red nail. Branna looked on with fascination, it was like watching a sweet coming-of-age movie.

The girl looked up. Shocked pale-blue eyes locked with Branna's. The girl reached into her skirt pocket, yanked out a small white cloth and with a quick swipe, wiped away all evidence of the red polish. Though the girl turned sideways, Branna saw her stuff the small bottle into her pocket. She waited to see what the girl intended next.

The teen moved aimlessly around the store as Branna opened the door to enter. Bells tinkled, announcing her arrival. Branna intended to rescue the girl. If she paid for the polish, maybe that would set an example, and she'd stop an innocent from committing a crime. She'd heard too many times to count, from her mother and family, about how she must set an example.

When she was barely two steps inside the store, the girl pushed past her at a run.

"Wait!" Branna started after her, but the teen turned the corner, vanishing into the alley.

But without her lace-edged hankie.

A smear of brilliant red marred the delicate, once pristine white cloth.

Puzzled, Branna picked up the fallen hankie. The girl had stolen the polish. Why? No money? Her parents didn't allow painted nails? Would the drugstore clerk know the girl? If she asked about her and the polish, would he call the police?

She tucked the lacy cloth into her purse. If she ever found the girl, they'd talk about stealing. But more importantly, did she have a responsibility to tell the girl's parents what she witnessed? That was something she'd have to think on.

The large clock on the courthouse clicked to one fifteen. She hurried toward the Magnolia Café, half way down the block. James sat on the bench out front looking relaxed in golf shorts, polo shirt, and sneakers. Did he have a tee time later?

"Have you been waiting here long?"

"A minute."

"Did you see the girl run from the drug store?"

"Yep."

"Which way did she go?"

"That a-way." James pointed in both directions like Scarecrow from the Wizard of Oz as a pair of joggers ran in opposite directions in front of them.

"You're no help. Seriously, this girl was young.

Early teenager with braided hair down to her waist."

"No, didn't see her."

Something about the girl and the polish just didn't sit right, but she couldn't figure it out. Lakeview wasn't that big; in time she'd find the girl and have a chat.

"You could've hollered at me when you arrived. I was only window shopping." She sat on the other end of the bench from James hoping he was ready to eat.

"I learned long ago never to interrupt a woman while she shops. Window or otherwise." He stood and walked to the door. "I'm starving. Let's eat."

She entered first, careful not to touch him, wanting to avoid the wonderfully strange sensations that only heightened the appeal of this man. If she'd met him under different circumstances, she just might risk going wherever the attraction would take them. But new job, new boss, new town, and old entrenched values kept her from reaching for him.

The coziness of the café invited folks to linger over a meal. Some tables had green and white checked tablecloths, others had traditional red and white ones. The lighting, fixtures crafted from antique gaslights, cast a soft glow. On the long windowless wall, a painted mural of a life-size magnolia tree laden with large, white velvety blooms wrapped upward and continued onto the ceiling. The mural created the illusion that diners picnicked outside beneath the tree.

"Please follow me." A hostess led them toward the back of the half-full café. The low din of chatter seemed to echo downward from the pressed tin ceiling.

Branna breathed deeply, taking in the aromas. Coffee brewing. Pie. Hot grease frying something. Not exactly the same scents wafting from Greta's Cajun cooking at home, but comforting all the same. Her mouth watered. When her stomach rumbled, she covered it with her clutch. If it weren't for the noise in the restaurant, James would have heard and that would be embarrassing.

She slid into the booth where the hostess placed the menus. James sat opposite her. A jean-clad waitress in a pink shirt with a red-and-white-checked apron tied around her waist plunked glasses of water down in front of them.

"Today's special—fried catfish with cheese grits. Coleslaw. Biscuit or cornbread. What can I bring you to drink?"

"I'm going to need a minute," Branna said. The waitress raised an eyebrow at James. When he didn't answer, she stuffed the order pad into her apron pocket and stalked away.

Branna studied the menu. She wanted one of everything. The scents coming from the kitchen made her hungry stomach nibble on her backbone. She was no better than a Pavlovian dog. As Grandfather Lind would say, "her eyes were bigger than her stomach."

"Never had a bad meal here," James said, folding his menu closed.

"Good to know. I'll bring my parents when they visit again." She continued her perusal of the menu. "Fried chicken. Pork chops. Pot roast. Burgers and sandwiches. And the list of pies looks..."

"Sara Nell won't come back until you close your menu."

"Oh." She folded the menu closed, mentally running through the list. Deciding would be impossible.

The waitress appeared in an instant. She looked

like the perfect candidate to work at a roadhouse. Blond, thin, yet shapely, with cleavage that made most men drool.

"I'll have the side salad, the garden salad sandwich and lemonade. Fresh-squeezed lemonade. You don't find that every day." She looked up into the waitress' plastic smile, then handed over the menu.

"Garden sandwich?" James asked. "Not the special? Don't tell me you're one of those women who only eat rabbit food. Or don't you eat southern?"

What did he mean by that? "Of course I eat southern cooking. I'm from Mississippi. My daddy's family is from Loo-zee-ana. My comfort food may be different than yours—there was no seafood gumbo or jambalaya or stuffed mirlitons on the menu—but I promise you my comfort food is southern. I happen to *like* what the menu says about the specialty sandwich." She cocked her head, daring him to challenge her decision.

"Mur-la what?" the waitress asked.

"Chayote squash or vegetable pear at the grocery store," James answered. "I want the fried grouper sandwich with fries, please."

"Sure thing, Dr. Newbern." Sara Nell smiled so brightly, Branna blinked to cut the glare.

"The Magnolia has the best fries in town. They peel, slice, and then bake the potatoes with a secret seasoning. The seasoning is the trick. That, and no frying."

"Fries that aren't fried?" She ran her finger down the side of the water glass, nervously wiping away the condensation. Silly, but she would probably always link condensation with her first meeting with James.

"I do watch what I eat." She tried not to sound defensive, but at five foot three, most of the world was taller than she, and she had no place to hide extra pounds. "And not that it's any of your business, but I want dessert. I *can't* pass up homemade pie. A meal is sometimes made up of a tradeoff of calories."

For some reason that made him smile. The one that melted her heart. Made it beat rapidly. When she looked away, James said, "I like to see a woman enjoy her food."

"Then watch me."

James raised an eyebrow.

She hadn't intended her response to sound like a challenge, but there it was.

"So let's get to the 'get to know you' part of this lunch. You went to an SEC school. But not Mississippi State. Why?"

"It's not where women in my family go." She hadn't expected twenty questions. She started to say she didn't base her educational needs upon whether or not a school was part of the Southeastern Conference. Nor would she mention the scholarship she turned down to another SEC school, the scholarship her mother had squelched with guilt. "I followed in the footsteps of my mother, grandmother, and great-grandmother. Ole Miss admitted women in 1882."

She wondered what else James knew about her.

Hearing the *swoosh* of the kitchen door opening behind the booth, she folded her hands in her lap. Sara Nell stood beside the table, arms laden with plates. With a *clunk* so forceful it made the bread on the sandwich jump, she set Branna's food down, then flashed another bright smile before gently sliding

James' plate in front of him.

"Ma'am, I made your fresh-squeezed lemonade."

Sara Nell's "Ma'am," dripped with sarcasm. There couldn't be much more than a year or two between them, so it couldn't be an age thing, but what? Not wanting to cause a scene, she ignored the rudeness and poured poppy seed dressing over her salad. The growls from her stomach demanded food. She might possibly transform into a snarling beast now rather than a pumpkin at midnight.

"Do you want *anything* else?" The waitress purred at James. Her lashes fluttered as though sending Morse code. What did the waitress expect James to say?

She couldn't remember when she'd experienced such poor behavior in a restaurant. But it would be impolite to point out to the woman the errors of her ways.

"No thanks, just Miss Lind's lemonade."

"You were born and raised here?" Branna asked between bites, wanting to shift the conversation. Sara Nell took the hint and trudged away.

"Born in the only hospital in town. Raised about thirty miles west. I'm curious. Why does one go from event planning to full-time teacher?" James asked, then drug one of his fries through ketchup before eating it.

"That was a smooth transition." She put her fork down. Through all she'd battled to get this job and leave home, no one until James had asked that question. "I love books and learning. I believe knowledge is power. I find it fulfilling to watch someone learn something new, and then have them discover how to use what they've learned to enhance their lives. I want to be part of that process." She'd never uttered those words aloud. Speaking them filled her with a sense of freedom.

"But event planning to teaching?"

"Do you doubt my ability?" she asked, worried that he might think her less than capable.

"Nope. Not one bit. You've got the education, enough experience, more importantly the passion—and we need that in classrooms. Just wondered about the leap."

What was it her father had asked when she announced she was leaving? Something about whether or not she was taking a blind leap into the shallow end of a pool.

"Ah, that. Well...let's just say my prior job was part of the family business." The last thing she wanted to discuss was family. Their ways weren't an easy concept to understand—a large extended one steeped in old traditions in a modern live-for-the-moment world where everything was expendable or replaceable rather than treasured like antiques.

"Part?"

"What did *you* do before you came to teach at the college?" she asked.

"I can take a hint. Family is off limits?"

"I thought the purpose of this get-to-know-you lunch was a professional one. I take it, you've seen my resume. I'd like to steer the conversation in the direction of LCC. That's the nickname for the college, right?"

The corners of James' mouth curled. He winked. "Yes. Questions are an occupational hazard of mine, Miss Lind."

His wink was an arrow to her gut. Tingles danced

in her veins, the same as when he'd held her hand while they'd danced last night.

What was happening to her? Better yet, what was wrong with her? He showed no signs of experiencing any odd sensations. He'd flirted a bit, but only a bit. The quivering in her gut made her want to run. She'd left Fleur de Lis in search of simplicity. Independence. No relationship tangles. Nor complicated emotions that made her squirm. That wasn't what she signed up for. Where did she go to unsubscribe?

Picking up her fork, she stabbed at the lettuce on the plate. Before the next stab, James tapped her hand with a single finger, and that mere contact sent a quiver up her arm.

"What would you like to know about your new job or the college?"

She raised her head to gaze at him. From across the table, he appeared totally at ease in his own skin while she twitched with panic in hers. She hadn't had a date with a man, not that this was exactly a date, since before her engagement. The only man she'd dined with, other than the ones in her family for the last eighteen months, had been Steven. "Tell me everything."

James wasn't flirting with her, just trying to put her at ease, right? She must have somehow misconstrued the signals. Dr. Brown had described him well—a mixture of ambition and easy charm. His kind of charm put her on edge.

Steven had shown great talent at turning his charm off and on, making his moods sometimes unpredictable. "Slick as owl spit" was how Grandpa Lind described him. She didn't know James well, but instinct assured her that he wasn't at all like Steven.

Which made him dangerous to her heart.

James was exactly the kind of man she intended to avoid. She needed carefree and casual, but did her heart have a different mission? "Tell me about the expectations you had when you started teaching and how those have changed. What about the difference between theory and reality in the classroom?"

She focused on her meal while James shared his teaching experiences.

The second she finished her last bite of salad, the waitress arrived to clear away plates as if she'd been hovering behind them, watching and listening. Sara Nell offered James a grin, then glared at her when James wasn't watching as though she were the enemy, before slapping dessert menus on the table.

Branna perused the pie list, but her desire had waned. She would have preferred lunch without a side dish of "waitress attitude."

"All the pies are made here. What. Can. I. Get. You?" Sara Nell asked, hiking the attitude quotient higher.

"They have a little elf-grandmother in the back who works her magic with pies," James said. "Ladies first."

Sara Nell stood beside the table, shifting her weight from side to side, poised with pencil and pad.

"I'll have sweet potato pecan, please," Branna answered, then closed her menu and slid it to the edge of the table without making eye contact with the waitress.

"Excellent choice. I'll try the lemon. If I share a bit of mine, will you share?" James said with a wink.

It made her breath catch.

"Fine. SPP and lemon." Sara Nell left in a huff. Branna expected to see a puff of smoke. Or at least steam coming from both of the waitress' ears.

"I considered the pumpkin," James said. "But I'm dubious about eating that after learning you shape shift into one at midnight."

"Cute." She leaned on the table and motioned James closer. "Do I have food between my teeth or something?"

"No. Why?"

"Does my perfume smell repugnant?"

James shook his head.

"Does she treat all female customers like that?"

"Sarah Nell?"

"Yes." Exasperated, she restated the obvious. "Sara Nell."

"Just ignore her." James patted her hand. "She and I never had a second—"

Before James finished his sentence, Sarah Nell appeared again. She plopped down their dessert plates and left in another huff.

Branna checked her plate to be sure it hadn't cracked in two. "Guess I don't want coffee," she said picking up her fork. "You never had a second what?"

"Date."

That explained everything. "Dr. Brown said you had a lot going for you. For the record, I think I should tell Sara Nell that *this* is the opposite of a date. This is lunch between two colleagues because *you* missed the official work one."

"I'm sure she'd be happy to hear that. But it won't make any difference where I'm concerned."

Taking a scoop, she spooned pie into her mouth.

The smooth texture and rich flavor of the filling combined with the crunch of the nuts made her taste buds dance. She closed her eyes to savor the flavor. It tasted like home. She took another scoop just to be sure her imagination wasn't playing tricks. She had discovered a slice of heaven...in a slice of pie.

"I don't know when I've ever seen a woman enjoy her food more."

Submerged in a sweet-potato-pecan-pie brain fog, what could she say? She wouldn't apologize for loving dessert, though she didn't appreciate the teasing. When their eyes met, admiration shone in his. He wasn't teasing, but totally serious. He enjoyed watching her eat.

Embarrassed, she shrugged. "I *love* this pie. If it wouldn't make me hungry all the time, I'd have candles that smelled like this in every room in my house. I'd bottle it and wear it as perfume. Pour it into my bubble bath. I always wanted to be the sweet-potato-pecan-pie queen."

James raised one eyebrow, then reached across the table and touched the corner of her mouth. A small piece of pecan dropped to the table as Sara Nell marched up. She gave Branna yet another glare and c*linked* the metal plate with the bill on the table between them.

"Call me," the waitress purred at James before departing.

Branna glanced at him, then to the spot where the waitress had stood before her departure. "The food's great. The service—not so much. If I brought Momma in here, she'd have the owner by the ear, then give the entire staff lessons in decorum."

"Sara Nell, her nose is a little bent out of shape. She's not usually this way. Besides, if you say something, you'll get the woman fired."

Branna shrugged. "I won't say anything, but she won't ever wait on me again." She didn't blame Sara Nell for trying. She'd been a fool for a man once, too, but once in a lifetime was enough for any woman. Besides, she wanted a man who was the strong faithful type. She wanted the "and two shall become one" in a relationship. Nothing smothering, but a man with whom life would have balance and would feel complete.

"Shall we take our tour?" James asked, rising from the booth.

Her radar blipped. She blinked. There was a smoldering tension between them. She recognized it now.

James was a problem. No handsome, southern charmer for her. She wanted a man-free life. Her brain reaffirmed that concept, but her heart waffled when James placed his hand in the small of her back and guided her toward the front door.

"That went well, don't ya think," James said. "How about if we try this again...soon. We haven't covered everything about the job, mostly hit the important highlights."

She saw mischief in his eyes. "Okay, sure...soon."

"Wait here a moment. I have an idea."

She stood outside the café as he walked down the street. Confused, she watched him go. Then her cell phone vibrated in her purse. She didn't recognize the number, but it was a local area code. "Hello?"

"Miss Lind, I was wondering if you'd like to go on a non-date?"

"James?" Half way down the block, she could see him, but he had his back to her.

"How about around seven-thirty this evening? A drive through the country to learn your way around and maybe a late-night drink? I know a place with a live band on Saturday nights. You'll experience local color. We'll do this for the LCC team."

"I'm not sure...that's such a good idea." He had walked away to call her?

"What if I promise, you'll be home before midnight? After all, I don't want to witness any shape shifting. I don't know if I'll ever look at pumpkin the same again, knowing you change at midnight."

"Dr. Newbern, I want to keep things professional." Was he afraid she'd say, no?

"Good. Then I won't pick you up. We're two colleagues getting to know each other better. Sort of a professional-bonding night. Where would you like to meet for a non-date?"

A non-date? She could handle that, right? She ignored the shouting voice in her head that told her to *Run! Run away*. Far away, from this man. The jitterbug dancing in her stomach threw a one-two punch to her head, which caused her heart to skip a beat.

James Newbern was not what she had anticipated in any way, shape or form.

"Why not?" she said finally. "You name the place." After all, she came to Lakeview for adventure.

Chapter 10

The tall wood-framed etched glass doors created an elegant entrance to the bar at the only hotel in town.

"Wow. The newspaper said this had a five-star rating." Branna stared at the beautifully crafted doors.

She'd read about the hotel's restaurant and bar in a local survey. That seemed like a reliable recommendation. After all, options weren't endless in Lakeview. Five miles west near the interstate, a handful of cut-rate motels for one-night-only tourists flashed *No Occupancy* signs on Saturday nights. None of them served food or adult-only beverages.

She spotted the Historic Register plaque on the brick wall beside the tall doors. The lodging establishment had remained locally owned since its opening. She had researched the place after James suggested meeting there, wanting to know what to expect, since she shied away from surprises. The building had antique character, and Lakeview folks might consider the 1900's construction ancient; however, Bayou Petite had signed its city charter almost a hundred years earlier than when Lakeview called itself a town.

James had made it clear their outing tonight fell under the heading of "colleagues bonding." It wasn't a date, and she wouldn't allow anyone to accuse her of not being a team player. A drive in the country would better acquaint her with Lakeview. The sooner she learned her way around, the more it would feel like home. She couldn't admit it to anyone, not even her cousin Biloxi, that she missed Fleur de Lis, the chaos of her large family, and Greta's cooking. She pulled the door handle to the hotel, grunting softly under its heaviness, and wondered if Dr. Brown had urged James to be more sociable to make up for his less-than-hospitable past.

Arriving early allowed her time to take in the surroundings and to nurse a drink before a drive into the countryside. The information on the hotel's website boasted a full-bar menu. Having one cocktail and a protein-laden appetizer would ensure that when she drove home in a few hours there would be little, if any, trace of alcohol in her blood. Just in case she was pulled over, though, that had never happened before. She always took every precaution. The world might end if she fell from her family's "good-example" pedestal. She didn't need that on her guilt-ridden conscience.

Besides, one drink would calm her rattled nerves, and she would insist that James drive.

Inside the bar, shelves crammed with leather-bound books lined the walls of The Library. A half-dozen pub tables filled the space between the shelves and the carved wooden bar. The scene transported her back in time to an old saloon, only one with books. The look of it appeared as though it had been plucked from an old movie set. The bartender in his white shirt, silver and black striped vest, and black bolo tie looked perfectly cast, just like gamblers she'd seen in old black and whites who won every hand of cards, swilled whiskey from a bottle, and drew can-can girls to them like miners seeking gold.

The only difference between the movies she'd seen and the place where she stood was the smooth jazz floating around her as if moved by air conditioning.

The bartender winked. "What'll ya have, little lady?"

She smiled and hiked onto a tall barstool. "Gin and tonic with a lemon twist, please."

"Happy to oblige you, sugar." Then he muttered something under his breath she couldn't quite make out about her and a "twist."

"Is there an appetizer menu?" she asked when he returned with her drink and set it on a square napkin in front of her.

"You could nibble on me, darlin', anytime." He flashed a grin and raised an eyebrow, then leaned on his forearm on the bar top as if posing for a headshot.

"Excuse me?" Though raised in the south where "honey, darlin', babe, and sugar" were not usually considered insults, but friendly greetings between those well acquainted—her practice was to ignore men who used those terms of endearment to suggest an intimacy that simply didn't exist. And while she hated confrontation, when the bartender licked his lips, she snapped.

"Do your regular customers like to be verbally mauled by you, *darlin'*?"

His grin dropped. His eyes narrowed. "Sorry." He pulled out a menu from behind the bar and slapped it on the bar top in front of her. "Order away, *ma'am*."

"Hey, Dave."

Startled by a voice behind her, she swiveled on the barstool to find James approaching.

"Is that any way to treat my newest colleague?" James' voice was more teasing than chastising.

"Branna Lind, meet Dave. Dave, meet Branna Lind. Nachos and a beer, barkeep."

Dave nodded, popped caps on two longneck bottles, placed them on the bar in front of James, and then snorted loudly and walked away.

"Be gentle with the natives." James chuckled. "Retract those Mississippi claws. We're civilized here. I promise."

"Hard to tell by that one." She scowled in hopes of driving her point home.

"Well, Dave took one look at you and saw a challenge."

"What?"

"An attractive woman comes into the bar *alone*, no wedding ring or engagement diamond."

She looked down at her left hand, then instinctively rubbed where a band no longer circled her ring finger. "I'm a target because I'm alone with no ring?"

"The combination is like waving a red flag at a bull. This is a small town. You're new and attractive."

"Women were liberated years ago, you know. What about just getting to know someone? Why is it men still have to act like Bubbas?"

James cocked his head, his brow furrowed deeply. "You don't look like that type."

"I'll probably regret this, but what type is that?"

Dave appeared and delivered a platter of nachos. He waited, clearly to hear James' reply.

"The militant-feminist type."

"Ya didn't look like that type to me, either. But it's true. Can't tell a book by its cover." Dave brandished his arms in a grand display noting the library of books around him. He shook his head and walked away muttering something she couldn't quite hear.

"Liberation doesn't mean militant." Her earlier snappy retort to Dave was the first time she'd ever done that. Usually, she played peacekeeper and set the example for her siblings and cousins. Maybe she could do with a little more feminist energy.

"So, you grew up here," she said, intent on changing the subject.

James slid the platter of nachos between them and placed one of the bottles beside her cocktail. "For you. Who drinks..." James pointed to her glass.

"Gin and tonic with a lemon twist."

"Yeah, that."

"A perfectly civilized cocktail."

"But who drinks that with nachos? The beer is Dave's way of making it up to you. He won't put it on the bill. He's not such a bad guy. You can't blame him for taking a shine to a pretty woman."

"Flattery from you? I'll thank him when he comes back. Do I look like the kiss-and-makeup type?" She didn't bother to contain her sarcasm.

"Yep." James said before taking a bite of the nachos.

Well, he probably had that right. She'd made up with Steven more than once. What she didn't know back then, Steven was also making up or making out with someone else at the same time. Steven and Dave were linked by the same gene pool in her book. That could doom all women-kind. Then, she reconsidered. Dave had to be more evolved than Steven.

"So you grew up here. We never finished that

conversation."

"Not Lakeview exactly." James took a bite of another laden chip. The remaining filling fell back onto his plate. She tried not to laugh when he scooped up the filling with yet another chip and popped the mess in his mouth. He certainly enjoyed his food.

"I grew up west of here in the next county. It was one of the last dry ones in Florida."

"Is that where we're going this evening?"

"No. Mostly for a ride to show you the countryside—that, and where and how your students live. Maybe we'll go over to the springs. Have you seen much of the area?"

"Very little." She'd visited her brother at college a few times, everyone there wore orange and blue, about fifty miles south of Lakeview. She'd heard about the crystalline natural springs nearby with their constant seventy-two degree temperature. Unlike her brother's time at college, she never had a free moment. Responsibilities at home directed how and where she spent time. The numerous holiday and celebration parties hosted at Fleur de Lis kept her busy. Those events helped pay the bills. Family tradition and family responsibility claimed all of her time. After college, Steven became a fixture in her world. Once engaged, she'd spent what precious few minutes she used to have to herself on planning her wedding with her mother. She and Steven weren't just getting married; their two families were merging as well. Between her extended family and his, the guest list had hit five hundred.

What a fool she'd been.

Thinking about it made her blood pressure rise. She downed her cocktail hoping the tang would wash away the residue of anger. A drive through the country sounded appealing, far more desirable than haunting old history.

She reached for a nacho and slid it into her mouth and chewed.

"Come on, woman. Eat up."

She *clinked* the longneck beer against James' bottle. "Just remember"—she grinned—"I have to be home before I turn into a pumpkin at midnight."

Chapter 11

James walked beside Branna into the cooling evening. "I'm in the parking lot across the street. I'll drive."

"Which one is yours?" In a grand flourish, she waved her arms at the parked cars.

"Guess," he said, grinning. His hand accidentally brushed hers as they crossed in the middle of the street. The pulse that radiated each time they touched no longer startled him. It had turned into an anticipation of delight. The familiarity of it was something he could get used to. No doubt about it. Branna Lind charged him up.

A passing truck honked and grabbed his attention. He waved as the driver waved to him.

"I guess I didn't think of Florida as the south," Branna said. "At home, we always wave to those passing by. It's considered polite, even if you don't know the person."

"North Florida is still pretty much old south. A rich Florida Cracker has two cars on blocks in the yard in front of his doublewide mobile home." He chuckled. "Go south, past Ocala, it's an entirely different culture. There, a lot of people are from out of state."

"You're a Florida Cracker?"

"Fifth-generation proud."

They reached the mostly-empty lot, only six cars

left. She walked away from him, pausing to look at the five vehicles on the left. James waited patiently with his hands in his pockets. He rocked back on the heels of his boots and tried not to give anything away.

At the end of the row, she turned around and faced him. "This one?" she asked pointing to a Ford Taurus closest to her.

"Nope. Want to guess again?"

She walked toward him, then stopped two cars away. "The Toyota?"

"Nope. Don't drive foreign."

"I drive a Volvo," she said defensively. "I give up. Which one is yours?"

He turned and pointed to the lone car on the right side of the aisle taking up two spaces.

"Yours? Wow. Nice." She crossed the distance to the rear of his car. "What year is this? Did you restore it yourself? Great paint job." Branna stroked the top of the trunk, then the fender of his red Chevy Chevelle.

"1968. The inside isn't completely finished. Waiting to install the back seat. A friend of mine is doing most of the work. Restoring cars is his winter hobby. I help when I'm able, but can't take any real credit for the work."

"It's spotless. The paint job is flawless."

The awe in Branna's voice surprised him. He cocked his head and watched as she walked around, her fingers trailing across the new paint job. Maybe she recognized quality workmanship on the classic. Maybe she saw the Chevelle as more than just an old car.

Maybe there was more to Branna Lind than he first thought.

"Let's go." He opened the door for her. When she

slipped past him and into the seat, a faint scent of flowers drifted to his nose. Nothing cloyingly sweet or strong, but soft and feminine. As she lifted her feet inside the car, her movements made him think of a dancer. Elegant. The denim skirt and gauzy white top she wore hugged her in all the right places. She even wore denim-trimmed sandals that matched her skirt. Where the heck did a woman find those kinds of shoes?

"You're probably going to think I'm odd," Branna said.

"Not odd. Just different," he teased as he cranked the engine. It rumbled, then purred. The air conditioner blew coolness around them.

"I know it's warm, but would you mind the windows down?"

"What about your hair?" he asked before he could stop himself. Didn't women hate the wind-blown look? He happened to love it on a woman.

"We're going for a drive in the country. I have a brush. You don't care what I look like, do you?" She shook her head. Short hair swished back and forth, then fell neatly back into place.

The strong urge to touch her caught him off guard. "No," he answered quickly.

"No, you don't care what I look like? Or no, you don't want to roll down the windows?"

James shook his head to clear the confusion. One beer with a plate of nachos wouldn't raise his blood-alcohol level a point. But Branna Lind had.

"Let's roll down the windows," he said, stealing a sideways glance at her as he pulled from the parking lot.

He'd made it to the bar early hoping for a snack to

stop the rumbling in his stomach. He had no intention of starving. Earlier, he had wanted to invite Branna for dinner and a drive, however, she seemed to think anything social, like sitting down to a meal, crossed the line away from professional. Luckily, his arrival at the bar came soon enough to save Dave from her claws— which he was surprised she had—and he saved her from more of Dave's tired come-ons. Before they left, Branna politely thanked Dave for the beer. They shook hands amicably. Dave assured her that he would remember his manners next time or provide his mother's phone number so Branna could call and complain about how poorly he'd been raised.

"Nice ride," Branna said. She tilted her head to the open widow and caught more of the passing breeze.

The breeze picked up as he increased their speed. They left town and turned onto the divided highway.

"Would you like to drive her?" James hollered.

"Maybe later. Music?"

"No stereo, yet. Bobbie, my friend doing the work, is still working on that. Hence the reason for the missing back seat."

They drove in silence for a while. He slowed to make a turn onto a two-lane blacktop with a thirty-five mile-per-hour speed limit.

"The fields are larger the farther we get from town. Mostly soybeans and corn," he explained. "Not much different than Mississippi, I guess. Except, we don't grow much cotton in Florida."

They passed a few houses where only rooftops were visible. Hedges and trees offered privacy and protection from rumbling traffic. As they drove, the scenery changed from wide-open fields to acres of densely planted pines waiting for harvest and marked for the pulp mills in Jacksonville. He caught whiffs of freshly mown grass. He did breathe easier in country air. The tension ratcheted tight in his body began to unwind.

"It smells different here," Branna said. "No hints of brackish water, like at home."

She reached her hand out of the window, as if trying to catch the wind. Her eyes were closed, though a half grin tugged at the corners of her mouth. The rigidness she'd exuded after the incident at the bar had disappeared, and with it went much of her high-maintenance demeanor. Relaxed, she was feminine and too appealing.

His body responded. He shifted uncomfortably in his seat. What he'd hoped would be a fun night with Branna might challenge all his restraint. The tension that had unwound—Branna just sent soaring.

How long had it been since he'd taken a woman for a drive for no reason other than to explore the countryside? Probably not since high school. Back before Lakeview even had a movie theater. Back when a Saturday night date meant bowling at an alley with only five lanes, and then making out by the Ichetucknee River. Back before Caroline.

"What type of music do you like?" Branna asked, her hands moving to her lap. "Do you have a favorite?"

"Do you mean, if I were stranded on a desert island and could have only one CD, what would it be?"

"Well, let's go with that."

"Something jazzy with blues. What about you?"

"Classical."

"Ahh."

Branna turned in her seat and faced him. "Ahh—what?"

"It makes sense. You look like the classical-music type."

"You are beginning to annoy me, Dr. Newbern. I'm getting a little tired of hearing that I'm some sort of a type. Like you've figured me out by pigeonholing me into nice neat categories. Is that what type you are? A pigeon-holer?"

He shrugged. "Never thought about it before. Don't you ever look at someone and size them up? By looking at them, you know exactly their nature. Maybe even their character." His guard edged back up. Of course she did. She had done that with him the first time they met. She still hadn't put two-and-two together to realize he was the same redneck she'd met at the Victorian.

"I probably do, but I try hard not to."

Now he'd hurt her feelings. "Didn't mean to offend you. But let's try a different approach. Can you guess what type of music I grew up on?"

Branna rolled her eyes as if she thought the question were ridiculous, or ridiculously simple. He only had to wait for a second for her answer.

"Country, of course."

"Nope."

"Country and Western? Is that what they called it way back when?"

"Wrong."

"Acid Rock? Heavy Metal?"

"Church hymns."

"You only listened to hymns?" she asked. Her eyes were wide with disbelief.

"I grew up singing in church. Not just with the

choir. I sang at weddings when I was young."

"Hymns. Really? You make it sound like you're so old. How old are you?"

Ahead, a caution light flashed stabs of yellow signaling a junction crossroad. Not even a town, just a collection of a half-dozen stores.

"See the flashing sign up there? Beyond that caution light is where we're headed." He pointed to the spot down the road.

"Are you changing the subject?"

"The subject being what?" he asked.

"Age. How old are you?"

He shook his head. "Are you sure you were raised in the south?"

"Of course," she snapped. "I'm as 'true-blue southern belle' as they come. Have the genealogy to prove it. Why?"

"If I tell you how old I am, are you going to tell me your age? You know a gentleman can never ask a lady about that."

Branna put her head back and laughed. Her shoulders shook as she continued to giggle. What had she found so funny?

"You are indeed old south, Dr. Newbern. You never ask a lady over the age of thirty how old she is. Under thirty, you have to make sure she's a lady first. That's the new rule."

"And of the two, which one are you?"

Glancing at her, he caught her narrowed eyes aimed at him. "You're the expert at types. You tell me, Professor."

He ignored her challenge as he pulled onto the gravel parking lot. Old telephone poles served as markers on the ground, roughing out the lot where spring weeds grew through the rocks. A few cars were there, but mostly pickups filled the spaces. He parked far away from the other vehicles. It would ruin his night if he came back to find a drunk had marred his restored baby. When he started to roll up his window, Branna did the same.

"Thanks," he said. "Nothing worse than coming back to a car full of bugs."

He started to step out of the car, but Branna's touch stopped him. His arm pulsed hot in that spot.

"Exactly where are we?"

Was that fear he read in her eyes?

Chapter 12

Warily, Branna glanced around as she carefully navigated the gravel lot. What had she gotten herself into?

"It's all part of the country attraction." James sounded smug.

The long building with faded gray siding had no windows. Old metal signs nailed to the exterior advertised Coca Cola, John Deere, Skoal, and Sunbeam Bread. A low-slung overhang protected a weather-worn wooden deck that surrounded the building. But for vehicles in the mangy looking parking lot out back, the place looked deserted against the backdrop of open countryside.

She followed James around the corner, picking her way in heels and trying not to turn her ankle, to what she guessed was probably the front side of the building since it faced the road. Worn wooden handles blended into the siding's seams, unless up close, she would have never known there were double doors there. "Tin" had been carved into one, "Lizzie" into the other. Even before James pulled on the door, she heard the throbbing music as much as she felt it.

"After you," James said. Then, he opened the door.

Music assaulted her. She flinched, but stepped across the threshold and into a small town honky-tonk. The band members wore boots, T-shirts with a band logo, cowboy hats, and twanged chords southern rock-n-roll style. The yeastiness of beer and hot oil popping corn scented the air. A step away from the front door, a burly guy dressed in black boots, black jeans, and a black hat—no one could mistake him for anything but a bouncer—shook James' hand, and then he rose from a barstool and pulled James into a bear-hug as though they were long lost brothers.

"Branna, this is Clyde," James shouted. She managed to hear him over the deafening music.

Clyde reached out and took her hand. She wanted to step away; it wasn't often she encountered someone so physically intimidating. He was the definition of a "brick wall," a tall one. Clyde held her hand lightly as though it was something quite delicate, and for a moment she thought he might kiss it. Instead, he grabbed a rubber stamp, turned her wrist and branded the inside. Black ink stained her pale skin in the shape of a horseshoe. She blinked and craned her neck to look up. Crystal blue eyes looked back at her. Clear and smiling.

"Charmed," Clyde said, and then winked.

Speechless, she let James usher her away, but not before she turned to catch another glimpse of the bluest eyes she had ever seen.

James located two stools at the end of a horseshoe shaped bar. She took the offered stool next to the wall, all the while wondering if her eyes were playing tricks. Was the blue of Clyde's eyes contact enhanced? She'd never seen a woman swoon, except in the movies, but she'd bet Clyde had a time or two or three, like whenever he turned those startling eyes on a woman.

A bartender laid down cocktail napkins in front of

her and James. "What'll it be for you, James, and the lady?"

She nudged James with her elbow. "Guess that answers your question from earlier. I'm a lady."

"I'll bet you are."

The bartender looked confused.

"Branna, this is Dale. Dale, meet Lady Branna."

Dale raised an eyebrow, clearly unsure if James was serious or not.

"Lady Branna, what'll ya have?" Dale asked as he popped the cap on a longneck beer bottle and handed it to James.

"I'm not sure yet. Give me a minute, please."

Uneasiness cramped her shoulders. This was exactly the sort of place she never dared go. The kind of place Biloxi and Camilla would sneak into back when they were in high school. Even when she was old enough to drink, she had never entered a "Tin Lizzie." In Bayou Petite, the news of her in a honky-tonk would have reached her parents' ears before she arrived home. As a child, she always hated the long lectures on decorum. The ones about how she had a greater responsibility to set a good example because she was the next Keeper. Therefore, always following the dictates of what was expected had made her life easier. She remained the proverbial good girl. Appearances meant everything.

But this wasn't Bayou Petite. No one knew her here. And better still, no one here cared whether or not she would be the next Fleur de Lis Keeper.

"Tequila!" In her mind, she shouted the word and did a hip-swinging, "ole," but the word never crossed her lips. "How 'bout a margarita on the rocks?" That would be safe. She wasn't brave enough to do tequila shots. Maybe she would try just one?

"Dale, a margarita for Lady Branna. Use the good stuff," James advised, then waved to a couple on the dance floor.

"Do you know *everyone*?" Branna asked.

James leaned close. His hand rested on her forearm. A delightful tingle shot up her arm. They were almost cheek-to-cheek when he whispered in her ear, "After thirty-plus years, don't you think I should?"

The warmth of his breath caressed her ear and caused a shiver to slide down her neck. His words barely registered in her brain. Had the world stopped moving? For a second, she imagined he wanted to kiss her. She held her breath and closed her eyes. But coolness touched her skin where his warm hand had been. A curl of disappointment formed in her stomach when he leaned away. Her cheeks heated from a flush. The fact that she had wanted James to kiss her left her fighting embarrassment.

Dale delivered a large, tall-stemmed, globe-shaped, salt-rimmed glass with slices of lime bobbing in pale green liquid. It was the interruption she needed to pull herself together. She would die if James discovered her secret thoughts. She did want to kiss him. And, maybe after some margarita fortification, she just might.

"This is big enough for four people to share."

She eyed it cautiously, tasted the salt on the rim with the tip of her tongue, and then drew liquid up through a straw. James looked on with obvious amusement. She took several sips, but the liquid level in the glass appeared to remain the same. At this rate, she'd be there all night if she ever expected to finish the drink.

Swiveling on her bar stool, she rested the back of her head against the wall. No one could sneak up behind her. The corner seat provided a panoramic view of the honky-tonk, and it gave her a sense of protection. Something she needed desperately in the moment. She actually sat in a joint that had been off-limits to her for all of her life. It was as though she'd disobeyed every elder woman in her family. She could hear their cumulative "tsk tsk" and shoved the thought away.

She didn't recognize a single face. Not that she would. However, people watching was fun. Drumming her hands on her thighs to the rhythm of the band's bass guitar, she allowed the music to wash over her.

"Let's dance."

Before she could stop him, James grabbed her purse and handed it to Dale, who put it behind the bar. "Save our seats," he told the bartender, laying a ten-dollar bill on the counter. He tugged on her hand and pulled her off the raised chair. She almost lost her balance. Then, they wound their way around through the tables to the dance floor.

The band announced the next song was the last one of the set. They wanted everyone out on the floor or they might not return after their break. The crowd roared when the guitarist picked the first strands of *Sweet Home Alabama*. Anyone not on the dance floor stood and cheered. Some banged bottles on the tabletops in time to the beat. The raucousness shot adrenaline through her body. If she'd been at the top of the Empire State Building, she'd swear she could jump and fly.

James never let go of her. There was barely room

to sway together, let alone dance, which protected his feet from another beating like they endured last night. She tingled all over from the throb of the music and from being in his arms. The energy of the crowd swirled around her, giving her the sensation of rising click-by-click, climbing the up-side of a roller coaster's hill. Giddiness washed over her as if she'd opened a door and stepped through to Never Never Land. A feeling of being completely alive.

The band continued playing the song, raising the pace of the frenzied crowd. She'd swear every single person in the room was moving their body. After a drum solo and a final guitar lick, the band bowed and quickly departed from the stage, leaving the crowd staring at the spot where they'd been.

"Oh, Lord! If Momma could see me now." She laughed, not caring who might hear her over the din of voices and piped-in muzak.

With James in the lead, their hands linked, she followed him toward their seats. Someone behind her bumped her hard. She gasped. Fell forward into James, almost sending him forward. She struggled to right herself with the rowdy crowd pushing all around her. Tremors of fear raced through her as she started to slip toward the floor. Panicked, she clawed at James' back.

James turned on a dime. Grabbed her, protected her from falling. He sheltered her from the crushing crowd, and held her steady as she caught her breath. The crowd parted around them as though they were a large boulder in the middle of a fast moving river. Shaken, she clung to him, then blinked when he leaned in and kissed her.

His mouth was warm.

Quivers raced all the way to her toes.

Wrapping his arm around her, he said, "Don't worry. I'll protect you." Then he wrapped her in an embrace, rested his hand on her hip, and guided her back to their spot at the bar.

Shocked by the kiss, a touch so light and quick that it appeared and disappeared so fast she could have dreamt it. She touched a finger to her lips. They were still warm where his lips had been.

"Who's going to protect me from you?" she whispered.

Chapter 13

James contemplated the woman beside him as Branna rested her back against the wall. Her gaze now landed anywhere but on him. Her eyes glittered, probably from excitement and maybe from drinking half of the oversized margarita so fast. The flush in her cheeks was probably alcohol induced.

Or could it be the result of their kiss?

He never intended to cross that line. Kissing a colleague would make for muddy business. Dr. Brown warned him to keep things professional. Why, he wasn't sure, since he kept to his own strict rule of no fraternization after watching other faculty members mangle their lives. He'd witnessed when a relationship ended badly—anger, even vindictiveness, showed up at work. Small towns had a way of breeding relationship-discontent. Maybe it happened in big cities, too, but there people had the luxury of anonymity.

However, the fact that he'd kissed her didn't bother him nearly as much as his reaction to the kiss worried him. When their lips met, the music died, noise went away, even the crowd disappeared. Only he and Branna were alive in the room. Time stopped. His heartbeat matched the rhythm of hers. Her soft feminine scent filled his senses. The caress of her lips made him a man dying of thirst...that only she could quench.

A second later, the reality of the bar, crowd, and

music crashed down around him. That moment of...unreality scared the living hell out of him.

He scooped a few peanuts from a bowl on the bar and tossed them into his mouth. Instead of discussing his spontaneous act and any reaction to it, for the last fifteen minutes, Branna had avoided all eye contact with him, even when she made small talk during the final minutes before the band started its next set. Weren't women the ones who were supposed to say, "we need to talk"?

The lights in the bar dimmed. A mirrored ball lowered from the middle of the ceiling and began to turn, casting prisms of silver light around the room. The band struck up a ballad. It was the time of night when people started hooking up, looking for love in all the right or *wrong* places. The blind-eye of alcohol made once unappealing partners look suddenly desirable. A curious pre-mating ritual that made him chuckle. Typical honky-tonk Saturday night.

All evening he had danced respectfully with Branna, like they were two friends out to have some fun, but in truth, despite his "no fraternization" rule, since the kiss, he'd strained to hold himself in check. The attraction pushed hard against his immoveable stand, so hard it made him want to set his rulebook on fire, watch it burn to ashes, and enjoy the release to freedom. Then, he wanted to kiss her again. And again.

"Let's dance," he said, not giving her an option.

Branna never let go of his hand as they returned to the dance floor. She snuggled close for a slow dance. Danger stepped closer. When she gazed at him, her eyes bright and half-shuttered, the effects of an alcohol induced haze, his heart and mind agreed that he needed her. Wanted her. His resistance drained further when he noticed a few grains of salt on her top lip.

"Lick, drink, and suck," he muttered several times, choosing to focus on the shot of tequila he'd order after the dance ended. He'd never had a woman drive him to drink before. Not even Caroline.

When Branna licked at the salt, the tip of her pink tongue entranced him. Everything in the room disappeared except her. He tilted her chin, ignored the question in her eyes, leaned in and pressed his lips to hers.

Her mouth was warm and pliant. She kissed him back. Kissed him as though she savored the connection building between them. Had it become his new lifeline?

Holding her close, swaying in place to the music, he continued exploring her lips. His hands moved down her back. Her softness aroused a hardness in him, and if she noticed, she didn't let on when she strained closer against him.

Branna's eyes remained closed as she clung to him. She swiveled her hips against his. The tip of her tongue rested at the peak of her top lip.

"Ohhh. God," he groaned. Could arousal actually kill him?

He'd tempted fate, then taken a leap off a cliff. But did Branna feel the same? Or at least something?

The only way to get closer to her, short of stripping naked and joining their bodies together, was to ravish her mouth. Thankfully, she didn't stop him.

When the song ended, Branna stopped moving, and then pulled back. "Why did you kiss me like that?"

He paused. His only excuse was lame. "Couldn't help myself?"

"What were you thinking, Dr. Newbern?"

"You have irresistible lips." He had only truth as a defense. Though it wasn't the complete story.

She frowned as though she expected some other answer. "Really? That's the best you've got?"

"Maybe I should take you home now. You've had too much to drink and drive. We can pick up your car tomorrow."

"I swear you sound just like my mother. Know this—I make my own decisions. I'm not ready to go."

Even mad she was beautiful. Her brow creased, and her eyes narrowed as she scrutinized him. Her mouth pouted in a way that only made him want to kiss her again. His gut clenched. Who was he kidding? He wanted way more than a kiss. Mentally, he tore his rulebook to shreds. "Another dance, then?"

When she turned to walk away, the band started the next slow song. He pulled her back. "I promise I won't do it again. Let's not ruin the evening. Forget that I'm a jerk."

She hesitated, but when he tugged her hand, she came easily into his embrace.

"I know a place not far from here," he whispered in her ear. "We can hang out there for a little while. Get a cup of coffee and something to eat. Make sure we're both sober before we make the hour drive back." He twirled her slowly, trying to get her to look at him. When she still refused, he let go of her hands and took a step closer. Nose to nose, with arms opened in surrender, he said, "I promise, you will be safe."

Questions, distrust glinted in her eyes. He waited for her answer. She paused for a long moment, then finally said, "How far are we going?"

"Not far, Cinderella. Besides, we can't have you turning into a pumpkin in front of all of these people."

"Oookay." Her voice warbled with hesitation.

He led her to the bar to claim her purse.

"It's Lady Branna, right?" Dale handed him the tab and motioned him closer. "As in, she's like one of those British folks related to the queen or something? I met a guy at a restaurant in Lakeview once. Someone said he was the nephew of a king in one of those little countries in Europe. He spoke American with a French accent. She's like him, right?"

James suppressed a chuckle. Branna wrinkled her nose and tilted her head as if she was trying to determine if Dale was teasing or not. Or maybe he made no sense to her at all. James couldn't tell, though he was amused as she drained the last bit of her drink.

"I mean, should I ask her for her autograph?" Dale held up a one-dollar bill. Ten years ago, when Dale first started tending bar for his uncle at Tin Lizzie, whenever someone remotely famous or noteworthy wandered in, Dale asked them to autograph a one-dollar bill. He framed it on the back wall of the bar. When the wall was covered, he then started stapling autographed bills on the ceiling, like the Irish pub over in Pensacola had done, until there was not a speck of ceiling tile showing. James had heard rumors that Tin Lizzie's ceiling was specially insured.

"Well, I don't know." James cocked his head. "I only met her yesterday. She said she's southern royalty. Who knows, maybe she is. I don't think she's the lying type. Ask her."

He watched Dale slide a dollar bill in Branna's direction and ask her the question.

"I'm not legally a lady..." She pursed her lips as if struggling to find the right words. She blinked a few times, then started again, "Well, I was raise to be a lady...but not the type you mean." She hiccupped. Confusion flashed across her face when Dale insisted again that she sign the dollar bill. Flustered, she wrinkled her face like a kid about to cry.

"Sign, then I'll give you back your purse."

James nodded, hoping to encourage her so he could get her out of the bar. She looked up at him wide-eyed. Her gaze locked on his as though she was drowning and needed him to toss her a lifeline. She licked her lips, then tried to shove her hair behind her ears. The large tequila drink had rocked her boat more than he'd imagined.

"Here." James handed over a pen. He moved closer to whisper in her ear. "Just scroll your name across the bill. You'll make the guy really happy. It will give him something to brag about."

As if under hypnotic suggestion, she moved the tip of the pen across the dollar, then handed it to Dale, who then, handed back her purse.

Pulling some bills from his pocket, James paid the tab, leaving a sizeable tip. He held out his hand to Branna, who took it and squeezed tightly.

Outside under the flicking floodlights, bugs bumped against the lights and buzzed. Gravel crunched under their feet as they made their way to his car. He kept her hand in his and helped balance her with his other hand in the small of her back. He felt her shiver. The evening coolness made him wish he had a blanket in the trunk. The river was not even a mile away. There, they could relax before the drive home. Who was he kidding? He had more than relaxation in mind. The outside air had not cooled his arousal.

They passed a crew-cab pickup with a couple in the backseat. The floodlight in the parking lot created a silhouette of a man and woman engaged in a fierce lip-lock.

"Getta-a-roooom!" Branna slurred her words.

"Com'on Pumpkin, we gotta go. That good ol' boy in that truck could have a shotgun. No sense in riling the natives." He hustled her along, then glanced back to the truck before he opened the car door for her. The couple inside the pickup gave no sign of hearing Branna's shout while they tore at one another's clothes.

Branna slunk down in the seat as though she had no bones in her body. "I've never been drunk before. So this is what it feels like."

She marveled at her own drunkenness?

He hooked her seatbelt, and then closed the door, rounding the car to the driver's side. He pulled from the parking lot with one eye on Branna, who attempted to open the window. Once she rolled it down, she laid her head on the frame and squealed, "Wheeee!"

"Never?" he asked incredulously.

"No. Never."

She giggled as though she enjoyed a private joke. He shook his head. Branna Lind was full of surprises.

Their outing had gotten out of hand. That was his fault. He'd take full responsibility, but more alone time with Branna right now would lead to serious problems. His brain shouted, "No!" His body, screamed, "Yes!"

He turned onto the road to Lakeview, a half-moon shone above. Except for an occasional farmhouse with a floodlight, the view everywhere now looked the same—empty darkness.

"Where do you live Miss Lind? Where is your house?"

"Remember...truck...last night? Beat up, white. Said you'd...introduce that guy. Interested in his house...but now..."

"What's your address Branna?" He slowed to the side of the road and leaned closer to hear her mumblings.

"I think..."

"Think what?"

Branna's head lolled to the side.

Damn it. She'd gone to sleep.

Chapter 14

Branna woke. Her body was limp and her brain enjoyed a pleasant haze as someone carried her. In the darkness, she looked up into James' barely visible face. His thighs bumped against her butt whenever he took a step. She circled his neck with her arms and would have gone back to sleep, except that the butt bumping made her giggle. The buzz from the margarita wrapped her in a state of relaxed surrender. And she couldn't deny it, the hardness of his body intrigued her.

"Pumpkins are lighter," James grumbled when they were a few steps from the landing at the front door.

"Huh?"

"Your midnight changing act. What happened to it? I'm not carrying a *pumpkin* up these steps. You look like a featherweight on your feet. But I have to say, you weigh more than a pumpkin in deadweight."

"Where are we?" Shadows surrounded them. Tree shapes created by moonbeams draped the darkness. She leaned back a bit to see the ground far below. Her brain began to compute. She was alone in the woods with a man she barely knew, and he was carrying her up to a cabin. His touch had produced the most wonderful quivers all night. Dare she admit to erotic stimulation? His kiss was smoother than satin. She had every intention of exploring the adventure of James. Once they made it inside.

But a headline about a dead college instructor flashed in her head. She tensed.

"Relax. You're safe. This is a protected place with coffee and food before the drive back. Listen, local cops sit and wait for drunks to leave the bars down the highway a mile. Neither of us needs to make the police-blotter list tomorrow."

When James got close to the door, close enough to press the handle, it poked her butt. The front door opened, and once across the threshold, he set her on her feet. She swayed, a definite margarita wobble. He caught her. Was this a game they were playing?

"Anyone home?" she called sing-songing-ly. When no one responded, she giggled. "No one's home. Are we breaking and entering? No. Couldn't be that because you didn't break anything. No door. No glass. Maybe your back. Carrying me up those steps. Are you okay?" She swayed. Being drunk wasn't so bad. She giggled, remembering the lengthy lecture her grandmother gave about the demons of alcohol.

Taking a step from the doorway toward the living room, she tried to balance on both feet, but swayed. James caught her, picked her up and plopped her on a couch that faced a large stone fireplace.

"I'm not a sack of potatoes." She frowned.

"Pumpkins. Potatoes. I could think of other ways of describing you."

He knelt in front of her, put a pillow on the armrest of the couch and guided her to lie back. He scooped up her feet, dropped her shoes, and let her stretch out long on the couch.

"You mean descriptions like the ones that sleazy bartender used at the Library?"

If he heard her, he ignored her question.

"I'll make some coffee and get us some food," he said.

She rose to sitting when he walked around the couch and toward the kitchen. The place had a definite cabin feel, but in Mississippi, houses built on stilts were called "camps" in the bayous and flood-prone areas. "Is there water nearby?"

"We're waterfront on the Ichetucknee River. This is my grandparents' escape."

She collapsed back down on the couch, her eyes too heavy to stay open.

A few minutes later she woke. The aroma of fresh-brewed coffee lifted to her nose, but she wasn't ready to let go of her margarita buzz. The mellowness relaxed her. All thoughts of anything else disappeared. But— the desire she experienced on the dance floor with James had not diminished a bit. She squeezed her legs tightly together, then stretched long. She had an itch that demanded scratching.

What would James think?

He appeared suddenly before her. She shuttered her eyes, almost squinting to see him. Could he read the need she was certain reflected in her eyes?

He placed a plate with hunks of cheese, torn bread, and fruit spreads on the coffee table. Due to her nervousness earlier, she'd not eaten much. She had cravings, all right, but food was not what she wanted.

Grandmother was right. Alcohol was indeed a drug. It had removed her inhibitions.

James reappeared with two mugs. He placed them on the table, then reached in his shirt pocket for individual creamers, and then retrieved sugar packets from his pant's pocket.

"I don't know how you take your coffee."

She scooted to sit with her knees bent. James sat on the couch beside her feet.

"Two creams. Two sugars."

James added the ingredients to her drink. He handed the mug to her. She noticed that he drank his coffee black and made a mental note. She snuck a few glances at him as she blew on the hot liquid in her cup. He seemed lost in contemplation. Since they'd crossed the threshold, the carefree ease they'd enjoyed before appeared to have remained at the bar. Maybe the hominess of the room had killed his mood?

"I'm sorry I fell asleep. This is nice, but we probably should be going soon." She couldn't look at him, instead watched the steam rise from her coffee.

"Actually, I think things work out like they're supposed to. Fate."

"Me falling asleep?"

She watched him ponder his response. His seriousness started to worry her.

"No, our meeting was fate. And *everything* since then." His chocolate brown eyes softened when he smiled at her. A quiver shot to her gut as he ran his hand from her knee to her bare foot. He stroked her ankle. She wanted to move, but couldn't.

"Our very first meeting at the bookstore definitely wasn't planned. James, you'd been avoiding me up to that point. But the rest of tonight? A non-date. The huge margarita—too much for one person to drink. Then, a place with food and coffee. You planned this, didn't you?" She looked at him warily. What had she gotten herself into? The more she learned about him, the more she wanted to know. But the closer they got, the more she wanted to run. How did he freeze her in place and at the same time, leave her wanting more?

"No. You're jumping to conclusions. I didn't—"

"Why did you kiss me back there?"

He went very still. Dangerously still. He put down his cup and locked his eyes on hers. Her breath caught. She stared back. She refused to back down.

The feeling that washed over her wasn't fear.

He angled his body, his shoulder against the back of the couch, then pulled her feet into his lap. His gaze kept her hypnotized. He spoke her name softly, "Branna."

"Uh ha?" Her heart raced. She set her coffee mug down.

"I'm gonna do it again."

She gulped.

He rose and picked her up, carrying her while keeping his eyes on hers. It was barely ten steps to the hallway. The moment at hand made her remember the kissing game she'd played in high school, "Ten minutes in heaven."

Down a dark hall, James turned into a room, then lowered her to a bed. Her head rested on a pillow. He sat beside her, their hips touching. He bent, and his lips hovered just above hers. His warm, strong hands cradled her face. The tingling from his touch intensified. Her insides quivered. If he didn't make a move, she was going to die.

His eyes searched hers as though asking a question.

She answered by rising to sit. Closed the distance between them. Their lips melded.

She kissed him hard. Desperately.

James deepened the kiss, sucking on her bottom lip. His tongue found access to her mouth. She wrapped her arms around his neck, and her body arched, pressing hard against his. An ache deep inside her grew, and she strained against him more.

Without breaking contact, he stretched out on the bed next to her, and then pulled her back beside him.

A voice she recognized in her head shouted for caution and reason, but she left the "good little girl" back in Bayou Petite. Here, she was a woman.

A woman in control.

She rolled on top of James, lying against the full, solid length of his body. She cupped his face with her hands and gently kissed him. He threaded his fingers through her hair, then rested one hand on the back of her head, the other beside her neck. The hard rise in his jeans left no room for doubt. He wanted what she did. She gyrated her pelvis into his, something she wouldn't have ever done with a man she'd only known a couple of days, let alone a man she'd never been out on a date with before.

"Branna?"

She tilted her head and then leaned close to him, her chin on his shoulder. His breath softly blew against her ear, and shivers reached her toes.

"You asked earlier, 'How far are we going...'"

He wanted to talk now? "Yes?"

James stilled. She could tell he held his breath.

"We're going to go as little or far as you want tonight."

Her insides melted. Desire magnified to full bloom. She pressed her lips to his, hard. Her hands reached for his, and she laced their fingers together.

Then, she whispered in his ear, "It's all or nothing."

Straddling his hips, she removed her blouse and unhooked her bra. A move she'd never made before. She pushed herself to standing on the bed, then stripped, dropping each piece of clothing in a pile on the floor.

Beneath her, James, his eyes trained only on her, wrestled off his clothes. They landed on top of hers.

As she lowered herself, James rose to a sit and ran his hands up her calves, and then her thighs. Heat from his tingling touch coalesced in the apex of her legs. The intensity made her weak. Had her bones melted?

She slid and straddled him. His hardness settled inside her. Her hips undulated.

Bravely, she faced him.

When his mouth captured her breast, she braced herself, hands on his shoulders.

The sensual stimulation was unbearable.

She'd lost all control of her body. She moaned, unembarrassed by the sound. She gloried in skyrocketing—all the way to heaven.

The moment was exactly what she wanted. She silenced the scold from the proverbial "good girl" in her head. Silenced it completely.

She stilled when James moved under her, wanting to experience each sensation.

They rocked together, up and back. Up and back.

Each move made her move more. Want more of him.

She tensed. Heaven exploded into bursts of shiny stars. Quivering warmth bathed her body. An experience so luxurious she never wanted it to end.

Later, when they lay tangled in the sheets, fingers threaded together, hip to hip, thigh to thigh, the clock by the bed beamed the time overhead. It was nearly two in the morning. She needed to go home.

Sitting up, she turned to reach for her clothes. James pulled her back and put his finger to her lips when she started to protest.

"Shhh," he said softly. "The next best part is yet to come. Just sleep with me for now."

He pulled her close, wrapped her arm around his waist, settled her head on his shoulder, then rubbed her arm in long soothing strokes. James had a power over her she wasn't in the mood to question. She drifted off, a deep contentment lulled her soundly to sleep.

Later, she woke with a start. Disoriented, she sat up, unsettled to realize her still nakedness. She grabbed the sheet to cover her body and looked around the bedroom.

Perfectly framed in front of three tall windows, was the silhouette of a man. James stood tall with his back to her. He was lean and muscled, and in the moonlight, looked like a god carved from marble. He appeared to survey the dark.

The proverbial "good girl" voice in her head screamed, *Now you've really done it!*

What had she really done? She looked around. A strange house. A strange bed. With a man who was nearly a stranger.

Oh God. She'd never drink again!

James must have heard her ruffle the sheets, or maybe he heard her panicked thoughts. He turned and faced her. Fear fled at the flash of his warm smile. The way it crinkled the corners of his eyes. All she could think when he walked toward her, moving with complete male grace, was that she had kissed him there, and there, and there.

When he reached her, he pulled back the sheet and exposed her nakedness. He kissed her softly at the base of her neck. Her pulse throbbed there. She couldn't breathe, not from fear, but from sweet anticipation. What would he think if she massaged him *there*, and then had her way with him?

"My turn." His voice sounded husky and sexy. "I promised. The next best part is yet to come."

He started a slow assault with his hands and his lips, caressing her shoulders, then moved to her chest, as though he treasured her body.

Delight tickled her insides. She gave in to the sensation of weightlessness. His mouth floated kisses over her breasts. His fingers caressed the inside of her thighs, moving in slow circles, inching higher and higher on her legs. In mere moments, he would have her drifting to meet heaven again.

The ecstasy was unimaginable. The craving was more than she could bear. Alcohol wasn't the demon addiction. Making love with James had to be.

James teased and tantalized her skin, stroked and sucked her body until she was begging for more and hanging on, trying not to fall off the edge of the earth.

He joined his body with hers. Filling her. They moved at a slow even pace, together as one. They rode the waves of pleasure.

He caressed her butt as they rocked. She grabbed tight to his shoulders for support and arched her back when he carried her to the top of the cliff of pleasure, the place where they both wanted to be...she felt his shudder as she heard her own long guttural moan.

Then they melted back to earth.

Had he somehow taken her bones?

Her body was so languid, further movement was out of the question—at least for another hour or so. Maybe the rest of the night. As her breathing returned to normal, James turned on his side, spooning her from behind. His hand draped, resting on her waist.

She never shared lovemaking with Steven that ever closely resembled what had just happened. And her "good girl" argument to Biloxi had been that sex couldn't possibly be satisfying outside of love...Well, she'd have to rethink that now.

She didn't have words for the experience with James, but that didn't matter. The corners of her mouth turned up. She was a late bloomer in more ways than one. She finally understood what Camilla had been telling her, about the burn, the need, and the euphoria so potent it was a drug. One that took you to the highest mountaintop, then launched you to the stars.

James was the perfect lover.

Had she really thought those words?

She had a lover?

She had a lover.

Oh, no.

Chapter 15

In the first light of early dawn, the room looked unfamiliar. Sitting up, Branna clutched a sheet to her chest. The banging in the kitchen had to be James, right?

What were you thinking? The "good-girl" voice in her head started to lecture, and her heartbeat zoomed to the edge of panic. Had she walked through a magical door in Lakeview or simply lost her mind? Maybe there was something in her drink last night. Otherwise, how could she rationalize, let alone explain that she'd been intimate with a man she barely knew.

Breathing deeply, trying to hold on to some semblance of calm, she gazed out the windows. When was the last time she rose to watch the radiance of a new day? When had she seen rays of light cast a glow that made the world look wonderfully refreshed? Certainly not since her engagement to Steven. Just how long had it been? Before college? For too many years, she'd juggled balancing school and duties at Fleur de Lis. Who had time for a sunrise?

The beauty of the golden light soothed the pounding in her heart. Tension eased more. Outside, squirrel leaped from limb to limb. The bedroom's second story windows offered a view like one would find living in a tree house. And through the trees, she caught a brief glimpse of light blue, the river flowed really close by.

Thankfully, there were no obvious neighbors in sight.

Hearing another pan bang against something brought uneasiness back to her gut. What had she been thinking? James was her assigned mentor. Their relationship had to remain professional.

She couldn't blame last night on alcohol, she was in enough control of her faculties that she could have stopped what happened. She didn't because...she wanted the experience. She wanted James. It was all about him. She and desire had climbed a mountain, reached the highest peak, then when desire demanded full attention, she was happy to oblige. Never would she regret making love with him, no matter how loud the "good-girl" voices wanted to shout her down.

But...after last night, James could peg her as another "type." If so, she probably wouldn't like the label.

She scrambled for her clothes, now neatly folded in a chair by the window, and then dressed. A second later, James entered the bedroom with two mugs. He handed her one.

"Two creams. Two sugars."

The timbre of his voice resonated low in her gut and sent a warming sensation lower. She barely managed to nod as he stood grinning at her.

She nodded again for good measure.

"Are you a morning person?" James asked.

Was he really standing there expecting a benign conversation? After everything that happened last night? In this room? In that bed? Not once, but twice. She blinked, hoping her voice would remain as casual sounding as his.

"Honestly, I love sleep. It's the greatest luxury in life. Sunday mornings, I get up for church at the last minute. I don't think Father John has ever seen me with makeup." She wanted to clamp her hand over her mouth. She was babbling. "A morning person by design, not voluntary."

"I see. Catholic or Episcopalian?"

"Hail Mary's and everything." She chuckled nervously.

His eyes never left hers. His gaze unnerved her. She raked her fingers through her hair, certain last night's makeup had smeared her face like a Jackson Pollock painting. Taking a step forward, she whispered, "Restroom?"

"Ah. Oh. Sorry. Through there." James pointed down the hall.

She took another step. Glanced at him. The door opening wasn't wide enough for her to pass with him in the way. He turned and raised his hands, holding his mug high above his head. She slipped by, making sure they didn't touch.

Inside the small bathroom, she stood in front of a pedestal sink and took a good look into the mirror. "Not *too* bad," she muttered while wondering how to disappear and reappear at home alone. Her actions last night would shock anyone who knew her. She had shocked herself. The discomfort that dawned with the sun was something she'd never experienced before. The idea of adventure suited her far better than the actual experience. Had Lewis and Clark felt that way on their Journey of Discovery to the uncharted west?

"Branna, are you okay? I can make breakfast or I

can take you out to eat. What's your desire?" James called through the bathroom door.

Desire had led to her current predicament—hiding out in the bathroom. How in the world would she face the man at work every day? His assignment was to show her the ropes on the job, yet he managed to educate her in several new ways that had nothing to do with what they did for a living. And, she'd be lying if she said she didn't want more.

"Branna, I'm starting to get concerned. If you don't come out, I'm going to have to come in. We can deal with the elephant in the room. We just have to talk about it."

Not only was James a good kisser, a wonderful lover, but clearly he had some measure of mindreading skills. That made him even more dangerous. Quickly, she washed her face, rubbed it dry, then slowly opened the door.

He reached in and took both of her hands, holding them as though they were delicate like porcelain as he guided her to the living room. Could she be growing accustomed to the quivering he sent though her body with a mere touch?

The man had the most unnerving way of capturing her total attention. As they stood before the stone fireplace, about in the same spot where everything had started last night, he looked deep into her eyes, as if looking for all of her secrets. She blinked.

"There are a couple of ways to look at this situation. It only requires an open mind."

Puzzled, she tilted her head and shifted her gaze from his eyes to his mouth.

"Yesterday evening was a non-date, but

somewhere between the 'non' and 'date,' it became an actual date."

She started to protest, but he squeezed her hands. "Hear me out. There was no way I could get you home by midnight, and we both know what happens then, so I brought you here, where no one—trust me on this—no one turns into a pumpkin at midnight."

She furrowed her brow and remained silent. So far, he hadn't said anything that she could argue against.

"Now, the way I see it, everything from *after* the Tin Lizzie to *dawn* was our first date, and I want today to be our second date, allowing us to dispense with all of the after-the-first-date issues."

It alarmed her that he was making complete sense. It wasn't lost on her that he didn't make specific references to their *activities* between midnight and first light. That would have sent her running.

"That's one way to look at it," she agreed noncommittally.

"Good, then on our second date, I want us to get to know each other better and decide on when we'll have our third date."

"*We*," she said. "We don't know each other at all!"

"*Au contraire, mon ami*. We know quite a bit about each other." He winked.

What craziness. Who was she? She went to bed with him, almost a stranger. And then he woke up and considered the new dawn an opportunity for a *second* date. The "good girl" warred with the "adventuring girl" in a heated battle. What should she do? James Newbern had an appealing charm. Many positive qualities. Who was she kidding? She'd lived more, drank more, and danced more with him than anyone.

He was the charge to her battery. He was sexy as hell. And, she never used four-letter language, yet the facts completely warranted it this time.

But in the light of day, her daring dwindled.

"I think," she started and offered a half smile. "I need to take a rain check on that second date. I'm not feeling too great. Plus, I don't mix business and..."

James grinned at her. "So. Much. Pleasure." He finished her sentence.

She wanted to slap the smile off his face.

"Hmm, are you one of *those*?" she asked.

He drew back. "One of what?"

"The type who blurs the lines between work and private life."

"I guess you'll just have to take a chance and find out for yourself, Miss Lind."

Chapter 16

A dream diffused into fractured images, and sleep slipped away. Startled awake, Branna looked around. This wasn't in her room at Fleur de Lis. Clarity settled in when she spied the green glow of the digital clock as it shined five forty-five a.m.

"Oh," she groaned. "Another hour...have to get up. Monday...school."

Closing her eyes, she slowed her breath, trying to coax her body to relax and her brain to quiet. She wanted to return to luxurious sleep where worries dissolved like sugar in hot tea. While Lakeview had washed her nightly bad dreams about Steven away, maybe her anxiety over James triggered them again?

Flashes of the nightmare came back to her. She found herself on stage at the Valentine's Day auction panicked and trying to cover her total nakedness with a large fan, one with feathers that a burlesque dancer might use. All of Bayou Petite stared at her, their jaws slack in stunned silence, while her view was of Steven's back as he abandoned her there, totally humiliated.

For months, unpleasant dreams had exposed her lack of invincibility and opened her eyes to her own fragile vulnerability. Steven's betrayal had crushed her confidence as easily as swatting a mosquito.

After that living nightmare, her choice to remain in Bayou Petite had locked her in a tug-o-war. Staying was a stand of defiance against him. However, staying meant she risked running into him in town and at local social functions. Unfortunately, their families traveled in the same circles, and even if they didn't, given the size of Bayou Petite, sooner or later, they were bound to meet.

She punched her pillow and flipped on her side. So what had she done about his...his philandering? Isolated herself at Fleur de Lis for months. That made her feel like only half a coward, but in truth she lived like one, rarely leaving the property and always in fear of running into the man who destroyed her well-planned life. She would not allow him to shatter her family with his promiscuous feats, thus she remained silent about *all* of the reasons she'd broken off the engagement.

In the end, her decision to face her fears and get on with her life drove her from home. Drove her all the way to Florida.

In an hour, she needed to rise from the safety of her bed, to start her first day of teaching. However, after Saturday night, she would forever associate *teaching* with James. In her brain, the two were intricately linked.

Frustrated that her mind continued to roam, she planted her feet on the floor, then padded to the bathroom. Turning on the light, she stared into the mirror. "You can't hide. You can't leave. You've got to face this mess, face James."

After squeezing toothpaste onto her toothbrush, she worked the brush in circles as her "good-girl" conscience berated her.

How could she have made love to him? A man

assigned to oversee her transition. Maybe he had a girlfriend. In that case, he was a louse. Or maybe he had something casual...like with Sara Nell.

Branna scrubbed her teeth harder. She had always laughed at the radio preachers shouting about the demons of alcohol, but now she understood firsthand—consequences came from exercising the elbow in a bar. In fact, a face-to-face with Steven again might be less uncomfortable than facing James at school.

The jitterbug that danced in her gut made her want to pack up and return to the safety of Fleur de Lis. Yet as much as that idea had appeal, if she dragged herself home, she'd forever be a coward and a complete failure. Such admirable qualities for the next Keeper of Fleur de Lis. Not!

Talk about morning-after regrets.

No, she wouldn't run. She could carry on as though nothing bothered her and reconcile that one night with James as a learning experience—one night of fun and pleasure. She, too, could act as though nothing out of the ordinary had happened. The façade of strength was better than a no-show of fortitude.

She finished washing her face, then took a deep breath. The more she tried to shift her focus, the more her thoughts drifted to James. The man took cool tingles and ramped them up to a hot sizzle. Could the magnetic attraction between them sit on simmer? It would take an ocean of self-control to keep her distance from him. The picture in her mind of James standing naked before the window in the moonlight made her dizzyingly hot. The heat of his hands on her body was more than a mere memory.

She fanned her face to cool the flush before putting

on her makeup.

At least this morning she finally felt human.

Not like yesterday.

The weekend had been wild, at least measured by her standards. How did her sister and Biloxi manage to party all the time? Did a person build up endurance to liquor, loud music, and dancing? Or did a hot-looking guy somehow trigger hormones that made a woman go crazy?

A chair held the clothes she laid out last night, but she went to her closet and searched for something different. A blue and white summer dress she'd picked from the Brooks Brother's catalog last year and had never worn.

"It fits fine," she said to her reflection in the mirror.

Partying as she had on Saturday night at Tin Lizzie would kill her before she could build up enough endurance to handle it on a once-a-week basis. How boring her life must seem to others. However, she'd take fine dining and a jazz concert over the raucous Tin Lizzie and bar food.

But as long as James danced with her, she'd probably follow him anywhere.

He'd brought her home yesterday morning, after a tall Bloody Mary with breakfast, rather than dropping her off at her car. Afterward, she slept most of the day, which helped her avoid the pounding in her head and the queasiness in her stomach. She rose once, thinking she might eat, but standing before the open refrigerator door, the idea of food made her first-ever hangover worse. She worked at rehydrating—all the salt on the rim of the margarita had made her thirstier than parched cotton growing in a drought. However, after hours of sipping only water, she could pass for a bloated fish floating in the Mississippi. She switched to club soda and washed down Tylenol. That had finally stopped the throbbing in her head.

And she would do it all again because?

Being in James' arms was like a fabulous vacation. One where she was wrapped in warm shearling before a fireplace while a blizzard blew outside, and at the same time, anticipating the thrill of racing fast to the bottom of a roller coaster's hill.

The idea was school girl silly, but so true.

However, yesterday evening, when she was barely feeling human, James had called and announced that he headed toward her house to take her to her car. A deafening silence hung between them on the trip. They barely made polite conversation. She sensed something bubbling beneath the surface of his calm exterior. Did it have anything to do with her? She had been too embarrassed to ask.

Late last night, Steven had texted her wishing her good luck on her first day of work. She threw the phone across the room. When would she ever get his thorn out of her side?

Branna pulled on her strappy sandals and took one last look in the mirror. She looked the part of a conservative college instructor. If she ever got a tattoo, which she wouldn't because it would literally put G.G. Marie in her grave, it would read "stupid" on her forehead. The "good-girl" rant was back. Might as well get it all out. Take the licks now, and then try to banish the voice in her head forever.

Could she have been more predictable than getting

drunk with a colleague, then falling asleep on him? To make her behavior even more egregious, she'd slept with him, a euphemism for sex, though they'd done some real sleeping, too. Yet, ever the gentleman, James had delivered her home. Walked her to the door and unlocked it after she fumbled the key. She found her bed, stumbled in that direction, and heard him close the front door. She barely remembered the sound of his car starting before he drove away.

What *type* had he labeled her after that?

Chapter 17

Branna's heels clicked in a hurried rush against the linoleum floor as she maneuvered through the classroom wing of the English Department's building. When she crossed the threshold to the instructor's suite, the carpet silenced the clipped-heel tapping. She shivered. A wall of cold air washed over her. No one could complain about heat or humidity while parked in the office. It was colder than the bookstore during the storm.

Sadie McGee, the department secretary, scurried toward her wearing a wide, welcoming smile. "Miss Lind! Bitsy called to wish you a happy first day. I have several other phone messages for you. I need to know what you prefer. Shall I keep them on my desk until I see you, like now? Or shall I put them in your mail slot? Or do you want them delivered to you?"

"Slow down, Sadie." Branna chuckled. "Good morning."

"Yes, good morning." Sadie bobbed her head. "Please excuse my exuberance. The first day of school makes me giddy, and I want things to run like clockwork."

She had met the secretary last month at the get-to-know-you luncheon when everyone but James welcomed her to the department. Petite Sadie looked years younger than fifty-five with her soft brown curls and slender figure. Amazingly, Sadie had been the department's secretary for, in her words, "Since God was a small child." Those years totaled twenty.

Sadie boasted that she knew everything about everyone and had eyed Branna suspiciously at the meeting, as though she sized her up, seeking the places where she kept her life's most private secrets. As if Sadie intended to ferret them out. She had also heard that Sadie had a can-do attitude, but that she smelled conflict the same way a bird dog instinctually pointed quail. Branna hoped the last part wasn't true. She wanted her private life to remain just that. Even more so, given the events of Saturday night.

"I like order, too, Sadie. I know I can trust you to show me the ropes about how the office runs."

"My desk is my command center. As for messages, I keep duplicate copies of all. In case you misplace one or accidently throw it away."

Sadie's desk sat in the middle of the large, square lobby surrounded by offices on three sides. Each instructor in the department had their own private one. She spotted her name on the door off to Sadie's right.

"Messages for me?" Branna asked, holding open her hand.

"I want to make things go smoothly on your first official day here." Sadie held tight to several pink slips torn from the message pad sitting on her desk.

"What's easiest for you?" She didn't want special treatment. What did the other instructors do? She'd have to remember to ask James later.

"Well, putting them in your mail slot is easiest," Sadie said, then twisted her mouth to one side, looking as though she wanted to suggest something different.

"But?" Branna smiled, still waiting for the slips of paper.

Sadie leaned in close. Her eyes darted from side to side as if scanning the room for eavesdropping ears or a spy. "I don't recommend *that* for *these* phone messages. Especially *private* and *personal* ones, like these." Sadie fanned the messages. The gentle movement of air fluttered against Branna's cheek. Then, Sadie handed them over, grinning like she'd landed the mother lode of gold.

Branna wondered about the secretary's trend toward the dramatic, though James had warned that the trusted woman considered acting her hobby. Sadie had often won the lead roles with the local theatre company. And, clearly, as Sadie stood before her now, Sadie thought she smelled a secret. Gossip.

"What *do* you recommend?" Branna asked, dropping her gaze to the caller's name on each slip of paper. Anger boiled up, but she immediately tamped down the emotion. When she glanced up, she caught Sadie's curious stare. She smiled, hoping Sadie would think the messages were completely unimportant.

Sadie leaned in close and whispered, "I can slide the personal ones under the door when you're not in your office. That way you'll maintain your privacy. I keep personal things very quiet, Miss Lind. I might *know* a lot of gossip, but I am *not* a gossip."

"Why, thank you." She'd heard Sadie's reputation was the exact opposite. However, since there were more men than women in the English department, she hoped the woman might be true to her word—the sisterhood and all. "For the information and for the messages."

Branna, fuming mad at Steven, stuffed the pink

papers into her purse and headed to her office. She slid her key into the lock, opening the door. When she turned to close it behind her, Sadie stood a breath away. Branna held the door for support, stopping herself from jumping back and screeching at the woman.

"I promise you, Miss Lind. I'm not a gossip. However, I am known to offer good advice about issues of a personal nature, if asked. I never give advice unless asked. I want you to know that I have a lot of experience in certain types of personal matters. After all, I've been married three times."

Had Sadie just suggested she would be a good source of relationship information, and in the same breath admit that she'd never experienced a long-term stable marriage? Branna paused before answering the petite woman. Seeking diplomacy—the last thing she wanted to do was begin her workday by alienating her new secretary, which would surely start fodder for the gossip mill—she chose her words carefully. "Sadie, thank you for taking the messages. I'll have a look at these, and if I need some suggestions, I'll ask. For the future, just slide personal messages, *like these*, under my door."

Sadie eyed her as if trying to decide if she meant what she said. "I will be certain to do that, Miss Lind. Now, I'll get back to work." Sadie pulled on the bottom of her sweater, squared her shoulders, and marched back toward her desk.

She watched Sadie's retreating back and mused that if Steven weren't already dead to her, she'd kill him.

After dropping her purse and tote on top of her desk, she tugged on the cord to the window blinds.

Clean morning light spilled in and lit the room. She rolled her desk chair out and plopped into it, intent on the view beyond the window of planted oaks and pine trees. Above the treetops, a large plane lifted from the runway at the airport. She wanted to put her anger on that plane and have the pilot jettison the bundle somewhere over the Atlantic. She hated that anything to do with Steven mined old emotions. Someday, the moment would come when his name no longer triggered any reaction. That moment when she would have only total ambivalence toward the man who trashed her self-confidence. The bit of lingering anger reminded her of how much a blow her confidence had taken.

After a few deep, calming breaths, she laid the pink slips of paper side-by-side on her desk.

Call me, please.

We have to talk. It isn't over for either of us.

I love you truly. Please call me when you get this.

She should've known he wouldn't let things drop just because she had moved out of state. He must have worked hard to locate her. She trusted her family. All but Camilla, whom she was never able to reach.

Like a staged play running in her head, Steven took center mark in her mind. How had she ever mistaken his arrogance for confidence? How could she ever have been flattered by all his attention and not recognize his controlling nature? She had years of proof of his behavior, from childhood. But worse still, how could she not have known, in the face of all the clues, Steven participated in extra-curricular activities that included gymnastics with other women?

The proverbial "good girl" was as gullible as she

157

was naïve.

Her jaw clenched as she remembered how she'd surprised him with a picnic dinner at his house and discovered him *in flagrante delicto*. The strange car in his driveway should have caused suspicion, but nooo, not for her. She used her key, thinking he would be in his office working too hard and in need of a break. Instead, she had found him upstairs, in the bed they were supposed to share after they married.

She had heard joined groans, moans, and cries as she climbed the stairs. When she threw the double doors open, she stared. She expected *Cinemax After Dark* on the TV. After a final thrust, Steven rolled to one side. When he noticed her, he frowned. A naked woman, still writhing in the sheets, grabbed for him, but he slapped her hands away. Rising from the bed, naked with a sheen of sweat, he grabbed clothes from a pile and threw them at the woman. He ordered Miss Hot and Horney to get out, his voice so cold that he could have been damning the devil rather than speaking to a sexpot with whom he had just exchanged bodily fluids.

Branna scrunched her eyes tight to block out the memory, but it was no use.

Shocked, she'd run downstairs. The woman scurried behind her, jerked the front door open, and laughed as though the whole event was some sort of joke. Stunned, Branna watched the hussy dress on the front porch, then climb into her car before driving off. For once, Branna was glad about the house's remote location. No prying neighbors to witness the surreal spectacle.

Boxer-clad and pulling on a T-shirt, Steven had descended the stairs. When they stood together in the foyer, she wanted to stomp her foot and shout the *F*-word, but couldn't bring herself to utter it. G. G. Marie would wash her mouth with soap for language unbecoming a lady. Regardless of the situation.

"I'm no worse than any other guy," Steven had said, matter-of-factly. "It's only *natural* for a guy to play around, especially before he gets married. You should thank me, Branna. It'll make me a better husband."

Had she heard him correctly? "Thank you? I should *thank you?* There have been others? For how long and how many?" she demanded. His response cut deep. Nothing in her usually organized, sheltered life had prepared her for his reply.

"Do you mean how many at the same time?"

She'd never, ever hit anyone before. Not even spanked her brother or sister when they were small. That day, she had launched herself at Steven, pummeling his chest and slapping him. Raking her proper, ladylike manicured nails down his face. Crazed, she roared and screamed like wild animal.

A hard crack against her cheek whipped her head to one side. Shocked, she crumpled to the floor in a heap. Tears welled, but she didn't give him the satisfaction of allowing a single one to drop.

The sharp sting of the memory had faded, but her mind replayed the events as though they had happened moments ago rather than last October.

She touched her left hand to her cheek. The heat of the slap and the flush that followed, along with the reverberating sting, no longer emanated into her fingers as though it had just happened. And thankfully, now, the weight of Steven's two-carat engagement ring no

Linda Joyce

longer weighed down her hand.

After the slap, she'd pulled the ring off, then picked herself off the floor, rising with as much dignity as she could muster. She laid the ring on the marble-topped antique server in the foyer, and then walked out. Steven shouted for her and ran down the steps after her. He had tried to stop her from getting in her car by grabbing at her keys and holding her hands firmly.

"Branna, don't. Once we say our wedding vows, I promise, I'll be faithful. Then I'll be a husband. Right now, I'm just a guy. Guys are stupid, you know that. Surely you understand. Com'on baby doll. Smile for me. Give me a kiss right here." His finger pointed to the dimple in his cheek, the one she used to love.

Limp, she leaned against her car. Steven reached for her, tried to pull her into a hug. The moment he released her hands, she shoved him away hard. Scrambled inside her car and locked the door. She started the engine, and backed out of the driveway.

Steven shouted, "You'll be back! You love me! You'll be back. You know your family wants me."

He was right. She *had* loved him.

Afterward, it took all the strength she had not to cave when their families got involved and pleaded his case. She never told anyone what happened. The shame was too much. Everyone chalked it up to pre-wedding jitters. Everyone took Steven's side.

Camilla had pushed hardest.

Branna tightened her fists in her lap. In her world, men weren't unfaithful to their fiancés or wives. An engagement was a commitment. An intention. If Steven couldn't honor monogamy then, she had no illusions that he would be faithful during their marriage. A

160

husband and wife, like her parents and all of her aunts and uncles, were a team who vowed to love and respect and honor. She had refused to marry Steven, no matter how much her broken heart nudged.

In the end, it was Camilla's advice that made her stand her ground. "I *know* he's been unfaithful. I *know* that's why you won't go through with it, but you have the greatest capacity to forgive. Forgive him. Besides, you always do what Momma and Daddy want."

"Not this time," Branna whispered as she stared out the window. There was only one way Camilla could have known about Steven's transgression...but was her sister a willing participant, or an innocent victim of the calculating low-life?

Steven's pursuit of her had lessened over the last two months. But how had he heard that she'd left Fleur de Lis? She never showed her face in town after the breakup. From where or from whom did he get her work number? None of her family would dare talk to him...except maybe Camilla.

Peaceful serenity filled her as she tore each message into tiny pieces. They fluttered like delicate pink snowflakes into the waste paper basket. Once she had finished, she slapped her hands together, happy to be rid of any evidence of her painful past.

She pulled out the roster for her first class to run through each of the names, practicing pronunciations, she hoped to speak them correctly in class. Half way through, the phone rang.

"Miss Lind," she answered, then made a check mark by a name on the roster to keep her place.

"Hello, gorgeous. How's my baby doll?"

Branna dropped the receiver as though it had

burned her hands. Jumping up, she rounded her desk and closed her office door. The last thing she needed was for Sadie's sharp ears to overhear whatever would come next.

She took a deep breath, calmly sat in her chair, then cautiously picked up the phone.

"Branna? Are you there?"

"Yes," she answered quietly.

"I'm calling to congratulate you on your new teaching job." His enthusiasm made her wary.

"Thank you."

"I could have gotten you a full-time position at the community college here. No more adult education night school for you. You didn't have to run so far from Bayou Petite."

What could she say to that? If she said he had nothing to do with her leaving, he'd never believe it. She had never made a habit of lying, however, her life was none of his business. In fact, it was off-limits in any discussion with him. "I have to go, Steven."

"I'm sending you a gift today. Please let me know when you receive it."

She could tell him she would refuse any gift, but it wouldn't do any good. His ego wouldn't hear of it. He had showered her with gifts for the first month after their broken engagement. She sent them all back. Each time he tried to see her, she'd refused. It had been a long uncomfortable seven months. Hearing his voice proved to her how much her heart had mended. She couldn't be swayed by his charm. Standing up to him, even if it was only over the phone, inched her confidence up enough that she could have scaled the Empire State Building without a superhero's help.

"Good bye, Steven," she said calmly and hung up the phone.

A second later, a knocked sounded at her door. "Miss Lind? I'm sorry to disturb you. I need a moment of your time."

She rose from her chair and opened the door for Sadie, then stepped into the lobby.

"Delivery men—I mean persons, it could be a woman—aren't allowed to roam freely on campus. There's a delivery for you at the front desk in the Admin building. Would you like to pick it up or shall I ask one of the grounds men to deliver it here to the office?"

"First, I need to ask. How do you receive calls for me—the messages?"

"Incoming calls go directly to your office number. They bounce to my phone if you're not in your office to answer, or you're too busy and choose to let it ring back to me."

"I see." Sadie had to be the one to provide Steven with the information. "About the delivery, do you know what it is?" She searched Sadie's face for a clue. Steven could be so persuasive. Could he have recruited Sadie to help him with his scheme?

"Yes, I do. Your caller, the one from the messages, told me to expect it. Told me several other things, too. Are you sure you don't want to talk to me about what's bothering you?"

"Sadie, thank you. I assure you, there's nothing bothering me, other than I'm trying to learn my students' names. If you know what the gift is, is it something that you'd enjoy?"

Sadie's chin dipped, her eye lashes fluttered, and

she smiled coyly. "I know you'll love it. I certainly would."

"Good. Have it delivered to you. I have a class. Whatever the gift, I don't want it. I guarantee you that."

"But Miss Lind?"

"No buts. Either accept the delivery for yourself or send it back. I don't care."

"All right." Sadie sounded tentative. "I'll go and get it myself." The woman did an about-face like a well-trained soldier and left.

As Branna turned, she spotted James at his desk through the sidelight window of the office. With one elbow resting on the desktop, he held the phone receiver to his ear as he talked, all the while fingering a silver object on his desk. His eyes were closed.

She started to tap on the glass and wave, but his expression shifted to one of pain. A sharp stab hit her gut. What might she do to bring a smile to the lips that had sent tingles shooting all the way to her toes when they last touched hers?

Chapter 18

"Caroline, why are you calling me?" James demanded, wishing he'd never picked up the phone. Their relationship was years over, but their shared loss still connected them more than their family's long relationship.

"James Dallas Newbern, that gorgeous house you bought would have been ours. You haven't invited me over. We would've raised our little *Katie* there."

He hated it when Caroline whined. She always used the "Katie card" when she wanted something. Caroline had not one nurturing bone in her body. That became crystal clear when she had demanded a full-time, live-in nanny for Katie before the child had been born.

"That's the past."

"Only three years. Dr. Simpson says that people grieve in their own way and mine is taking longer than some, but not as long as some of his other patients."

"I'm sure he appreciates the weekly paycheck." He figured the doctor would announce Caroline was healed or recovered or whatever as soon as her money ran out. He also heard the pout in her voice and could picture her stomping her foot. In the early stages of their relationship, he'd found her little pout cute. However, he'd grown to hate that about her by the time Katie was born.

"There's no need for sarcasm, James. After all, *we* were Katie's parents."

It seemed so long ago, a different life. When they were a couple. A different time. He was a different man back then, and set on disproving the old saying, "You can take the man out of the country, but you can't take the country out of the man." For the life of him now, he couldn't remember why he thought that. There was nothing wrong with being successful, and being a country boy, too. He still wanted it all, career, family and his own home in the city, though he didn't admit it to anyone.

And, he'd mistakenly thought he'd have all of that when Caroline walked into his life, or rather she backed into it.

Women drivers. He had backed out of a parking space, then she backed her car into his. It was during his college years. The campus police said they were both at fault. He'd offered to buy her a pizza to get her to drop the whole thing, there was barely a dent in either car. Her coy grins brought out the apples of her cheeks and showed off her dimples. Long, curly blonde hair, crystal blue eyes. Everything to like. Their family had attended church together for years, but until then, he'd never really looked at her. That day, she batted her long lashes at him, and his hormones answered. After that, his obsession for her was beyond anything he understood.

Looking back, if someone suggested the connection between them was the result of her being a vampire *and* his maker, he couldn't argue with that. She had sucked the life out of him.

Within a month, he'd bought a one-carat solitaire

engagement ring. When he proposed, she said yes, but wanted a bigger diamond before the wedding. He promised her one as soon as he could afford it. Her mother insisted it would take a minimum of a year to plan a proper wedding, and pointedly suggested he have the new ring by then.

The night of their engagement party, after they dined with a hundred well-wishers, he'd taken her to the river. Under the stars at the water's edge with the soft lap of the water, they made love.

What came next shouldn't have been a surprise.

Caroline waited until she was more than three months pregnant to tell him or their family. Her mother, the devout Southern Baptist, wanted to move up the wedding date, no grandchild of hers would be born out of wedlock, but Caroline's will proved stronger. She demanded a couture gown in white and a wedding she'd always remember. She wouldn't get married until *after* the baby was born.

He always wondered if she'd done that to keep him dangling.

The months were torturous. Caroline grew more contentious and demanding as her body changed and grew. At first, he chalked it up to hormones, pregnant women had those problems, but she acted as though she wasn't pregnant. Whenever he tried to talk about their baby, Caroline would change the subject. She never even admitted her waist had spread. Denial. At a level he'd never seen before. Pregnancy brought out the worst in her. And, she never let him touch her again.

Then Katie was born. Caroline wouldn't even look at her.

Yet, he was in love the minute the nurse put Katie

in his arms. That first contact lasted a few moments, but he had bonded with her. He never wanted her to feel alone. He never wanted her to feel unloved. Never wanted her to have an apathetic mother. Maybe Caroline really couldn't help it. According to her shrink, she was a complete narcissist. Caroline somehow misconstrued the diagnosis and considered it a high compliment.

He and Caroline never married. Her true colors glowed during her pregnancy. He suggested counseling before they considered taking another step in the direction of marriage. Their pastor insisted on counseling, but Caroline refused.

The worst of it was the day Katie came home from the hospital. Caroline acted as though she'd dropped a watermelon in a field and after that, it was someone else's responsibility. Instead of a wedding, he and Caroline worked out a custody agreement with Katie living with him.

His little Katie never made it to her first birthday.

"James? Are you listening to me? James?"

He picked up the polished silver rattle on his desk. Light glinted. A reminder of his daughter. Hard to believe Katie would have started preschool this year.

"No, Caroline, I'm not. Not anymore." He hung up. Katie might be gone, but he had other kids in his life. Kids with hopes and dreams. That's what he loved about teaching. Helping others take another step on their journey.

He grabbed a binder and a pen and left his office. In the past, the first day of classes always lifted his spirits. Maybe today it would be the same. He looked around. Sadie wasn't at her desk. Usually, he let her know where he was headed. It was odd that she wasn't there, but maybe she slipped away to make copies or visit the ladies' room. He scribbled a note and left it for her.

As the class before his let out, he slipped between small groups of students. Waving to the instructor wiping the white board clean, he took the middle seat in the back row of the room and waited.

Students' nervous chatter came with the first day of classes. For most, his class would be their first taste of college ever. He enjoyed the newbies, though the freshman that delayed starting college until fall often appeared more attentive. Something happened between high school graduation and their first day of community college that washed away half of their arrogance. Those students seemed to embrace a fresh view of the world.

The incoming students found seats and paid him no attention, an old man in a class of teenagers. It didn't surprise him that not one student sat in the front row. He tracked the time on his watch since the classroom clock hung on the wall behind him. When his watched showed a minute past nine fifteen, he stood up.

"This is Communications 101, an entry-level, first-year class," he said. All eyes turned to him. He took his time making his way to the front of the room. The thud of his boots echoed in the silence as he walked behind his desk, then paced in front of the white board. He had their attention.

When he turned to face his audience, they looked back with surprise, curiosity, and a few challenging stares.

"You," he barked, pointing to a young man slumped in his seat at the end of the second row. The student popped upright.

"No sleeping in my class. Please close the door."

The young man obeyed and hurried from his seat.

James scrawled his name with a blue marker, along with the name of the course on the whiteboard. He tapped the board to make his point. "This is my name, Dr. James Newbern. You may call me, Dr. Newbern. If you're not here for communications, please leave now." Then he picked up the student roll and walked in front of his desk. Leaning against it, he crossed his booted ankles.

"Good morning and welcome. If this is your first college class, congratulations! You're no longer in high school. I believe you must be smart because you've made the decision to further your education."

A few students shifted and sat upright in their seats.

"What do I expect from you? I require your best. Nothing less will get you successfully out the door at the end of this semester. I hope you find the material useful in your everyday life. Maybe even enjoyable." Twenty-one pairs of eyes focused on him. A few other pairs looked anywhere but at him.

"I'll take attendance this week. I'll know your names before the week is out. If I butcher your name when I call it the first time, correct me. I apologize in advance if I get it wrong. If you have a nickname or something else you wish to be called, *if it's publicly appropriate*, I'll be happy to oblige." That remark triggered a few snickers and giggles, like it had every semester in the past.

He intended his opening speech to set expectations, and hoped a bit of humor would put them at ease. For some of them, even though Lakeview was a small community college, it signified a huge accomplishment. In rural communities, some students' families could barely afford tuition. That fact was never lost on him.

"And since this is my class, you follow my rules. I'm a totalitarian. If you don't know the meaning, look it up. I'm willing to listen to reason, not excuses. Answer when I call your name and let me show you to your new seat."

Loud groans rolled back to him.

"What? You don't like your first assignment? No worries, this won't be the only seat change this semester. Change brings chaos. Chaos causes growth. You'll sit in several seats before you're done and get to know all of your classmates."

As he began to call names, he pointed each student to their new seat. Some students showed more reluctance than others.

"Buddy Davis?" James called out.

"Bubba." A young, tall, thin guy rose and moved into the seat where James pointed at the end of the first row. "Bubba, it is. Cheryl-Lynn Fenton? Start the next row."

More than halfway through the list, James called out, "Andres Parker?"

A stout, brick-wall-type of guy near the back of the room raised his hand. "Bubba," he said. Giggles circled the room.

"Naw, he's already claimed 'Bubba.' Give me another name or we'll have Bubba 1 and Bubba 2. Or B1 and B2. You get the picture. It's your nickname. You two work it out and let me know what you want to do."

Andres scowled. "Parker," he growled. "*You* call me Parker."

"Okay, Parker it is." James wrote the name on the seating chart. That was one name he'd not forget. "Now, for more alliteration. Where's Pamela P. Preston?"

A pretty blonde in a pink tennis outfit sat in the middle of the second row and gave a princess wave. A diamond bracelet dangled on her wrist. She stood, gathered her bag and moved as though she might be an actress making a grand stage entrance. She walked to the front of the room, where she stood next to him. She almost reached his full height of six feet. He wondered how she had decided on Lakeview for college.

"Miss Preston, please take a seat over there." He pointed to the third row.

"I prefer Bubba." She spoke with a pronounced drawl and batted her eyelashes.

James met her gaze. "You prefer him, or to sit by him, or you prefer to be called Bubba?" The class burst into giggles. Ms. Preston wasn't fazed.

Buddy "Bubba" Davis, seated at the end of the first row, leaned over and pulled the desk next to him closer. He patted the seat, inviting the blonde to sit. "Why honey, you look more like a 'Barbie' than a 'Bubba' to me."

The class roared with laughter.

James managed to keep a straight face. "Miss Preston, do you have a nickname you'd like me to use?"

She lowered her eyelids until they were half closed, and then she purred, "Barbie will do just fine."

This group would make for an interesting six

weeks. Good thing, because he hadn't planned on teaching summer school, but thanks to Dr. Brown's mentoring assignment and the hiring of Miss Lind, if he had to show up four days a week, this class would make it worth the while.

He finished checking the student roll, then said, "Now that I have your names, including Bubba's and Barbie's, let's get down to business. Each of you will stand and give us a speech. At least one minute long. I'll time you. Tell us where you're from and what you want to do when you graduate from this place."

He coached a few of his shyer students through their impromptu speech. A few he had to rein in, though he managed that with nothing more than a stern glare. He was pleased when the students needed no encouragement from him to applaud for their classmates.

"Next item, here's the syllabus. Pass it around." He handed off the stack of paper to Barbie. "This is a new communications class. There will be several projects, speeches, presentations, and a couple of short papers. This class moves quickly with only six weeks to cover what is usually done in fifteen or sixteen. You cannot afford to fall behind. Class participation is part of your grade and I guarantee, I'll call on each one of you at least once in every class. Read chapter one for Wednesday." Murmurs filtered back to him along with the sound of rustling paper.

"Individual speeches, group speeches, methods of electronic communication..." Bubba read aloud. "A pantomime presentation? What the heck is that?"

With an exaggerated shrug of his shoulders, James stretched out his arms, palms up, then put an index finger to his lips. Next he turned, then lifted his foot knee-high and stepped an exaggerated step, each step taking him closer to the door. Soundlessly, he pointed to the hall. He gestured with his hands, encouraging his students to leave.

Barbie took the hint first. She picked up the paper from her desk, her tote bag, and gathered her purse. Laughing, her classmates lined up as if following a mother duck. James waved goodbye as each student crossed the threshold. He grinned until he looked from the doorway into the hall where Branna stood.

"Of course," she said. "Laughter *would* be coming from Dr. Newbern's class. He would be that *type* of teacher."

He considered a snappy retort, but a second later she was gone. "Miss Lind, you are an irritating, but unforgettably-hot type," he sighed, remembering the heat of her kisses. Obviously, when it came to her, he'd thrown all professionalism out the window.

There was nothing left to do but go for it.

Chapter 19

Branna gave three light raps on the closed door. She hadn't intended to kick a man when he was down. Their exchange in the hall bothered her, and she needed to clear the air.

"Enter."

"Am I disturbing you?"

"No, come on in. What's up?" His mouth curled into a grin, but it didn't reach his eyes.

"You look like you could use a friend. I was only teasing a few minutes ago in the hall."

When she sat in the chair next to his desk, a silver rattle with a pink bow tied around the handle caught her eye. That was the object she saw him with before. Was there a connection to the person on the phone and the rattle? Did James have a child? Maybe a niece or nephew?

A second of panic hit her. Surely, he didn't have a wife. No, if he were married, the honorable Dr. James Newbern wouldn't have been out with her, let alone done everything else they'd shared. She relaxed. James wouldn't cheat on a woman. He wasn't Steven.

"Really? A friend?"

"My first class is starting in ten minutes, but how about lunch when it's over?" Maybe she could cheer him up. Maybe she'd regale him with funny stories about Fleur de Lis, which could make him smile and help ward off the homesickness hanging in her heart.

Bang!

The glass doors to the office suite rattled as if someone shoved them open so hard the handles had hit the wall. The vibration reverberated through the room. Immediately, James rose, and she followed him out of his office.

In the lobby, Sadie struggled with a huge vase, the size of an urn, filled with red and pink long stemmed roses in a mass with white Baby's Breath. With one hand, Sadie tried to maneuver paperwork out of the way on the top of her desk. She clutched the vase close to her chest, trying to keep it balanced. James rushed to help. He grabbed the vase and lifted it out of the way. With a quick flourish, Sadie shoved everything on her desktop to one side.

"Miss Lind, aren't the flowers beautiful? Did you two have a fight?"

Branna looked at James. "No. Why?"

"Then why wouldn't you want these lovely flowers from your fiancé?"

Confusion flashed across James' face. His eyebrows rose, silently asking the unspoken question.

Why did he always think the worst of her?

"I do not have a fiancé. I am not engaged. See"— she raised her ringless left hand and wiggled her fingers as evidence of the truth—"no ring. I'm not engaged."

Sadie's doubtful frown focused on James then back at her. "Miss Lind, I don't think I mixed up the details. Steven definitely said he was engaged to you."

"Oh? The optimal word in that sentence is *was*. As in, 'not any more' for seven-plus months. I will never marry that man."

"Well, Steven told me—"

"Sadie, believe me when I tell you, you can't believe what he says. I learned that the hard way."

Sadie shrugged. Her brow creased in doubt.

Branna tried to hold on to calm. Would she ever escape the tentacles of Steven's charm? Her immunity to him had finally reached maximum capacity. What he did or didn't do, didn't matter one whit to her.

With anger simmering below the surface, frustration overflowing, her eyes watered. She sniffed deeply, then doubled her resolve. Annoyed was the only reaction she'd allow to his interference. At some point, her continued rejection of him would penetrate his ego, right? Then he would pursue someone else. Someone *not* in her family. Hopefully, that would happen sooner than later.

"Enjoy the flowers, Sadie. I'm off to my first class. It's going to be a great day." Turning from the two doubting faces, she stepped toward her office for her tote bag. Grabbing it and hoisting the strap over her shoulder, she made once last glance before turning out the light. The door clicked locked when she pulled it closed. James and Sadie stood before her in the exact same spot as before still wearing the same doubting expressions. She couldn't make them believe her. Time and truth were on her side.

"James, my offer for lunch is still open. Let me know."

Pushing open the glass office door, she crossed the threshold and strode down the hall. Her short-heeled sandals *tip-tapped* as she strode purposefully down the hall. Meandering students cleared a path. She ignored the bashful glances and the occasional stares.

177

"If Steven thinks he can needle his way back into my life, he needs medication. The strong stuff," she muttered as she trekked. "Who does he think he is?"

But she knew. Steven Sterling was everyone's darling in Mississippi. He came from a family with old money and an antebellum home, plus all the bucks in the world to keep the place as a private residence. Unlike Fleur de Lis which, though still a private home, offered access to the public as a way to offset upkeep expenses. Strangers often roamed the property. They liked to escape from the tours. Once she found someone in the restroom upstairs, an area marked off-limits with a sign and velvet rope.

But not so at Steven's family's home. First rate antiques and accessories her family would never own. The Sterlings kept three housekeepers on staff. Not to mention the gardeners and a cook.

Steven's parents and grandparents had spoiled him. He was too charming for his own good. He had a respected legal practice. As far as she knew, he conducted his business ethically. But that ego of his— as wide as the endless horizon of the Gulf of Mexico. Steven once bragged there were two types of attorneys. Ones who got ulcers from trying to do the right thing. The second kind, like him, were tigers with the killing instinct and went into law to stay out of jail.

Well, there was no law that prevented an engaged man from sleeping with other women, however, his cheating certainly killed their engagement. She'd never ever trust him again. There were many reasons she'd remained silent about his misdeed, including her inability to withstand "poor Branna" sympathy everyone would heap on her. Better for everyone to think she broke the engagement because of cold feet. She didn't want her family on the pity train—the truth of Steven and Camilla's fling would energize the gossip loops for months.

However, she was done with hiding, trying to make nice, and trying to protect everyone else. Steven's long-arm-of-the-law created a problem that required a head-on approach. Months of avoiding him, then moving several states away hadn't guaranteed a private life. Still he insisted on inserting himself into her world. But why?

With Sadie's affinity for gossip, she expected news about her and Steven would spread like sand in a windstorm across campus.

She also expected Sadie to judge, but James? His scornful look hurt. She couldn't deny that, but she'd done nothing wrong. She wouldn't defend herself when no crime had been committed. If James Newbern thought he would have another pigeonhole to stick her in, he was flat wrong. She absolutely was not the type to lie about relationships. She didn't lie. Period.

Fully charged with determination, she reached the classroom and a cacophony of chatter. She flipped on the overhead fluorescent lights, marched to her desk, and dumped her tote. Grabbing a black marker, she scrawled her name in big letters on the white board along with the name of the course. She drew in a quick breath, then blew it out before turning to face her class.

Mingling students migrated to their seats. Chatter quieted. Her heartbeat thudded double time to the clicks from the second hand on clock hanging on the back wall.

"Welcome to Interpersonal Communications. I'm

Miss Lind." She scanned the room. Chairs were set up eight across and five deep, yet she only had twenty-five students. The front row was bare, though she spotted a few eager beavers in the second row, textbooks and notebooks open, with pens in hands ready to begin.

"Good morning. Welcome. Education is the best way for you to invest in yourselves. You pay to sit here, so you can sit where you want. If you want to get the most for your money, move down front *and* participate." A handful of brave souls rose from their seats and parked themselves in the front row.

"I'm making a seating chart. For the next two weeks, please sit in that same seat. After that, you can test me. If I've got your names down cold, feel free to move about the cabin. Going across the front row, give me your name. Let's start with you."

"Me?" The young man in the AC/DC T-shirt looked behind him.

Branna nodded and tapped the end of her pen against the paper to urge him along.

"Chuck Lyons."

"Thank you, Chuck. Next."

She completed the seating chart, then handed out the syllabus. She kept the banter light as she moved into lecture mode. Noting items of importance from the textbook, she watched students take the hint. Her first lecture as a full-time college instructor filled her with a new sense of confidence.

Before the class ended, she went to the board and wrote "pan" in large letters. "Class, we use words to communicate, but words can cause communication failures. By a show of hands, how many think this word means something you put butter on in the morning after you've toasted it?" She counted the three raised hands. "Okay, a few. Now, how many of you might do this to find gold in Alaska?" More hands shot up.

"Most of you. Now for your homework for Wednesday—" Groans rose from the class and harmonized. She hid her grin.

"The three that think 'pan' is for toasting, stand up and count off."

Once the task was completed, the three students glanced at one another and shrugged.

"You three are group leaders." She pointed to each one. "The rest of you count off 1-2-3. Then, get together in your respective groups. Communicate, so that all of you are clear about the different definitions of p-a-n. Then, come up with ten other words that have different meanings—using 'pan' as an example. And, read chapter one for tomorrow."

Pride in a job well done brought a smile to her lips. Solid communication had to be the cornerstone of any relationship, including hers with her students. Giddy didn't begin to describe the joy running through her.

As she gathered her things and followed the last student out of the room, she reached to turn off the lights. James waited in the hall. With arms crossed on his chest, he leaned back with one knee bent and his foot braced against the wall. His expression had changed from the one he'd had earlier, now he wore a humbled grin. A misbehaving lock of dark hair fell over his forehead. She stopped herself from touching it, touching him. His smile made her heart beat quicker.

"Miss Lind, I apologize for jumping to conclusions earlier. If the offer's still open, I'll meet you back at the office at noon for lunch."

An apology? James couldn't be more different from Steven. "Sure, I'll see you at lunch."

She could understand how James might be curious about her version of the facts differing from what Sadie offered. Lunch would provide an opportunity to work on her own interpersonal communication skills. Besides, she wanted to know about the phone call that morning that appeared to cause him so much pain. And why did he keep a silver rattle on his desk?

Chapter 20

James grabbed the phone on the first ring. "Hello."

"JD, I need your help. You available to make a run with me on Friday? Keith's gone again. Chasing some tail or drink'n himself to hell."

James listened to Bobby Parker, his friend since forever, plead his case. Bobby was the only person he allowed to use his childhood nickname.

"What do you have in mind?"

"It's a straight run down and back."

"What do *I* get out this?"

"Man, I helped you drag that four-hundred-pound safe into your house yesterday, when you couldn't find anyone else strong enough to lift it."

He imagined Bobby, on the other end of the phone, flexing his muscles to prove his point.

"Your prize—you get my company for almost twenty hours," Bobby said.

"Not good enough."

"I can't pay you until the end of the summer."

"Yeah, well, last time you cheated me out of my pay. I've got a different proposition for you."

"Shit, Professor, when you use them big words, I know I'm gonna be had."

"Yeah, right." He chuckled.

Bobby liked the world to think he was a poor Florida Cracker with barely two nickels to rub together.

In truth, he had graduated with honors with a degree in agriculture from Florida's Land-Grant College. He owned several hundred acres and leased even more for growing hay.

He and his father ran a small crew to harvest crops, however, hay required cutting, fluffing, and bailing every six weeks from spring to late fall. Bobby rotated his stockpile and trucked dry hay once a month to the Florida Keys, where a feed store on stilts that had survived every hurricane since 1900 bought all the Parkers' hay.

"How about a trade?"

"Trade what?" Bobby's voice carried suspicion. "Last time you twisted my arm, you had me planting impatiens and sea grass for half a mile at your Momma's. Then, made me drink water instead of beer."

So Bobby *hadn't* forgotten their agreement from last fall. He imagined wheels turning in Bobby's head, trying to figure any angle to get out of the deal.

"I prepared you for what comes next. The outside painting is done, as is the landscaping. You never showed up to help with either of those jobs. Now, I need a barbeque pit. Brick. In the backyard."

"Shit, JD. I'm not a cook. I *am* a Cracker. Or have you forgotten that since you moved up in the world? My idea of a barbeque pit is a hole in the ground lined with rocks."

"Your elbow grease works fine in the city."

"You mean slave labor, don't ya?"

"Do we have a deal or not? Your call. I can meet you at the interstate rest stop at five a.m." He waited. He'd give Bobby a few minutes of silence to do his thinking. Let him stew and make up his mind, then

Bobby couldn't claim coercion. Or if he did, it wouldn't matter. "Call me back if you need more time to decide. You do have another option. Put out a missing persons report on Keith and wait for him to show."

"Naw. I'll do it your way. Some friend you are, never invite me over to your new mansion unless you need a favor."

"Stop whining. We'll go south on Friday. No partying this time. Then you spend Sunday indentured to me."

"Okay, but Charlene wants us to go out next Saturday night. You been nice to any ladies lately? One that might wanna go dancing with you?"

"You tell your bride that I'll call her. If I don't have a date of my choosing a few days in advance, I'll let her set me up. Again. God help me."

After the last disaster, he swore he'd never ever agree to another blind date. Charlene meant well, but she didn't understand that when he said he wanted to discuss books with a woman, he hadn't meant cookbooks. He hoped Branna would not demur.

"You ought to thank my wife for caring enough about your sorry ass to try to find you a girlfriend."

"I appreciate her efforts. I'll buy her flowers or something."

Charlene had always set him up with good-looking women. And she tried for substance to go along with the outer package, but he'd decided that the women Charlene knew fell into only two types. The obvious ones on the troll for marriage, or the secretly manipulative ones hoping to hook a husband. Either way, those women reminded him too much of Caroline.

"See you this Friday before dawn."

He hung up the phone. Would Branna have an interest in experiencing more local color Saturday night? She and Charlene might not have much in common, but Charlene had never met a stranger. She made friends like bunnies reproduced. And she was the most loyal, faithful woman he'd ever known.

But maybe Bobby hadn't snagged the last good one.

Maybe.

Chapter 21

Pine bark mulch crunched beneath Branna's shoes as she picked her way beside James. They headed to the Eatery in the Student Union. Her sandals were not a good choice for walking on the uneven surface.

"Let's slow down," James said.

"No need. I can keep up." She stepped carefully, looking down to watch where she placed her feet. The last thing she needed was to fall face first. With her luck, if she fell, some student would capture it on video with their phone, and she'd make a splash on evening news. Or even worse, on *YouTube*. The only alternate way to the Union was the long continuous sidewalk connecting each building on campus, however, that would make the trip longer. By then she'd be completely melted from the rising humidity. She refocused her attention on the information James was dispensing.

"The student's Halloween Ball is our most popular and well-attended event. We banned cellophane as a costume a few years ago. Students from the golf course program—big-city, south Florida types rather than local ones—had the idea to use cellophane as a costume."

"Cellophane?" He had to be kidding, right? She patted the moisture on her forehead. Though pine branches shaded the path and protected her from the hot noontime sun, the humidity made her wish for an old-fashioned lace hankie. That would look far more feminine than wiping her forehead with the back of her hand. Air conditioning couldn't be reached fast enough. The thought of cellophane against her body made her shudder. Was she sweating more?

"Hard to believe." James held the door open to the Student Union for her. A blast of cool air brought her temperature down a notch.

"In this swamp? At least in Bayou Petite, evening breezes coming up from the Gulf and cool things down."

They stepped to the end of the food line and waited their turn to order. The aromas of fried chicken, sizzling burgers and hot grease made her stomach rumble.

In front of them, a female student turned to James. "Dr. Newbern, I heard you're going to take over as faculty consultant to the student newspaper."

"Not exactly. I've volunteered to assist Ms. Moore with production—layout and design—*if* she needs it. Reporting assignments will remain between her and the new student editor."

"I'm thinking about joining the staff in the fall. I was hoping I would be able to" —the girl flashed a coy grin—"learn from you."

"Working on the paper is a great experience-building opportunity. I'm sure Ms. Moore would love to have an interested and dedicated student like you, Beth. Have you met Ms. Lind? She's teaching Interpersonal Communications this summer."

Beth's composure shifted from demure to annoyed as she adjusted her books in her arms.

"Hi, Ms. Lind. I took that class last semester. I have only one more semester after the summer and I'm done." The young blonde looked more like a junior high girl with her plaid shorts and pink polo shirt than a young woman headed for her junior year in college.

"It's nice to meet you, Beth." Student-teacher relations were a serious matter, and she watched the changing expressions on Beth's face with curiosity. The young woman's behavior bordered on inappropriate as she tried flirting with Dr. Newbern. It was painful to watch.

"What are your plans after graduation?" Branna asked. She hoped her insertion would distract the student.

"Next!" the counter help barked at Beth.

Beth gave a weak shrug, then turned to give her order. Afterwards she said, "See ya later, Dr. Newbern."

Branna grabbed a tray and handed it to James before pulling one from the pile for herself. She gave her order to the woman behind the counter before the woman barked, "next" to avoid the annoyance.

"Adoring co-eds must be an ego boost. Benefit of a small town campus?" she muttered, fully expecting James to hear.

"I heard that. I'm not that type. Nor is anyone on this faculty that I know of. There are rules, and then there are laws. This institution upholds both."

"Have you seen someone for your affliction?"

"What affliction?"

"Typing."

"Like on a keyboard?"

She counted to ten. "Is everyone a *type* to you? Is each person you meet stuffed into a cubbyhole with a label for future reference? You just described yourself as not being 'that type.' For the record, I'm more than a *type*. I'm more than some label you want to pin on me."

The food-service worker gave her a curious glance when handing over her plate. Branna set it on the tray next to her drink, shrugged, then paid the cashier and headed for the dining area already crowded with students and other faculty members.

In the far corner, she spied an empty table. She made her way through the maze and sat. When James arrived, a table of co-eds erupted into giggles. They whispered and cast glances in his direction.

"You asked me to join you for lunch, not psychoanalysis, Branna. I'm not willing to discuss your theory here. Let's find something else to talk about for now."

"Like the giggling co-eds eyeing you?" She smiled brightly at the girls sneaking glances.

"No."

"Like the silver baby rattle on your desk?"

He straightened in his chair. Had she hit a nerve?

"No."

"Then, what would you like to discuss?"

"Do you want to meet some friends of mine for a beer next Saturday night?"

"Is it a date?"

"Just a night out with friends."

"Not a date? Then exactly what *type* of evening are you talking about?"

He clearly ignored her dig. His eyes twinkled, though he tried to hide a grin. "I guess you'll just have to come along and find out."

Chapter 22

Branna jerked back the shower curtain and yanked a bath towel off the shelf. Last night, she'd fallen asleep before setting the alarm. She hated being late for anything; it was a sign of disrespect. Echoes of G.G. Marie's "tsk tsk" whispered in her head.

Wrapping the towel around her body, she stepped from the tub and grabbed a hand towel for her dripping hair. From her bedroom, her cell phone chimed. Clutching the towel to her body, she dashed to check caller ID, but she had no time talk to anyone, including her cousin, who hadn't called back last night.

She blamed Biloxi for her need to rush. "If you'd have called me back, I wouldn't have forgotten to set my alarm," she muttered tersely.

The phone chimed again. As she reached for it, movement outside her bedroom window stopped her cold—a silhouette of a tall man wearing a baseball cap. In a few quick steps to the window, she intended to flip the plantation shutters closed. She recognized the person peering inside, his nose pressed against the glass.

"Oh Lordy! You scared the crap out of me!" She hollered at Bill, the painting contractor. Yesterday afternoon, she'd inked her signature on a contract for him to paint the outside of the house.

"I rang the doorbell. No one answered. I knocked.

You didn't come to the door. Your car's still in the drive. I knew you had to be here. I came to see if you were dead or something."

She winced. Bill yelled loud enough for the entire neighborhood to hear.

"Are you a painter or a peeping Tom? I'm in a hurry. Can't you start painting in the front of the house?" Precious minutes were tick by. She had to hurry or she'd arrive late for class.

"Would love to, but your import is in the way. Don't think you want the metallic blue dotted with white house paint."

"Please, just go wait in the drive. I'll be about fifteen minutes."

She snapped the shutters closed and finished drying off. Her clothes, she'd draped them over the chair last night, a habit she perfected so she never had to think about what to wear before her first cup of coffee, made dressing easy. This morning she prized her organizational skills and reached for her skirt and top.

Blow-drying was quick work with short hair. She finished with a paddle brush, then stood over her antique vanity, a gift from her Covington grandparents, to apply makeup, which timing herself, she managed in under two short minutes. Finishing with a soft peachy lip gloss, she ran to the bathroom to wash foundation her fingers. She'd never gotten the knack of using a makeup sponge. When she grabbed the cold-water tap and twisted, the faucet came off her in hand. Water sprayed a steady stream, down her turquois blouse and brown skirt. Water gushed. She froze and stared.

Her reflection in the mirror showed disaster.

Makeup ruined.

Hair wet.

Clothes needed changing.

Panicked, she bent to look under the sink, found the shut-off valves, and cranked them both until the water cut off.

Ding-Dong. The doorbell rang.

Her cell phone chimed again.

"Crap!"

She raced to the front door, her clothes dripped water along the way. "I told you that I'd be fifteen minutes. Can't you keep your pants on?" she shouted, pulling open the front door. Her next-door neighbor, the elderly and very proper Mrs. Campbell, stared back.

"Oh, gosh. I'm sorry Mrs. Campbell. I'm running late for work. How may I help you?"

"I just wanted to be sure this man wasn't trying to break into your house. I already called the police. Are you sure your all right?"

"The police?"

Branna opened the door wider, stepped out onto the porch next to Mrs. Campbell, and waved Bill over.

"Mrs. Campbell, this is Bill, my painter. If the police come, please tell them it's a case of mistaken identity. He's legit. Now, I've got to change for work. Sorry about the confusion. Have a nice day." She closed the door on the pair and headed for her bedroom. Her darn cell phone started chiming again. Annoyed, she shoved it into her purse. Whoever called had to wait.

After handling details with Bill and finally dressed for work, she took a deep breath and turned the key in the ignition. Her old Volvo started with a purr. She put the car in reverse and backed down the drive. If she hurried, she might just make it on time. If nothing else, the adrenaline running in her veins would push the car to the college. Tardiness was an embarrassment she wanted to avoid. Especially on the second day of school. She was probably more anxious than her students about the semester.

The bright morning sun shone in her eyes as she drove due east. She flipped the visor down and turned the radio to classical music, something to settle her racing pulse. Checking the speedometer, she slowed. A speeding ticket would definitely make her later. As a distraction from the 35 mph speed limit, she checked her cell phone log.

Steven. Steven. Steven.

Couldn't he take no for an answer? She had bigger issues to deal with than his ego, like finding a plumber. She'd ask Sadie or James or maybe Vivian for a recommendation. If luck smiled on her, though after the morning she'd had she wondered if luck had left her high and dry—more like low and wet—the plumber could meet her at the house at lunchtime.

Once on campus, she turned into the closest commuter parking lot and found the first empty space. As faculty, she had a reserved spot in a designated lot, but that was on the other side of campus. Not enough time to drive there and hoof it to her class on time. She parked, then sprinted across the street to bypass her office, and made a beeline for her classroom. The *clack-clack* from her heels ricocheted in the mostly empty hall, which required careful navigation to avoid falling on the newly polished floor. Pausing outside the classroom, she took a moment to catch her breath. When she had changed from a skirt to pants, they called for much higher heels. That made staying upright and movement beyond a turtle's pace difficult.

"Good morning class." She breezed in across the threshold. "Let's get started."

The students' chatter continued as though she hadn't spoken. A female student from the first row jumped up and grabbed something from the back of a seat. She met Branna at her desk as Branna pulled the roll call list from her binder. The student hovered close. So close that Branna could smell the lilac soap and mint mouthwash on the younger woman.

"Miss Lind. I don't want to embarrass you, but please take my hoodie." The girl's face reddened.

"Excuse me?"

"I'm Crystal Cabot, Miss Lind."

"Thank you for the offer, but I'm perfectly fine. It's not cold in here." She started to move around Crystal to the front of the desk, but Crystal grabbed her arm. Behind her, the students were quieting. Someone snickered, which caused the hair on the back of Branna's neck to rise.

"Miss Cabot, is there a problem?" she asked warily.

"It's not me Miss Lind. It's you." The girl raised her hand close to her chest, wiggled her fingers and pointed discreetly to the front of Branna's pink blouse.

Branna looked down and gasped. Dampness had seeped from her bra on to her shirt and made two prominent darkened spots. Shaken, she grabbed the hoodie from Crystal.

"Thank you." She pushed her arms through the sleeves and zipped up the jacket. How silly of her to think that being late would be her worst embarrassment of the day. Luck had abandoned her without so much as a backward glance. Thank goodness the damp shirt scene happened here rather than Bayou Petite, otherwise, it was one more thing she'd never live down at home.

Crystal smiled and nodded, then took her seat. Branna hoped no one else had noticed. An older male student winked at her when she leaned against her desk. To hide the rising heat in her cheeks, she held the student list in front of her.

"Please answer when I call your name." Professionalism dictated that she ignore her own embarrassing discomfort and teach.

The time couldn't pass fast enough for her. In the final minute before class ended, the older male student raised his hand.

"Miss Lind?"

"Mr…?" She scanned the seating chart. "Mr. Ashford. Yes?"

"Are we going to discuss nonverbal communication?"

Was she walking into a trap? Was he somehow baiting her? "It's covered in the syllabus, Mr. Ashford."

"I know." The man grinned. "I just thought maybe you were trying to get to the topic sooner. You've provided a good example today all through class."

There were several snickers.

"Class dismissed."

She left the room ahead of her students. When she reached the English department's office, she pushed open the door and stopped. Sadie sat at her desk with her fingers flying over a keyboard as though an accomplished pianist. She sported a new short haircut that looked all too familiar. However, it made Sadie's face look much rounder.

Flattered, Branna grinned. "Good morning, Sadie. I need advice." She headed for her office with the key in hand.

Sadie jumped up and followed. "How can I help?"

"By the way, like your new haircut. I need the name and number of a plumber. I have a situation with my bathroom that needs immediate attention. You know everyone in town."

"Well, there's good. There's fast. There's good and fast. Which do you need?"

"Good to know there are three plumber options. I need the one who's going to be at my house at twelve fifteen so I can let him in, trust him alone inside, and fix my bathroom faucet without breaking anything. Oh, and do it for a reasonable price."

Sadie looked up at the ceiling, puffed out her cheeks, and tapped her index finger against her pursed lips. Branna squelched a giggle. Sadie looked like a middle-aged chipmunk with a bowling-ball haircut.

"Lester Sullivan."

"Lester Sullivan it is. I'll take whomever you recommend. I trust you. Please give me his number, and I'll call him now."

"Well, since it's a bit of an emergency, I'll call him for you. That way he's sure to show. He's my brother-in-law. You can trust him. I promise."

"Thanks for handling that for me. It is above the call of duty. I've another class next period, but I'll be there by twelve fifteen. Let me make it up to you, I'll buy you lunch tomorrow."

"No lunch. This is the least I can do after our

misunderstanding. You know. About your engagement."

Branna nodded and hoped Steven would never come up again. "I insist. Let me buy."

"Well...if you insist."

"Done," she said. She opened her office door and stepped inside. Paper crunched under her heels. More messages from Steven? She closed her door halfway and hobbled to her chair to pull the papers off her heels. The harassment had to stop. She needed to figure out a way to handle the man's unwanted attention. If she continued to ignore him, he'd push until he sweet talked Sadie into something drastic. He'd pulled stunts before. Would reason work with him now? If the past was any indicator, probably not.

If not, she'd call Uncle Peter again and ask for more advice. Last time, she'd hired "the Big Gun," her nickname for Uncle Peter, he had a chat, attorney to attorney, with Steven. Afterward, her ex-fiancé had left her alone...for a while.

Steven's stunt last November had scared her and sent her running for the Big Gun. She remembered the incident all too well. A rainy night after she had finished teaching a class at the Senior Center and only a few students mingled in the hall, she investigated someone whistling an eerie tune. The sound echoed from the hall into the classroom where she sat reading essays. When she stepped out of the room and into the hall, the man continued to whistle as he strode purposefully in her direction, as though he had waited for her to appear. He carried folded papers.

"Branna Lind?"

"Yes," she answered hesitantly.

"You've been served." He handed her papers, then walked away whistling a funeral march.

She'd listened enough to Steven's "attorney-speak" to know what "served" meant. She glanced over the papers—suit papers—alleging breach of contract. Steven wanted a million dollars! Stunned, she raced home to Fleur de Lis and called her father who was at their beach house in Biloxi. He calmed her down and agreed to meet her at Uncle Peter's law office.

The next morning, after a sleepless night, her anger burned on a short fuse. She marched in and took a seat in the chair in front of Uncle Peter's desk. Her father sat next to her and patted her hand. When Uncle Peter read over the papers, he chuckled. She wanted to hit him.

"Start at the very beginning and read this document. This is Contracts 101," Uncle Peter instructed.

She glared at him, but did as told.

"Steven Sterling, Plaintiff, versus B. Noel MyLove, Defendant." She stopped. "What in the world? I'm not a lawyer, but this can't be proper form."

"Darl'n," Uncle Peter drawled, "I think the man is desperate. He wants your attention. This looks like a lawsuit. Served it like a lawsuit—well, maybe—and written like a lawsuit. But it's not."

"But..." she sputtered. Leaning forward she tossed the papers back on Uncle Peter's desk.

He laughed.

Her father sighed, crossed one ankle over a knee, and sat back in his chair. "Peter, explain."

"Uncle Peter, what can I do?" she interrupted. "I'm done with that man. I'm sick of the harassment. Jewelry, flowers, cards, phone calls, and now this! A fake lawsuit? Served where I work! Isn't there a law against that? He's invading my space. Ruining my life."

Her uncle sat back in his chair and steepled his fingers. "Branna, there's no law against a man trying to win back the woman he loves. I can see how upsetting this is to you. I'll give him a call and ask him politely to stop. How would that be?"

"Can I have him arrested?"

"How about we try it my way first?"

"*Humph.* Charge your billable hours to him!"

That had ended Steven's attempt at wearing her down. Until recently. She hated that she had let him upset her. She didn't want another empty apology from him, then or now. She promised herself, after a month of crying every day over that man, she would never cry over any man again. So far, she'd kept that promise.

"Excuse me." Sadie interrupted her thoughts. Standing in the doorway she said, "Lester will be waiting for you at your house at lunchtime."

"Thanks very much, Sadie."

"Good morning," James said as he walked into view behind Sadie. "Will you need a ride to your house or do you have a rental?"

"What?"

"Do you need a ride home? At lunch today?" James spoke slowly, as though she might not understand English.

"Why would I need a ride?"

"Because your car got just towed from the student parking lot."

"I thought my decal was good for any spot, except the ones reserved for Dr. Westcott and Dr. Brown. Someone towed my car?"

"Correct. You can park anywhere, but those two spots, and your car was towed. I thought you had mechanical problems or something, thought that was the reason for the tow truck."

"I own a Volvo. I don't have mechanical problems," she insisted.

"Well, your car just got towed. I saw the tow truck pull out as I pulled in. No one else I know has a metallic blue Volvo with Mississippi tags."

"Oh, yeah, got to change those...What was the name of the tow company? Where are they taking my car?" She rose. Was James joking around? Her car towed? No. It had to be there.

"I'll call campus security to see if they know anything. Maybe security can stop them before they get past the front gates." Sadie scurried to her desk.

James appeared deep in thought, as though he scanned his brain for data. "Best Boys," he finally said.

Confused, she shook her head. "What are you talking about?"

"The name of the tow company is Best Boys."

She yelled, "Sadie, the tow company is Best Boys." She dashed for the door. Her high heels slowed her pace when carpet transitioned to tile. Changing from a trot to a fast walk, she called over her shoulder to James, "Are you coming to help me or not?"

When she arrived at the spot where her car had sat, her feet ached from pounding the sidewalk in heels. Campus security officers blocked the entrance and exit of the student commuter parking lot. Red lights flashed. She scanned the parking lot.

No tow truck.

No Volvo.

But in the spot where she had parked the Volvo less than two hours ago, a new Mercedes sedan waited with a big, red bow on top.

"Ma'am, please stand back." An officer—an older, heavyset man with white hair poking out from under his cap—hitched up the waist of his pants. "Is your name Ms. Lind?"

"Where's my car?"

"Are you Ms. Lind?"

"Yes. Now where is my car?"

"I found this addressed to you and taped to the door handle of this here new vehicle." The stern looking man offered a red envelope.

Anger burned in her gut like an exploding volcano. This was the second time in her life that she wanted to slap Steven silly. How dare he humiliate her at work.

She refused to touch the envelope. Instead, she raised her hands to shade her eyes from the bright sun. "But my car? Where has Best Boys taken my car? And why?"

"I've been told your fiancé authorized it." The disapproval that etched the man's face said he had better things to do with his time.

"Officer"—she looked for his nametag—"Officer Hutton, I don't have a fiancé." She flashed the back of her ringless left hand and wiggled her fingers as evidence.

"What?" Shock registered on the man's face.

"Ms. Lind says she's not engaged. With whom did you speak to about her car?" James asked as he drew closer. A few students gathered in the parking lot appeared to be straining to hear the conversation.

"A man called, said he was Ms. Lind's fiancé. He

arranged for a tow truck to deliver her new car. He said it was an engagement gift, and that he had arranged to have her old car picked up."

"And you let him?" she cried.

"Calm down, Branna. I talked to the dispatcher at Best Boys. Your Volvo is waiting in your driveway."

"Oh great! Now it will end up with paint on it!"

James' furrowed brow told her he didn't understand.

"A painter is there today, painting the exterior of my house." She turned to face the older man. "Officer Hutton, you've been had. I don't have a fiancé. And if my Volvo has paint on it when I get home, you're going to need to arrest me for killing Steven Sterling!"

"Yeah, that was his name. Mr. Sterling. Said he wanted to surprise you."

"Surprise me? I'm going to surprise the hell out of him!" She reached in her pants pockets. No cell phone. It was in her purse, in her desk drawer. She couldn't call Steven or Best Boys or even Bill to ask that he tarp the car to protect it. She couldn't leave work to chase down the tow truck. She'd have to wait until lunch...then she had to meet the plumber.

Nauseous, she laid her hands over her stomach. Never in her life had she experienced so much chaos in such a short time. If only she could crawl back into bed and start the day over.

If only.

"Hey! I gotta go to work. Are the cop cars gonna move?" a student shouted from the sidelines of the gathering crowd.

Officer Hutton waved to the second officer at the end of the parking lot, who hopped into his car and drove away, lights no longer flashing. Hutton laid the red envelope on the trunk of the Mercedes. "Take this. It's yours."

He walked to his patrol car, grumbling about something, and never looked back. The only word she understood—"Women!"

Storming over to the car, she yanked up the red envelope, scrunching it in her fist. There was more than a note inside. She felt the outline of a key. She headed toward her office leaving James in the parking lot. "I'm going to show all you men what kind of woman I am."

Chapter 23

As she pulled her purse from her desk drawer, someone in the doorway cleared their throat. Branna looked up. James leaned casually against the doorjamb, but his furrowed brow and frown looked anything but relaxed.

"You're really taking that present home. Interesting. It's none of my business. I just didn't think you were one of those women."

She wanted to scream that he was wrong, she wasn't *that* type—the kind to accept expensive presents from a man she abhorred, but since she wasn't the "screaming type," she picked up the keys from her desk hoping to convey an air of calm control. James backed out of the office as she approached the doorway. Too angry to speak, she wore her poker face, the one she'd perfected that showed no hurt or pain, the one she owed to Steven.

James puzzled her. Away from work he was fun and engaging. Yet, for such a smart guy, he lived in a world of absolutes, little room for shades of gray. She could understand if he was one way or the other. The duality left her confused.

Until her split with Steven, rules ruled her life. Only recently, since her break with family tradition, had she discovered how colorful life could be when one colored outside the lines. James would have to discover that on his own. No books...or woman could teach him that lesson.

"Sadie, I'll be back. Going to meet the plumber," she called out as she left the office tugging securely on the purse strap hanging over her shoulder.

James' words ran through her brain, up and back, like a pianist practicing a musical scale. She'd refused his offer of a ride, choosing to take the Mercedes—her choice was not to inconvenience him. Not be a burden. His response hit her like a punch.

"It's none of my business. I just didn't take you for being one of 'those' women."

His tone rubbed her wrong.

Judgmental.

Opinionated.

Dismissive.

What she hated was the fact that in the green polo shirt that hugged his chest so well, his eyes looked a deeper brown. The timbre of his voice vibrated in her gut. He was way too sexy for his own good. That's what she hated.

"He's right! It's none of his damn business," she gritted out, then tightened her grip on the steering wheel. "A car is just a car. Just transportation. And mine's been hijacked by a manipulating jerk. Steven Sterling, you're vile."

Turning the corner on to her street, she spotted a plumber's truck parked by the curb. She pulled the Mercedes in front of it and sighed with relief at the sight of her Volvo. The tow-truck driver had unloaded it in the drive, but close to the street, far enough away to avoid any painting mishaps. Now all she had to do was show the plumber inside, store the Mercedes in the garage—until she figured out what to do with it—and make it back in time for her next class.

She parked and climbed out of the car. Maybe the plumber would ratchet up her low opinion of men. The male species had three strikes for today—the painter, the ex-fiancé, and the college professor.

"You'd be Miss Lind?" A man approached, carrying a battered toolbox. His shirt showed a white embroidered "Sullivan's Plumbing" insignia.

"Yes. Thank you for coming on such short notice."

"I heard your house might be flooded."

"Not exactly. That's what I'm hoping to avoid. I turned off the water before it made *too* much of a mess." Had Sadie exaggerated the circumstances to get her brother-in-law to drop everything to make this appointment? "I'll show you."

She stood outside the bathroom door and let the plumber enter.

"Ah." He nodded. "You need to replace the faucet. I can remove this one. In order for you to use the sink, you'll need to provide a new one for me to install. I don't carry that kind of stuff on my truck."

"Oh. Hadn't thought of that."

"This job won't take long, but..."

"You need the new faucet."

The man grinned. "Sadie said you were smart."

"And I thought I left household repairs behind in Mississippi. Fleur de Lis was always in need of something," she muttered under her breath. Then, brightening she asked, "If I pick up a new one after school, when would you come back and fix this?"

"I'll be here before you leave for work in the morning."

"That's a plan. Thanks for your help."

The man let himself out while she rushed to her bedroom for a dry bra. Then she searched her closet for a blouse. In the past, any public embarrassment would've put her over the edge. Too much had happened in such a short time. That left no opportunity for a mental flogging about her impropriety. After all, it wasn't like she could hide from her students. She had to roll with the scene. She conducted herself professionally, and since she acted as if nothing out of the ordinary happened, most of her students took the cue. If she ever looked backed on today, surely she would laugh. Surely.

Crystal deserved a reward for her quick thinking. A gift card in the pocket? Branna planned for it when she returned the jacket to the student tomorrow.

Heading back to campus, she patted the top of the dash of her Volvo. "I won't part with you. You've been steady and reliable. Never left me stranded. You've listened to me complain. Never judged or offered unsolicited advice."

She turned on classical music and watched her speed. "But what do I do about that silver *thing* in the garage?"

The corner of the red envelop that the security officer left for her peeked out from her purse. Red made her think of red eyes and all the tears she'd shed after she discovered Steven's betrayal. Knowing him, he considered the red envelop to be a romantic gesture. But red matched the color of blood, and it was the color of a matador's cape used to piss off a bull. At the moment, she'd match her anger with any angry bovine. The note said that the car was intended as a wedding present, however, he hoped she'd accept it now—as a re-engagement present.

"Not before he crawls over glass on his hands and knees down Main Street!"

And then...

Not even then.

But she had to find a way to deal with the deeper pain Steven injected into her family. The ragged rip in their lives left by Camilla. She had to call her sister. Camilla had to know that she had forgiven her.

As Branna drove east bound on Highway 90 and approached the turn-off for the college, the roar of a small jet buzzed in her ears like the whir of a blender. She made a right on red as the plane's continued drone hit her last nerve. The noise grew louder and louder. Whenever she traveled the road to and from the college, planes racing down the runway, whether taking off or landing, made her flinch. The short distance between the end of the runway and the road was too short for comfort.

Barely able to think over the noise, she glanced to the right just in time to see a small plane bump off the runway.

It headed straight for the road.

Straight for her car.

She slammed on the brakes. Braced her grip on the steering wheel. Where to go? Not to the right—that would take her in to the plane. Trees loomed on the left. Stomping her foot harder on the brakes, she covered her face with her hands.

Whomp!

A tree stopped the car. The impact jerked her forward hard. She struggled for breath as force flung her backward in her seat. Friction from the seatbelt abraded the side of her neck. The windshield cracked, splintering into a spider's web that looked like a mosaic. The tip of the plane's wing protruded inside her car on the passenger's side.

She gasped for a full breath and panted. Her chest hurt. Her head throbbed. Stunned, she couldn't move.

The buzzing grew louder. The plane's engine still rattled, along with sirens and clanging bells. An acid taste clotted at the back of her throat. Her hand trembled as she tried to unbuckle the seatbelt. A blur of black popped down on the hood of her car, jumped to the ground, and raced away into the woods. She blinked. Her eyes refocused, but the throb in her head made her squint.

"Over here!" a voice shouted next to her car.

She looked in the direction of the shout. A man yanked on her door. Two more men appeared.

"Unlock the door! Unlock the door!"

Hot tears slid down her cheeks. Twisting slowly, she tried to open the door. Before managing the orders, a crash exploded behind her. She jerked against her seatbelt. Wrapping her hands around the back of her head, she rested her forehead on the steering wheel as a man bashed out the window of her Volvo.

Beside her, the door opened. Someone fumbled with the seatbelt. Two men reached for her. Gingerly they helped her out of the car and to her feet. When she turned to look at her Volvo, she crumpled. Strong arms on either side of her carried her away from the crash and set her down on the ground.

"Branna!"

She couldn't see him, but she heard James' voice.

"Where is she?" he shouted.

"Over there," someone shouted back. "Ambulance is on the way."

Detached from reality, she observed the activity before her as though watching a play. More men appeared on the scene. Men in black jackets, a few with guns drawn. They headed into the woods. Overhead, a helicopter *thwopped* through the air, hovering above treetops.

Had someone forgotten to tell her about a filming of a new *Bond* movie? She laid back and covered her eyes with her hands to block out the sunlight. Her body ached. Her head hurt. Her neck burned.

She would definitely be late for class.

Chapter 24

"Branna, can you hear me?" James called. Screams from the ambulance's siren split the air as the large vehicle turned off Highway 90. Kneeling beside her, he checked the left side of her neck for a pulse. The seatbelt had rubbed a burn on the other side. Her stillness frightened him. When he put his other hand on her chest, trying to determine whether she was breathing, she swatted his hand away. Relief hit him squarely in the gut, but then he saw the blood in her hair.

"Hang on, Baby. Help's coming."

He leaped to his feet when the ambulance stopped behind her car.

"Over here!" He waved both hands to attract the emergency crews' attention over the fire truck's blaring sirens and flashing lights. When the driver waved back, he knelt again beside her.

"Miss Lind, I know you're not the type to give up. The EMS guys are here to help you."

He rose and stepped back as men with equipment packs rushed toward Branna. He went to her Volvo and gathered her purse and other personal items. Her vehicle was DOI—dead on impact. Given her professed fondness for the car, the sight of it would be a big blow. The insurance company would surely total it; shattered windshield, crunched front end, and engine fluids making a puddle on the ground. Luck had protected her. She'd barely missed being DOI, too.

His heart pounded triple time, so hard it hurt. What would he do if he'd lost her? She wasn't what he expected, and everything about her drew him to her. He'd dreamed of feeling her nakedness again, but had put up his usual barriers, not only because she was a colleague, but because she was attractive, and he'd safeguarded his heart against beauty since Caroline. Branna Lind challenged him in every way possible when it came to a male/female relationship. He'd stubbornly married old notions and hadn't realized it. Until now.

There was more between him and Branna than he'd been willing to admit.

He wouldn't lose her.

Standing discreetly out of the way to allow the emergency crew to do their thing, he moved close enough to reach for Branna's hand. He squeezed it gently. Her eyes remained closed, yet she squeezed back. He was certain she knew it was him.

"Branna, I have your purse and things out of your car," he told her.

"My poor car," she said, though her eyes never opened. "It didn't deserve this."

"Miss, we're going to move you now." The EMS guys carried the gurney until they reached the road, then dropped the legs on the table and rolled Branna to the ambulance.

"Miss?" A uniformed police officer stood next to the gurney.

"Her name is Branna Lind," James told him, but what he wanted to say was, *"I'm here because we're close. We're lovers."*

"I'll follow you to the hospital. I need to ask you some questions," the officer said.

Branna nodded slightly, but James wondered if she really understood.

"Branna, I'll follow you there, too," he told her before the ambulance doors closed.

He ran to his car. Trying to maintain the speed limit as the ambulance raced ahead, he considered the enigmatic Miss Lind. While bright—truly book smart—and dedicated to her new job with zealous enthusiasm, she possessed an air of innocence, too. She'd lived a sheltered life, it seemed to him, to remain a role model for others. Family name and reputation signified a way of life to her. She couldn't separate one from the other.

At first, it was hard to believe that she'd never been to a roadside bar before, but from her reactions, it had to be true. At the time he hadn't believed her, but after careful consideration, he'd decided she'd never been drunk before either. She trusted him. Otherwise, though she wanted "carefree" and "adventure," her ingrained manners and values wouldn't have allowed her to untether from the rules she lived by.

He ran through a yellow light to keep the ambulance in sight. "Let her be all right," he prayed.

She'd made love to him openly and freely. That had to be a sign of her faith in him. A belief that he wouldn't take advantage. It could be a sign of more. Hope rose in his chest.

Miss Branna Lind had gotten under his skin. The first time they met, she'd snubbed him, a dirty redneck farmer. However, the second time...during the storm, they connected in a weird intimate way. Any sane person would think him crazy. Later, when she'd danced with him at the faculty party—without knowing who or what he was—she'd delighted him. Her unabashed laughter made him feel lighter—happy even. An emotion he never considered owning again. The tinkling sound of her giggles—purely feminine.

When she gazed at him with a sparkling glint in her eyes, he wanted to be worthy of her esteem. She made him feel strong and bold. She made him laugh. And, her willingness to work at dance steps she didn't know rather than shying away made her adventurous and appealing.

Ahead, he watched the ambulance turn right. He followed the flashing lights when he reached the intersection.

So what did it matter that she accepted a car from another man?

Who was he kidding? It mattered.

The car represented a tie. A link. Maybe even a commitment. But she denied it. Why? And it mattered that she could be swayed by material things.

Would she, too, manipulate him like Caroline had?

Maybe.

"She's not Caroline!"

He'd risk it for a chance with Branna.

She had to heal and make a full recovery.

He couldn't lose the first woman he'd loved in years.

Chapter 25

"Looks like I need a ride after all, Dr. Newbern." Branna offered James a sheepish grin when the nurse finally allowed him to enter the hospital's examining room. She touched the small butterfly bandage at her hairline on the left side of her head. "They're letting me out of this place with a mild concussion."

"My car's out front. Wouldn't want you to take a taxi."

"I'm not the taxi-type," she chuckled.

James frowned.

"Don't you think that's funny? If I don't laugh, I'll cry." Her head pounded, but if she didn't stay on the light side of things, she'd break down in front of him. She had enough pain to produce enough tears to fill a wash bucket. Not a pretty sight under the best of circumstances, and these were anything but.

She laced her fingers together in a tight clench. She itched to call Momma, who would fuss over her and take care of her every need. Maybe even call her brother and order him to fly her home to Fleur de Lis. Never before had she understood the privileges bestowed upon her because she was the next Keeper. Selfishly, she had viewed it as a sacrifice, a mantle yoked around her neck. Why had she never understood that she could pick up the phone and call *anyone* in her family, and they would move heaven and earth to make sure she was safe and cared for.

Thankfully, James had her cell phone. That prevented her from allowing her resolve to melt like ice on hot asphalt. She could stand on her own.

"I guess making jokes is a good thing. A smile is nice. I'll try to think of a few knock-knock jokes while I drive you home." The scowl he wore suggested her humor should wait for a more appropriate time.

On the short drive from the hospital to her house, she clutched the door handle in James' car with one hand and held the seatbelt away from her neck with her other. Though the bandaged burn on her neck was on the left side, the idea of a seatbelt against her skin made her woozy.

Lightheaded, she blinked to bring the world into clearer focus. Tears pooled, her vision blurred, but she refused to give in to weakness and vulnerability. Much had happened in a short time, processing reality required focus she could barely muster. However, one thought made a continuous loop through her mind.

She could have died today.

The fact that she'd survived made her grateful for each breath she took. Her heart ached because of all the worry she'd caused her family. And, beyond all else, she had to make things right with her sister. She had the power to change the relationship with Camilla, maybe even convince her to come home.

Tucking the seatbelt under her arm, she wiped her eyes, then quickly grabbed the strap again. The feel of it against her body produced a newfound panic.

"Is there someone I can call for you?" James asked in a calm low voice. The tone of voice a man might use when he was scared a woman might fall apart. "Your parents? Sister? Someone?"

"No...no one. The closest family in distance to me is my brother. He's in college down in Gainesville. I can manage this on my own. I expect to be as good as new in a few days."

"Guess brothers aren't much help, are they?"

"For some things, but not this."

"I'll be happy to call your parents. I think someone needs to stay with you."

"No. No, thank you. Really, I can manage." How could she explain that she had to do this on her own? Since she wasn't dying, this was a chance to prove she was capable and strong. She fell apart when Steven betrayed her—she wouldn't do that today, though her inner child was wailing for her momma.

James' car approached her house. She couldn't wait to get inside to rest. Squinting, she shielded her eyes from the evening sun's rays that lit the sky. Above the treetops, pink, silver, lavender, and gold reflected off the clouds. A beautiful, yet ordinary day. Her day had been anything but. Obviously, she had not one drop of clairvoyance in her body. If she'd had any inkling about the twists and turns that faced her, would she have bothered to get out of bed that morning? Everyone gets to be an ostrich and hide their head in the sand sometimes, right?

The painter's truck parked at the curb had the windows rolled down and the radio cranked with the bass booming, rattling glass. The vibration beat in her head as though the pounding originated there. She winced. Nausea hit hard. Bill ran up when James opened the car door for her.

"Miss Lind! Are you okay?"

"Yes, but, would you turn your radio down?"

"Oh, sure!" Bill said, and then disappeared.

"Take it slow," James cautioned as she stepped back to close the car door. "Where are your keys? I'll get the front door unlocked."

Bill returned and danced around her like a nervous puppy. "Did you hear? It's on the news! The accident. You're a hero—well, not a guy hero, but a girl hero."

"What?" She leaned on James for support as she dug in her purse and fished out her keys.

"Yeah, the DEA and local Feds, they found the guy—the pilot—in the woods. Got the dogs out on him and everything. The pilot is a drug smuggler. It's on the news. You're famous!"

"Ah, thanks, Bill. I need to go inside." She couldn't compute half of what he said.

When she moved, pain zigzagged through her chest, and her breath caught in her throat. The doctors said she'd be bruised and sore, but they never said the pain would bring her to her knees. The meds weren't doing their job. Or maybe their full punch required more time to work?

She sagged against James, who scooped her up and carried her. The jarring from each step made her head hurt more, but if she had to walk the twenty feet, it would take her all night.

"Hey, Bill. Make yourself useful. Unlock the door for Miss Lind," James told the painter. "Keys are in my back pocket."

Bill grabbed the keys and raced ahead. He swung the door open wide. "I stayed around to see how you are. I'll be back to finish painting tomorrow."

"Sure," she mumbled before Bill took off again.

"The couch?" James asked. "It's warm in here. Do you want the air conditioner on?"

"Bedroom first. Yes, A/C. Tea, please."

James placed her gingerly on her bed, then headed back down the hall. She heard the air conditioning click on before he entered the kitchen. She rose slowly and inched her way to the dresser. Her reflection in the mirror confirmed that no one looked good in a hospital dressing gown. She'd used it to cover her bloodstained blouse. It could be a wardrobe prop for a zombie movie.

She managed to stand, undress, and toss the wadded up blouse into the corner near her closet. Carefully, she pulled on yoga pants and eyed her bed like a kid eyeing a candy counter.

Maybe the painkillers and muscle relaxers had kicked in. That could be an explanation for her desire to have James undress her, and then crawl into bed beside her. Under other conditions, modesty would prevent her from asking for his help. The drug-induced relaxation wiped away inhibitions. In fact, she could make a sound argument that he *must* cuddle with her, the warmth of his hands on her body would calm her nerves. He had a healing touch.

In slow motion, she pulled on a loose fitting shirt, an old cotton one of her father's. She left a couple of buttons undone at the top and the bottom. Taking a step, she wobbled in her bedroom doorway.

"Let me help you," James said.

"Don't pick me up," she begged.

He walked her step-by-step to the living room, allowing her to take the time she needed. She sat slowly, with his support, at one end of the couch, then lifted her legs, stretching them out long. James disappeared down the hall. He returned with pillows from her bed.

"There's a quilt in the hall closet." She pointed. Homesickness trumped bravery. She needed a reminder of home. Comfort. The handmade quilt had been a gift from Great-Grandmother Marie. The faded squares sewn together, with their washed-in softness, would ease her pains.

"I raided your kitchen. Here's some chicken broth and tea." James set a cookie sheet with two cups of steaming liquid on the table in front of her. "I do pretty well as a cook."

He must have seen her wince and thought it was because of his offerings.

"Would you like something else?"

"No. Thanks. This is fine. Tea for me."

Wearing a curious expression, James cocked his head and looked at her as though he contemplated something.

Had she spoken her reply or just heard the words in her head? The drugs provided an "out-of-control" sensation, and if she ever thought to audition for a role in *Dr. Who*, she could call on this experience for help.

"I'm just killing pain with humor. Or maybe killing humor with drugs? I don't know which."

Shaky, certain that at any moment might she break down, she fought to hold back tears. She wanted her mother, wanted comfort and support, but she had to navigate a recovery without leaning on family. She could do it. The emotional need pounding in her heart was not a life or death matter. Grown women weren't supposed to cry for their mommas, right?

Sitting in the chair across from the couch, James

rested his forearms on his thighs and scrutinized her. She shifted and pulled the quilt up to her neck, then reached for the cup of tea.

"I appreciate your kindness. You don't have to stay. I'll be all right."

"I could call Sadie. She'd come and stay with you. If you'd feel more comfortable with a woman."

"No. I can't ask her. It would be awkward."

"Then, I'll stay."

"I'll be fine. I promise."

"Okay. Be fine with me here." He laced his fingers together and put his hands behind his head, making himself comfortable in the chair. "Here are the facts. You're on drugs right now that reduce your ability to think clearly. Also, they can impair your physical abilities. I won't leave. We can't have you drown in a tub or fall down, knock your head, and bleed out."

Her bottom lip trembled. She took a sip from the cup, then drew a ragged breath. "I keep thinking that I could have died."

Immediately, James rose. He motioned for her to make room for him on the couch. He sat, then scooped her up and held her. He cradled her with one arm and with the other, wrapped the quilt around her back, tucking her into a cocoon with him, her head on his chest.

"It's okay to cry, Branna." His words were almost a whisper.

Her body started to shake. Tremors passed through her, but she fought against the tears.

"Let go," James urged.

Her first wail sounded foreign to her ears. The next few came in a wave. She tried to catch her breath between each raspy sob. Inhaling was more like hiccupping.

"I'm here. I'm here," James whispered.

His words became a healing mantra as he gently rocked her. She cried until she was cried out. The heat of his body soothed her. When the tears finally stopped, she snuggled close and rested her head on his shoulder. Not many men could handle a woman's tears as he had. She didn't care if he thought she was childish or not, as long as he continued to hold her.

Forever might not be long enough.

Chapter 26

James closed the shutters in Branna's bedroom and pulled back the covers on the bed. He returned to the living room and carried her to her room. Hopefully the prescription drugs would do their job, and she'd sleep undisturbed. At least until he had to wake her according to doctor's orders. As he pulled a sheet and blanket to her chin, she puffed out little breaths while lost in deep sleep. She'd never looked as vulnerable as she did then. That vulnerability tugged hard at his heart. The usually commanding Branna Lind now looked angelic, and that pushed all of his protective buttons.

"Sleep, sugar. I'll be right out there," he whispered for his ears only.

He'd done everything backward with this woman. They were lovers when they were barely friends and barely friends before they were technically colleagues. Their night of lovemaking was more than a one-night stand to him. But could he convince her of that?

"Christ, we were supposed to be only colleagues," he muttered.

Walking back to the living room, he looked for insights into the woman that had given his heart a jolt. Everything in view appeared in its proper place. She was neat and organized. A decorator probably had a clever technical word for Branna's style. A mix of modern and antique furnishings. The room exuded comfort without being feminine fussy. It was a place where a guy could hang and feel at home, even put his feet on the old trunk used as a coffee table.

The artwork over the fireplace drew his attention. Vibrant colors, a type of abstract. A street scene obviously in New Orleans' French Quarter. A Creole cottage with shutters next to a two-story building with lacy ironwork rails. The painting reminded him of Branna. Colorful, detailed, and full of movement.

With nothing else to do, he settled on the couch, picked up the newspaper, and started to read. The letters blurred. His eyes couldn't follow the words. He leaned his head on the back of the couch to rest.

When the phone rang, he snapped awake, then sprinted toward the kitchen to find it, hoping it wouldn't wake Branna.

"Hello?"

"Dr. Brown here. Branna was gone by the time I arrived at the crash site. How is she now? May I speak with her?"

"She's sleeping."

James noted the long pause on the other end of the line. He wondered what Dr. Brown was surmising. About Branna. About him.

"I see. Tell her I've worked out a schedule to cover her classes for the rest of the week. Do you know anything about her condition? Will she be back next week?"

A muffled ring caught James' attention.

"Gotta go. Her cell phone's ringing. Don't want it to wake her up."

"Call me back if I can do anything."

James hung up and sought out the sound, hunting it

like a bird dog follows a scent. He ran to the bedroom and closed the door, not wanting anything to disturb her. Grabbing Branna's purse from the chair, he pulled the ringing phone from it. The shrill of *Fur Elise* blasted loudly.

"Hello. Branna's phone."

"Who is this?" a woman's voice on the other end demanded.

"James Newbern. A friend of Branna's. To whom am I speaking?"

"I'm looking for my daughter."

"Ah, Mrs. Lind. Well, she's had a slight accident."

"An accident? No! How is she? Who…who did you say you are?"

He kept his tone level in hopes of conveying the information so she wouldn't be alarmed. No need to frighten Branna's mother.

"I'm James. Branna and I are colleagues at the college. She's going to be fine, but she's sleeping right now. She sustained some minor cuts and bruises, and a mild concussion. Mostly, she's shaken up from the car accident."

"Oh, God! Where is she? In the hospital? How'd this happen? When?" Then he heard a muffled plea on the other end of the phone. "Charles, come quick. Branna's been hurt."

"You're on speaker phone," a man's voice said. "Who are you?"

"I work with your daughter. I'm Dr. James Newbern, Professor. Branna is resting at home. She's asleep. The doctors say she'll be fine in a few days. She needs some rest."

"You're sure?" Mrs. Lind clearly doubted his

word.

"Yes ma'am."

"This is Charles Lind, Branna's father. How did this happen?"

"Well sir, I didn't witness the accident. Came upon it afterward. A plane ran off the runway and hit Branna's car."

"A plane?"

"As I understand it, she swerved to avoid it, left the road, and the impact happened at the tree line. Branna's car hit a tree, and the plane hit her Volvo."

"Oh, Charles! I can't believe this. I have to go to her."

"This happened on the road to the college?" Mr. Lind asked.

"How seriously is she hurt?" Mrs. Lind pressed.

"She needs a few days to recover. No complications are expected. Mr. Lind, an airport runway runs perpendicular to the road leading to the college. You'll both be happy to know, Branna's become a local celeb—" The doorbell interrupted him. "Hang on. Someone's at the door. I don't want them to wake Branna up."

He raced to the front door and opened it, ready to tell the intruder to lay off the bell. Sadie smiled widely and offered up a pot that smelled a lot like chicken soup.

"Let me in. A van pulled up. There's a reporter and camera crew on my heels. We can talk to them together after I put this pot down."

James moved aside. Sadie slid past him as he stepped outside and closed the door behind him. He tried to wave away the TV crew rushing toward him.

"Peter Simmons with WTFL news. I would like to speak with Ms. Lind."

"She's not available."

"What's your name?" The news reporter asked as he stuck a microphone in James' face.

"Ms. Lind isn't at home. I suggest you call before coming back. Please leave."

"Who was that woman who just entered? Was that her?"

"No. Now, if you'll excuse me." James turned to open the door.

"Aw, c'mon man. The lady's a hero! It's not often a woman single-handedly stops a drug smuggler's plane in our neck of the woods."

"You aren't from our neck of the woods. You're from a TV station down in Gainesville. We *do* watch TV up here. Now, once again, call before you come back. If the lady wants to talk with you, she'll let you know."

"Give her my card."

James took the card, then entered the house. Sadie met him with a frown. "Why didn't you wait for me? They could have interviewed us together."

"They didn't interview me. I've got Branna's parents on the phone." He spoke into the receiver. "Sorry about that, Mr. and Mrs. Lind. I guess you heard most of it. Our administrative assistant, Sadie McGee, is here. As soon as your daughter wakes up, I'll have her call you."

"Yes, please do. It doesn't matter the time," Mr. Lind said.

"Charles, I'm going to her as soon as I can pack a bag. I'll have Gill fly me over. I can't wait for a phone call."

"James, we'll call you back if Mrs. Lind decides to come," Mr. Lind said.

"I want to assure you, she'll be fine. However, I'll help on this end in any way I'm able." He closed the phone when Branna's parents ended the connection.

"I've got biscuits in the car. Sweet potato pecan pie, too," Sadie said.

"Let's wait a while, wait for the van to leave. You know food won't cure what ails her."

"Maybe not, but it can't hurt."

The doorbell interrupted them. "What now? If it's that TV reporter, I'm going to call the police."

Sadie grinned, "You know my cousin is on the force. I'll call him while you answer the door."

"Who aren't you related to in this town?"

James looked through a side window. It presented the perfect vantage point to observe anyone on the front porch without being noticed. Cars lined the driveway and blocked his car, while others parked at the curb near Sadie's minivan. A contingent of women, most of whom he recognized from the society page of the newspaper, stood on the porch.

"Sadie, you field this crowd. Don't let them in. I'm going to check on Branna. Then, I'm going to find a screwdriver and dismantle that damn doorbell."

Sadie headed for the door as he eased down the hall toward Branna's bedroom.

Turning the knob gently, he opened the door. Branna still slept. He sat in the chair across from the bed. The bedroom faced the back of the house and with the door closed, most of the exchange between Sadie and Lakeview's social elite do-gooders sounded only a decibel above a whisper.

He squinted and waited for his eyes to adjust to the darkness. Outside, the setting sun had slipped below the horizon, and the treed lot blocked most of the final rays of light. Blinking again, he fixed his attention on Branna, who struggled to sit up. Jumping up to assist, he grabbed an unused pillow and plopped it on top of the one behind her back.

"I thought it was all a bad dream," Branna murmured.

"For your sake, I wish it was." He hunkered into a squat because sitting beside her on the bed seemed too personal.

"How did I get in here?"

"I thought you might rest more comfortably in your own bed. You were asleep when I carried you in."

"Professor, for someone who doesn't like my 'type,' you've been most gallant. Thank you. Thank you for your help before, and thank you for now."

"Well, let's just say it's part of the service. After all, Dr. Brown assigned me to mentor you through your adjustment period."

"I doubt he ever intended *this* kind of service."

Her chuckle set him at ease. Humor was a cure-all, as much as chicken soup. If Branna could joke, she must be on the road to recovery.

"If you're hungry, Sadie brought soup. Better than the broth I heated up. She says she's got biscuits and pie in the car."

"Sadie's here?"

"Yeah. She's outside with local ladies of charity who've come to crown the town's newest heroine."

"Her family needs her. Please encourage her to go

home. I'll be fine. I don't need a babysitter."

"I'm here." Sadie appeared in the bedroom doorway. Light from the hallway fell across the bed. She flipped on the lights.

"Oh! Turn it off. Please," Branna cried. "The light hurts my eyes."

James rose and turned off the bright overhead light and switched on the lamp beside her bed.

"See, you do need me. I brought the rest of the food in from the car. Would you like a bite to eat?"

"No. Not now. Sadie, your family needs you. Thank you for the food, but please go home."

"Not until you're up and out bed."

"Well, I think I can do that."

Branna gently moved the covers aside. She planted her feet in the spot where he'd been sitting. Under her own power, she rose to standing, more mechanical-like than with fluidity. She looked at her feet, shuffled a few short steps, and grabbed for the doorjamb. "There, I'm up and out of bed. I'll see you out."

"I don't think it's a good idea," James cautioned.

"Please, let me try." Branna's imploring eyes made him move out of the way. He offered his arm for support, but she pulled away.

Sadie took the lead and headed down the hall. Branna followed, mostly sliding along the wall, using it for support. He trailed one step behind, ready to catch her if she tumbled, all the while praying she wouldn't.

Helpless, he maintained a watchful lookout as she reached the living room. With steadier feet than he'd imagined, she crossed the space, grabbed for the back of the couch, and followed it like a railing. About fifteen feet separated the couch from the door. She managed the expanse a half step at a time. When she reached the door where Sadie waited, he let out a breath in relief.

"Sadie, thank you again. I'm sure the food is wonderful. You're very thoughtful." Branna flipped the switch for the front porch light and opened the door. James stood beside her, willing her strength, though he didn't dare touch her, but if she fell and injured herself again, what would he tell her parents?

Sadie hugged Branna tight. "So, you're tougher than you look, I'll give you that. But I think Dr. Newbern should leave, and I should stay."

Branna closed her eyes and sucked on her bottom lip.

He couldn't decide if she was about to explode or cry.

Rather than wait for Branna's reply, he jumped in. "Sadie, I've got this covered. I have to call Dr. Brown back, and I promised Branna's parents I'd call them back, too." He used his professorial lecture tone, one that he knew Sadie wouldn't argue against.

"I promise, I'm fine." Branna smiled weakly.

"All right." Sadie frowned, apparently reluctant to leave. "You've got my number Dr. Newbern, if you need me."

After the secretary was safely in her car, he turned off the front porch light, closed the door, and then assisted Branna in her shuffle back to the couch. He located her cell phone in the kitchen, intending to make good on his promise. "I answered your cell phone earlier."

"My cell?"

"I didn't want it to wake you up."

"Ever hear of voice mail?"

Sarcasm was a type of humor. He hoped it was a sign of her continued recovery.

"Your mother called. Then your father got on the line. They're worried. They want to talk with you. Especially since I told them what happened. And...if you don't call them, I have to. If you truly don't want your mother hiring a pilot to bring her here, you'll talk to her."

Branna heaved a sigh. "You told them? Oh. You don't understand," she wailed.

"I know that I'm a man of my word."

"Maybe so, but *your word* created an obligation for me."

"Just call them. Tell them you're fine. What's the big deal?"

"My family's complicated."

Branna held out her hand, and he plopped the phone into her open palm. She pushed a button on the keypad. She had the phone on speaker. He listened to the other line ring and Mrs. Lind answer.

"Momma? It's Branna."

"Branna!" Her mother called for her father. Then she continued, "I'm coming as soon as I can get there."

"No, Momma. James may have exaggerated a bit out of concern for me. I'm fine. Not that I wouldn't love to see you, but how about next weekend? Could we plan for that?"

"I don't know...how about this weekend?" Her mother's concern came through loud and clear.

"Momma, I swear I'm fine."

James glared at her. "You have"—he pointed to her head—"a concussion. Not to mention bruises and other

233

small cuts. And, that thing on the side of your neck."

"You're being hardheaded," her father insisted.

Astonished that Branna would lie to her parents about her injuries, he rose to leave the room, seeking to give her privacy. Branna tugged on his sleeve, then patted the couch beside her. He gave in and sat.

"You have to trust me when I say, I'm fine. If you don't trust me about this, how will you ever trust me to run Fleur de Lis?"

"That's different, Branna."

"No Momma, it's not. If I can't run my own life, stand on my own and make solid decisions for myself, how can the family ever trust me to be a good steward of the estate? You want me to lead, but you don't let me."

James cocked his head. Had he overheard correctly? Estate? Well, that answered a number of things. Estates usually equaled big money. Branna an heiress? If so, an expensive car as a gift was something she probably expected in life. But then, why did she drive an old Volvo?

Sitting beside her made eavesdropping unavoidable. He turned his attention to the photos on the side table. He guessed the group shot was of her family—a very big family. He picked up the framed photograph and studied the faces. She looked a lot like her mother. The two could just about pass for sisters. And there was another woman who closely resembled Branna. A sister, maybe. She and Branna looked to be close in age. The two elderly women in the center caught his attention. Twins?

"James?"

"Yeah?" he said distractedly. When she tilted her

head and peered at him with the phone resting in her lap, he asked, "Is your mother placated?"

"For the moment. Could I bother you for some tea? This," she said lifting the cup from earlier, "is cold. And it needs sugar. Would you like something?"

"A little Captain Morgan to take the edge off," he muttered. "I'll make tea. Would you like some of Sadie's soup? I'll ladle you a bowl."

"Just tea. I'm too tired to eat."

He slapped his thighs and rose. Branna stretched out on the couch. He covered her with the quilt, tucking it under her feet.

"I didn't mean to complicate things when I answered your phone. And, darn. I didn't think to lie to the folks on the other end of the line."

"I didn't lie. I played the incident down. My family is—"

"Don't say complicated again."

"So much is expected of me. They treat me like I'm...in need of a nursemaid and in line for the throne, when what is needed is a strong leader."

"But aren't you?" he called from the kitchen.

"I'm the proverbial good girl. I'd never colored outside the lines until I dumped Steven and moved here."

"So, you're saying you hit your rebellious streak late? That happens to the good-girl types. I hear it's not fatal. Cream? Sugar?" he called over the kettle's whistle.

No answer.

"Branna? Do you want anything in your tea?"

Was that a sob?

"Branna?"

Yep. Definitely a sob.

He moved the whistling kettle from the stove, turned off the gas, and quickly made his way to her.

"Hey, what's wrong?" Sitting on the floor, he was eye to eye with her as she lay on her side with only her face peering out from beneath the quilt. She looked like a lost soul.

The depth of her fragility hit him. His gut tightened. Branna's tears were drops of pain and each one branded his heart.

"You don't understand anything about my life. Yet you keep judging me. I'm this *type* or that *type*. Your low opinion oozes out. You don't even bother to try to hide it."

"Wait. Look—"

"Are you always so harsh?" Branna sniffed.

Harsh? No. Cautious? Yes. Judgments weren't always a bad thing. In the past, an error in judgment had cost him dearly. But Branna wasn't Caroline. His head had taken a while to catch up with his heart. "I'm sorry I seem harsh."

Their gazes locked.

Branna nodded. "Apology accepted. One sugar and one cream, please."

Had that been Caroline... No. He had to stop that. No more comparisons of anyone to Caroline. That was a piece of bad luck he could finally shake off.

He returned with mugs of tea, steam rising from each and curling together. Branna scooted and leaned against the armrest of the couch. She took a mug and blew on the liquid. Traces of tears had made barely visible tracks down her face.

He took a seat on the opposite end of the couch,

near her feet. "Branna, if you'd like to talk about..." He started to mention her parents, but changed his mind. "The accident or anything else, I'll listen."

"Oh James." Branna plopped the mug down on the coffee table. Tea sloshed over the side.

She pushed her feet out from beneath her and surprised him by cuddling close, practically gluing herself to his side. Soft sobs started. Her body trembled. Tears soaked the front of his shirt. The helplessness that had engulfed him when Katie died now blanketed his heart.

He put his arm around her and hugged her close. What could he do? What should he do? Was her flow of emotion the result of the concussion? Did he need to call the doctor, or better yet, rush her back to the hospital?

"Branna, it's okay. Whatever it is, I promise, it'll be fine." Maybe she needed more rest. A good night's sleep cured many things. It could make the world a wonderful place.

"I'm here. Let it all go."

He let her cry. After several minutes, when his shirt was soaked and her tears lessened to a slow dribble, she sniffled. He offered her a tissue from the box next to him, then turned and patted her shoulder as she held the tissue to her nose.

If blowing one's nose could ever be described as dainty, Branna managed it.

"Another tissue, please."

He pulled four from the box and handed them over.

Branna's gaze met his. "So what type am I now? The foolish crying type?" she whispered.

Her accusation stung, but he deserved it. "No. Not

at all. You have the wrong idea about me. Look, we really don't know each other that well. Unlike you, I keep my life uncomplicated. By your own admission, yours is not."

"Humph."

"What does that mean?"

"You've been hurt. Now your armor's hard. Do you have compassion for anyone?"

"What? Yeah I do. If I didn't, I'd have left you at the door when you said you were fine and could manage by yourself."

"Maybe you have an over developed sense of...duty, or misguided ideas about honor. Maybe that's why you're still here."

James paused. The last thing he wanted was an argument with her. He softened his tone. "Branna, you needed me. I wanted to be here for you. What you experienced today was scary stuff, life threatening. Someone needed to stay. I decided that someone would be me."

He couldn't bring himself to say that the accident scared ten years off his life, and that his heart had fallen in love, even if his brain resisted. The thought of losing her scared the shit out of him.

"I'm fine now. Thank you for the use of your shoulder. You can go."

The flashes of anger in her eyes bothered him more than her punctuated angry tone. Was anger a cover for pain? Fear?

Her blotchy, red, tear-stained face wouldn't win her a beauty contest, but she still looked lovely. Vulnerable. Gentile. The pain in her eyes made him want to hold her until it all melted away like the sun rising to push away a dark nightmare, making it fade away forever. She made him want to be the man that made everything in her life turn out all right.

"No."

"No?"

"I'm not that kind of guy, Your Highness. I'm not leaving you alone. Tell me what I don't understand about the complications of your life."

Chapter 27

Loud banging woke James. Disoriented, he pushed up from the floor to sitting, then rested his back against the couch. Morning rays of light seeped in from around the drapes, but gave no clue as to the time. He glanced at his watch. It showed six thirty a.m. He'd slept all night on the floor.

A soft low groan behind him drew his attention. He turned and looked over his shoulder. Branna appeared deep in sleep, though agitated by a dream. Sleeping had brought color back to her cheeks. She looked irresistible. Sweet. Warm. Womanly. Dare he sneak a kiss? He could enjoy waking up beside her each morning. He craved a deeper connection with the woman who had haunted his dreams.

Running his fingers through his hair, he let out a low growl. Who was he kidding? He wanted more than a kiss. He wanted to pick her up, take her to bed, and make love to her—all day. Some knight in shining armor, taking advantage of a helpless injured woman.

What was wrong with him? She needed help, not lust.

When the banging started again, he jumped up and ran for the front door. Whoever was making the noise had to stop. Branna needed sleep. They'd talked off-and-on until two in the morning, until neither of them could stay awake.

He yanked open the front door, stepped outside, and pulled the door closed. "Stop that!"

The banging continued.

"What the hell are you doing?" he called to Bill, who pounded the rim of a gallon-sized bucket of paint.

The painter stood at the rear of his van, the back doors opened wide. Several five-gallon paint buckets surrounded him like a drum set. Inside the van, a blend of colored paints puddled on the floor.

"Sorry, man. Did I wake you?"

"Never mind me. Branna's sleeping."

The painter eyed him up and down. "Yah, man, whatever you say."

"Don't give me crap. Paint if you're going to, but stop the banging noise. The lady's had a rough night. Yesterday was tough business."

"Is she doing okay? That was something, though. Did you see the video of the crash on the news last night?"

"No. What video?"

"Some college kid films planes taking off and landing for some docudrama he's making. He happened to be in the right place at the right time. Got it all on tape. Miss Lind will be the FBI's star witness in the drug smuggling case."

"I don't know if she saw anything other than the plane. Anyway, look, no noise. Okay? Let's let her sleep."

"Sure. No noise."

When he returned to the house, Branna remained asleep on the couch. The aroma of brewing coffee greeted him, and he followed his nose to the kitchen. Last night, he'd set the timer on the coffee maker after

Branna directed him to coffee and filters.

Anticipating the hot dark liquid that dripped into a glass carafe, the fog in his brain started to push aside. Black and strong. That's how he wanted his coffee this morning. He needed a massive caffeine jolt if he intended to make it through the day. Waiting for his liquid addiction-of-choice, he thought about the things Branna had shared between her catnaps and bites of Sadie's biscuits.

At first, it was uncomfortable to hear such intimate personal information about her, after he'd resisted intimacy for so long. He engaged in deep discussions about politics, philosophy, books, and even religion once in a while, though he usually avoided those discussions also. Never had a woman exposed her most deep-seated emotions and layered them with logic as Branna had done.

"I wasn't born with a silver spoon in my mouth," she had said.

"Well, this one isn't silver either. However, the pecan pie is gold-medal worthy. Take a bite." He held the spoon to her lips, and she tasted the pie.

"Mmm, this is good. I was born with a yoke of responsibility. I'm the oldest female in my generation of the family. Do you know how many generations are living right now on my mother's side?"

"No."

"Four. We're a huge group. I have a sister and brother. And there are five cousins. There's my parents' generation, a total of eight adults. My grandparents' generation. There are three of them. And finally, there are the Old Aunts. My great grandmother and her twin sister are the matriarchs of our family." Branna pointed at the family photo on the table next to him. "And I'm expected to run Fleur de Lis and pass it on to future generations. Until me, every previous Keeper had the benefit of the Old Aunts' wisdom. In my lifetime, at some point, the Old Aunts will pass away. They are, after all, in their nineties."

"Well, there's not enough pie for all of them, so we won't share. And what exactly is Fleur de Lis?"

"Home. It's an antebellum estate built by the Old Aunts' grandfather before the War Between the States. Don't think there's money just because it's a grand old house. It's our legacy. My family works hard, and everyone contributes to upkeep, but each family also has a home of their own—some in Mississippi and others in Louisiana. My parents live at the beach in Biloxi. Fleur de Lis barely pays for itself. For example, we remodeled a couple of years ago with the help of an architect." She scoped up a bit of pie. "Yum... So we added an elevator when it became clear the Old Aunts found navigating stairs a problem. That construction project was a huge ordeal because the house is on the historic register. We put the elevator in the old cistern and built a connector to each floor between it and the house. The architect designed the connectors and made them look as though they'd always been there. That wisdom about remodeling—expect to pay twenty percent over the quote and double the time to finish the project—we had overruns and missed deadlines."

"Estate equals land. Does your family farm or something?" He took another bite of pie and said a silent prayer of thanks for Sadie's baking skills.

"Over the years, most of the land was sold off to provide funds for upkeep of the house. Any day now, I expect to get a call about the heating and A/C problems. That'll be twenty-thousand dollars or more. Just keeping the house clean is a full time job. We have Greta, she's part of the family after all these years, and she takes care of the Old Aunts who are, since I'm gone, the only permanent residents in the house. The house is too large for one woman to clean, so Greta hires help now and then, and more frequently when the entire family is in residence."

"The entire family? That must be some house."

"Not everyone makes it all the time, but mostly for the big days. Thanksgiving, Christmas, New Years and Mardi Gras. Oh, and everyone is always there for the Valentine's Ball."

He finished his pie and contemplated her family. They sounded very Norman Rockwell. "So, I'm waiting for the other shoe to fall. The downside of this life *is*?"

"Can you imagine how much laundry there is after the family vacates? Do you know, we put in a second dishwasher to handle dishwashing for family weekends? Even that's not enough. Without multiples, someone would slave in the kitchen washing dishes and glasses and missing out on fun."

"Your problem is laundry and dirty dishes?"

"The responsibility for the house belongs to my mother right now. She passed the baton to me. I've been groomed for the job since I was knee-high to a grasshopper."

He chuckled. He hadn't heard anyone use that expression in a very long time.

"It's not funny. How would you like to be saddled with a property that you had to care for and preserve, not just for your immediate family, but for generations to come? How about holding a position that requires committee approval to do anything? You're just the minion with the elbow grease to carry out the committee's commands." She yawned.

He knew all too well. He'd grown up on a farm. One that his much-older brother stood to inherit. "What I don't understand is why you're here, if your life is already planned."

"My mother, my beautiful mother whose shoes I'm supposed to fill, drives me crazy. She expects me to step up while refusing to face the fact that she really still wants to run the place. She orders me around as though I'm a lady-in-waiting. She called me from her nursery, the plant kind, at least twice a day to check up on things when I lived at Fleur de Lis."

"Sorry, but that doesn't seem so bad."

"I had to get away...to know that I'm capable of making good decisions. After all, my choice of a potential groom flopped dismally." She fidgeted with the edge of the quilt covering her lap. "There's more."

"I've got all night."

"My breakup was acrimonious. I have called that man names in my head that I didn't even know I knew. He made me doubt myself. Made me question things I've never questioned before. I've always done the expected thing. If I'm going to run Fleur de Lis, I have to know I can handle my own life, one that's never truly been my own. Until now, every decision I've ever made put family first. It got to the point that I wondered if I existed other than to serve my home. And, there's so much I've never done because it was done for me. Like bake a cake. Mow a lawn."

"Hmmm."

"That's all you can say? Hmmm?" She yawned again.

"Hmmm, for you and the pie. Take another bite. Breathe. I see your point. But that still doesn't explain about the guy and the car."

"The guy is the ex-fiancé. Our parents pushed us together for years. I haven't told anyone what happened. Let's just say I discovered that his desires were varied. He's not who everyone thinks he is. And, I'm *not* keeping the car. If you don't believe me. Just wait and see." Branna's body sagged. She lowered her gaze. Her eyelids closed as though she'd lost the last reserves of her energy.

"I believe you."

When she didn't answer, he touched her arm. She had fallen asleep.

Last night gave him a lot to think about. More than how much he wanted to kiss her silly, or when he could tangle in sheets with her next, which he intended to, just as soon as she was well. In the meantime, he would ensure she healed and would protect her at all cost.

But how would he ever compete with the magnetic pull of Fleur de Lis? Was there anything he could do to make her stay with him? He'd willingly follow her back to Mississippi, if she wanted. If not, what the hell would he do?

Chapter 28

Clack. Clack. Clack.

Branna woke. Confused, she sat up and shook her head to clear the fuzziness. How did she get in her bed? Her last memory was drifting off to sleep on the couch cuddled next to James. The pounding in her head made her lie back again and close her eyes.

Surprised to hear a soft snore, she peered through the dimness in her room. James sat in a chair pulled close to her bed. His feet rested on top of the covers near hers.

Clack. Clack. Clack.

"Huh? What?" James muttered.

"What *is* that noise?" she asked.

It sounded again.

"The painter. I think he's playing with his ladder. Raising and lowering it to get it to the right height." James stretched his arms and yawned.

"How did I get in bed?"

"The painter woke me up at six-thirty this morning. I brought you in here so you could sleep undisturbed."

"I must have been really out of it."

"Lots happened since six-thirty. The plumber came and left. He brought a faucet and installed it. Said it went with the house. He also said he saw you on TV last night, which made him think that you wouldn't be running out to get a new faucet at the store."

"Thoughtful man." She yawned. "What time is it now?"

"About time for me to go. Near 10 a.m. Do you need food before I go? I can scramble an egg. Do you want me to have Sadie come sit with you for the afternoon?"

Her stomach rumbled. "I'm feeling well enough to get up. I can manage. I don't want to impose on you more."

"Dr. Brown called. He's covered your classes for the rest of the week. Wishes you a speedy recovery."

"I hate missing work. I'll manage fine this afternoon. Maybe I'll feel well enough to return to classes tomorrow. Maybe—"

The doorbell interrupted her.

"I'll get that." James rose and left the room.

As she pulled her robe tighter around her, she heard the front door open, then James said, "Come on in."

Moving slowly, she shuffled down the hall. When she made it to the living room, a jean-clad guy with a T-shirt showing off the college's logo set two potted plants decorated with big yellow bows on the floor by the door. On the coffee table, four large flower arrangements hid the entire tabletop. The fragrance of roses wafted to her nose. Then, as if on cue, the sound of *Fur Elise* floated around the flowers. Somewhere hidden beneath the arrangements, her cell phone rang.

She started toward the table, but stopped. James closed the door behind the departing delivery guy, then reached between the flower pots and vases and retrieved her ringing phone. He handed it over.

Without looking at the number, intuition told her

the caller was her mother.

She was right. "Hello, Momma."

"Branna! How are you feeling this morning?" Her mother's voice sounded a pitch too high and too bright. Something was up.

"Good. Momma, let me call you right back." Branna closed her phone and turned to James. "I'm grateful for the help. You've got stuff to do, so please don't feel obligated to stay." In truth, she hated to see him leave. Being close to him, despite her injuries, made her pulse beat stronger. Faster. Harder. She could finally admit to herself there was only one reason for it, even if she wasn't ready to speak the words aloud.

"I'll have some food delivered for you. I've a class this afternoon. I'll call you later this evening."

He surprised her when he moved close and cradled her face with his hands. His warm lips pressed firmly against hers. She leaned in and kissed him back, wishing she could melt into his arms and hold him tight forever. The accident had brought focus to her mind and clarity to her heart. Being near him heightened each of her senses. Her toes curled. In his arms, the connection to him ran deep.

He touched her as though he cherished her. Tender and light. She loved that about him. Her heart skipped several beats. Quivering sensations flooded her body.

This was love. The real thing.

James owned her heart.

When he pulled back, his eyes reflected puzzlement, or maybe surprise. She hated coolness touching her where he had touched before. He pulled back farther until an arm's length separated them, but he held her hands. Was he as reluctant to leave her as she was for him to go?

Before he let himself out, he turned back to her. She blew him a kiss. He beamed. Was that true happiness on his face?

What *type* was she now?

After the *click* of the front door closing, she returned a call to her mother. When the phone's ringing stopped, but before her mother could answer, she said, "Sorry for the wait. How are you?" If she kept the conversation routine, her mother would hopefully remain calm.

"Honey, Steven called."

The hair on the back of Branna's neck prickled. That was the last thing she expected to hear. "Oh?"

"He's very concerned about you. Your accident yesterday hit the internet news. He mentioned something about it being a good thing that he gave you a car...and he's optimistic that the two of you might reconcile. He said the car was one you'd admired."

"Momma, don't build false hopes. Steven and I won't, under any terms, ever be Mr. and Mrs. Sterling."

"I would like to understand what came between the two of you. Steven said—"

"The painter needs me, Momma. I'll call you back later."

"All right. I'm happy to know you're okay."

Branna pushed the "end" button and wished there was one she could use on Steven. If she ever saw that man again, she'd probably need an attorney, because she'd be going to jail for murder. What nerve to involve her family!

Of course he did. He was Steven Sterling. He'd do anything to win his case. She was nothing more than a challenge to conquer, then push aside for the next. She knew his routine.

After a cup of tea and a small bowl of cheese grits, she popped a classical CD into the stereo and lay on the couch to rest. Her body ached. Heaviness in her limbs made it hard to want to lift a hand. Her muscles argued when she fought against relaxing.

She focused on the melody. In her mind's eye, she read the individual notes on sheet music. She flexed her fingers as though she played the piano and hoped losing herself to the sounds of piano and strings would erase the sadness embedded in her chest. When she broke her engagement to Steven, she hadn't considered how hard it was for her mother, and now that Steven had planted hope, she had to be the one to squash it. How would her mother feel about Steven and Camilla?

When the home phone rang, she looked at caller ID. She reconsidered before answering. How did he get her number? What lie had he told to some unsuspecting person to gain the information? Or had her mother caved?

The ringing stopped as she reached for the phone. Then started immediately again. If she didn't pick up, he'd call back again and again, ruining any chance of resting. Maybe call blocking was the answer.

She grabbed the phone and firmly pushed the "talk" button. "Hello, Steven."

"Branna, I'm so relieved to hear your voice. Your mother said you were fine, but after seeing the photos of your Volvo on the national news...anyway. You're sure you're okay?"

"I'm fine."

"I wanted to fly out there the minute I heard, but..."

"But what? You were too tangled up with your current lover?"

"That's not nice. There's no one but you, Branna. I never loved another woman."

"Don't you mean, 'other women'? As in the plural form of the word. Are you so in the habit of lying, Steven, that you're incapable of honesty? I know your clients benefit from your skill at sidestepping the truth, but it doesn't work with me."

"Baby Doll, I'm sorry about the past. I'm asking you to forgive me. I thought you might have since you never told your family—at least not as far as I can tell—about our little issue. All of your family still talks to me."

"As long as they don't talk to you *about* me, I'm fine. Besides, you have a professional relationship with Uncle Peter. I didn't want your Robin-Hood lawyer image ruined just because you can't keep your pants zipped."

"It was one time, Branna. It's not like you to carry a grudge. The Branna I know would forgive me."

"That naïve girl is gone. Had it only been *once*, I *might* have forgiven you. But Steven, I know the whole truth. And I will not let you destroy my family. Words of warning. Stay away from me. Stay away from my family." She ended the call.

Calmness claimed her. No more uncontrollable rage. Only serenity, like gentle waves lapping against white sand on a sunny day at the beach. Sure, she had a touch of anger, a cupful compared to an ocean, but Steven no longer had a hold on her heart. She was completely free.

"Freedom!"

She'd experienced it with James. Her one night with him had been the exact opposite of anything she'd ever done before. In James' arms, inhibitions dissolved, spontaneity and desire flowed. She was a woman who knew her own mind and understood she had value as a person. They were equals *and* lovers. Well, one night together might not make them lovers. She'd have to work on that.

She'd never enjoyed a sense of ease with Steven even though she'd known him forever. Looking back, a much defined set of expectations came with a relationship with him. Much like a checklist of acceptable behavior with a report card given once a week.

"Proper. Pretty. Propriety," she repeated to herself.

Maybe he felt as trapped as she had? Maybe that was the reason for his wandering, and he just didn't understand the root problem. He hadn't always been so heartless.

"A devilish smile, seducing eyes and athletic body...and those first twinges of real desire," she muttered, remembering him in high school.

But he was two years ahead of her. They only dated in her mind. She worshiped him from afar. During her final year of grad school, they worked together on a charity fundraiser—one of his mother's famous causes. Steven had noticed her then.

Their chemistry left her breathless. The Prim Princess—folks called her that behind her back—bent herself into a pretzel to please him. How could she have been so stupid? The result of naiveté? Having never been in love before Steven, he consumed her world.

A few weeks after they started dating, he had

called late at night and woke her. He whispered as she lay in bed cocooned by darkness. His soothing voice directed her where and how to touch herself. He made her whisper where and how she would touch him. Hearing his climax shook her as much as the intensity of her own. Afterward, there was an awkwardness between them that never truly went away.

The first time they made love, it was hot and fast, and over too soon. His touch made her feel uncomfortable in her own skin. He ridiculed her lack of experience. She had blamed herself.

How sad that their best lovemaking had been that one time of phone sex.

Still, nothing had prepared her for the letter she'd accidentally found when she'd gone to clean out her things from his condo in New Orleans. Steven's current legal case had taken him out town for depositions, which allowed her privacy to pack. She'd loved the cozy intimate space in the heart of thriving French Quarter action. She took her time and prepared a farewell dinner for one. While chopping vegetables, she managed to slice her finger. She searched the medicine cabinet in the bathroom for a bandage, and a letter fell out. She opened it.

In a feminine scrolled handwriting, a woman begged Steven not to let his engagement stand in the way of their relationship. After all, she had a husband. The woman still wanted him, and had forgiven him. She'd seen him in April at the beach with yet another woman—a woman who wasn't Branna.

The woman confessed to being pregnant and not knowing the true paternity of the unborn baby. The letter closed with a threat. As long as Steven remained in her life, she wouldn't tell his ex-fiancée's family about him sleeping with both sisters.

The news had knocked Branna to her knees. The paper slipped through her hands. She knelt in front of the commode, not sure if she would be sick or not. The question of the pregnancy mattered nothing compared to the reference of "another woman last April" and "sisters."

That "*April woman*" referenced in the letter was Camilla. Her sister. She knew exactly when it happened—during Camilla's spring break.

Steven slept with her sister while she'd been buried in wedding plans. Camilla had acted strange, but she chalked it up to her sister's changeable moods. Then, after she called it quits with Steven, Camilla disappeared. Her sister had hinted about an incident, but when she pressed her for details, Camilla had shut her out and taken off.

She could never reveal Camilla's involvement with Steven. Never tell her parents or any of the family the reason for the breakup or why there was no chance of any reconciliation ever. Camilla's betrayal would pit family members against family members and destroy the family bond. Everything in her upbringing honed her instincts to protect family and Fleur de Lis. A split in the clan could be fatal to their legacy. She wouldn't allow that.

Steven had used Camilla.

Eventually everyone would discover Steven's predilection for indiscretions. As Granddaddy Lind said, "A leopard doesn't change its spots." Steve's true nature would be revealed someday by a woman claiming child support. Or a jealous husband. Branna had decided long ago to take the high road and remain silent.

And now she could see the amazing grace of her loving family. Everyone questioned, but no one pushed. Well, no one except her mother. No one judged. Why couldn't she see that at the time? They would have protected her *and* Camilla from him.

She missed her sister. Ending the engagement had been painful, yet the true deep sadness came from the rip in the relationship with her younger sister. Branna had stayed at Fleur de Lis longer than she wanted, hoping Camilla would come home. She'd forgiven her, though the wound still needed more healing time. Camilla was just a pawn in Steven's world, and her sister, even with her wild ways, hadn't stood a chance against skilled seduction.

Could she have possibly forgiven Steve for an affair? Maybe. But never could she look at him again knowing he'd seduced Camilla.

Moving to Lakeview had brought the closure she needed, given her heart wings. Steven no longer had a hold on her. In time, she'd rebuild the damaged relationship with her sister.

First, she had to find her.

She chuckled and murmured, "Will Steven see the humor in my decision if I give his car to Camilla?"

Chapter 29

Hot water, Epsom salts, and aromatherapy oils that Momma had guaranteed would relieve aches and pains filled the tub. Branna slid down in the luxurious water. Drifting scents of wintergreen, peppermint, and eucalyptus relaxed her. She dunked a sponge and squeezed it, sluicing water over her body. If the salts worked their magic, she'd feel like a new woman by the time she got out of the tub. All except for the cut at her hairline and the healing abrasions on her neck. She winced when she patted her neck with the sponge.

Thursday had stretched long. She napped between watching replays of the accident recorded on a DVD. After viewing the same footage for hours, the time spent had lessened her panic. It wasn't that she had PTSD. Still, desensitization to the accident had to be a good thing, especially when catching a glimpse of the bruises on her body made her squeamish.

Reporters doing follow-up stories had interrupted her self-therapy. Finally, she'd unplugged the phone when people she didn't know called to talk about the accident. Some were certain she should have died. Several people were looking to find a way to grab fifteen seconds of fame at her expense.

Sadie had dropped by after work to check on her and brought ice cream to share, then insisted on inspecting Bill's paint job when he finished for the day.

He received Sadie's final approval, and only then did Sadie let her write the check, after which, Sadie confided that reporters were still calling the office seeking interviews.

The accident was more than seventy-two hours old. It must have been a slow news day if they were looking to drag out leftovers.

Branna soaked the sponge again and squeezed. The warmth from the water ran over her. "Ahh. It's heavenly to be alive."

She slipped lower into the tub until the water covered her body and closed her eyes to let her imagination carry her away. She imagined James in the tub facing her, her foot seductively stroking his inner thigh, inching higher and higher, hoping for hard evidence of his desire. It was her tub fantasy. Anything she wanted could happen, right?

Next, he would take her foot in his hands and begin to massage, massage his way up her leg pulling her closer and closer to him. He'd massage all the way up to...there.

She squeezed her legs together tightly, and a shudder ran through her. She ran her hands over her breasts and lower to her stomach, resting her hands on the insides of her thighs. She massaged until the tension melted away.

If she could make James appear, she'd make sure they'd share a bath he'd never forget.

When the doorbell chimed, she jumped and splashed water over the side of the tub. The clock on the counter showed eight p.m. She wasn't up for visitors. Maybe if she ignored the noise, *whoever* would leave her alone.

Bang. Bang.

Clearly, *whoever* was insistent. Reluctant to leave her watery cocoon, she rose and toweled off, still hoping the annoyance at the front door would disappear.

Bang. Bang. Bang.

"All right! I'm coming."

She slipped on a sage green robe she'd bought at the day spa in New Orleans. With another towel, she dried the wet ends of her hair as she walked to the front door. She peered through the peephole, then drew back. The one person in the world she wanted to see stood on her porch.

"Hello? Branna? It's James. Are you okay?"

She flipped the towel over her shoulder, then opened the door before he could bang again.

"Whew. You're okay. I tried to call several times, but the phone went directly to voicemail."

"I turned it off. Too many interruptions."

He hoisted a grocery bag before her. "You've got plenty of flowers already, so I thought—food. I know you haven't had a decent meal since before the accident. I brought steak and salad."

"Then get in here and cook for me," she teased and grabbed for his arm. "And they say the way to a *man's* heart is through his stomach. My masculine side needs some attention. Flowers, even the edible ones, aren't very filling. I need protein, then chocolate. Steak. Is. Good." Her stomach rumbled loudly as though to second her decision.

James closed the door behind him. "I'm glad I got here in time."

"I'm so hungry I could probably eat half a cow."

"That could be arranged. I know a farmer. But for now, sit at the counter and direct me. I'll take care of everything."

A jolt spread through her when James put his hand on the small of her back and guided her toward the kitchen. Despite her hunger pangs, she had the urge to throw open her robe and ask him to devour her. In the past, that notion would have lived only in the fringes of her mind and never lingered. G.G. Marie would call her a hussy or a floozy, if she knew. And, she never would. Which was good, since not only did the image of her and James linger in the forefront of her brain, she also pictured herself in a cowgirl hat straddling his buff, nude body. They could play her version of "ride 'em cowboy." Her cousin would be shocked to know that she could tell Santa she'd been naughty *and* nice this year when they made their annual Christmas Eve birthday photo with the red-suited man who came to Fleur de Lis' holiday party each year.

"I'll be right back," she told James. She detoured to the bathroom to wait for the heat of her blush to cool. She fluffed her short damp hair, then placed the towel on the rack.

"I found the frying pan," James called out.

"Yee haw," she said low enough to ensure that he couldn't hear. Wetting a washcloth, then covering her face with it, she hoped the cool dampness would lower the fever James had brought on. If he had noticed, he hadn't commented.

On her way back to the kitchen, she grabbed a box of matches from the hall closet. Candlelit ambiance with dinner would create the mood she desired. Life had to be lived to the fullest, right?

Yesterday had proven that to her in a whole new way. She would balance her happiness with family responsibilities. She had a right to come first, especially when it came to love. Her mother put love first. Her aunts and uncles too. Why had her family foisted expectations on her unlike anyone else in their family?

She lit candles in the living room and the large one on the dining table, before she put several jazz CD's in the player, then hiked herself up on the swiveling barstool at the counter.

"It smells awesome in here." Her stomach gurgled embarrassingly loud, enough to be heard over the sizzle of meat.

"Sounds like you have an appetite. I would've brought wine, but in case you're taking pain meds, alcohol would be ill-advised."

"I took a muscle relaxer, but not the painkiller. I agree, though. Not a good idea to mix."

She didn't need drugs or alcohol to experience the high that came from the company of the man she loved. How would he respond when he discovered that fact?

When the steak reached doneness, and the salad was mixed, James put plates of food on the counter and handed over silverware.

"We could eat at the dining table," she offered, hoping for a candlelit dinner.

"Is there something wrong with the counter? No need to mess up a linen tablecloth."

She shrugged, relenting, and wondered how to go about seducing him. There, her education was lacking, save watching Victoria Secret models on commercials.

"This is so good. I guess it's cozy at the counter," she said between bites. The domesticity provided a sense of belonging. A contentment she longed for. She could imagine many dinners sitting side by side with James. "How was class today?"

"They grumbled about their homework for next week. They have to come up with a list of at least ten books that define who they are."

"Hmm. I could start with *Gone with the Wind* and *Divine Secrets of the Ya-Ya Sisterhood*."

"My students weren't so quick on the draw."

She gazed at him. His eyes crinkled in the corners from his warm smile. His hands, strong and steady, cut steak with a knife and fork. When he licked his lips to catch a dribble of juice, she fumbled her fork, almost dropping it.

"You're really invested in your students. A great quality in a teacher, James." She ran her hand from his shoulder to his elbow. When she looked up, his brow was furrowed, and his mouth quirked to one side as though he were perplexed.

"Last year, a student I'd had during my first year of teaching came to see me. He'd graduated with honors, then had gone on to a university and received his Bachelors in journalism. He said as quirky as some of the homework was, my class was the one that helped him the most. For me, the reward doesn't get any better than that."

"Clearly you have lots of talents." She paused. Hearing her voice practically purr was a little unsettling. Gathering up their plates, she asked, "Adult beverage? I have a bottle of wine. Just because I shouldn't imbibe, doesn't prevent you. I wish I had thought of that with dinner. Or, I have some Basil Hayden, if you prefer."

"Branna, are you sure you're okay?"

"Yes." She hoped that didn't sound as overly bright to him as it did to her.

Wariness in his eyes let her know of his skepticism. "I feel like I should check your temperature or something."

She wanted to say she was definitely hot, but not due to any infection, unless a cocktail of love and lust was her virus. "Let's go sit in the living room and enjoy the music."

Though he hadn't asked, she brought him a glass with two fingers of bourbon whiskey and set it on the coffee table.

"No," she said shaking her head. "Please sit over here." She pointed to the other side of the couch. If he remained where he was, she couldn't cuddle close to him without aggravating the abrasions on her neck. The other side would be perfect. And if he couldn't take the hint when she curled up to him, after he finished half of his drink, she'd unbutton his shirt.

Would he need a clearer clue?

When he settled into the couch, she snuggled close. He lifted his arm over her shoulder, which made their bodies fit closer. He raised an eyebrow, but kept his question to himself, and instead started talking about upcoming summer events in Lakeview.

Contact with James, as always, fluttered her heart and produced racing quivers through her body. Sometimes soft and pleasurable, other times, more intense. When the intensity cranked up, the current running through her always seemed to converge in the apex of her legs. Like now.

She shifted her hips, seeking a more satisfying

position. Though her muscles ached, that only made the quivering sensations more desirable. Like the contrast between sweet and salty.

Each minute that passed seemed more like five or ten. She tried to keep up with James' discussion of "Things to Do in Lakeview," but as it dragged on, her impatience rose. He, of course, probably thought he was being helpful while she waited for an opening to tell him she loved him. But with little experience in seduction, would she come off sounding like a silly high schooler? If she put a sexy, full-court press on him, he'd probably freak and tell her she wasn't that type, which was only half the problem. The other part—the good girl voice in her head sounding like G. G. Marie yelled, "Floozy!"

A confession of her feelings needed perfect timing. However, maybe it was time for "show" rather than "tell."

"What was it like growing up in a historical landmark?" James asked. He took a final sip of the bourbon and drained the amber-colored liquid.

"Wonderful," she said, lifting her face to his. "James," she whispered, ignoring his obvious choice of subject. "Would you like another drink?"

"No."

"Do you want me to change the music?"

"No."

"Do you want to help me feel better?"

"That's why I'm here."

She smiled. With nimble fingers, she maneuvered the bottom button on his shirt undone. When he didn't move, she unbuttoned the next button. Excitement made her shiver. Breathless, she reached for another on his shirt.

"Branna?" James halted her crusade to free his buttons. "As much as I want where I think this is leading, I'm not comfortable. You had a harrowing experience yesterday, and you're still healing."

He kissed her nose, then lifted her chin and pressed his lips to hers. A chaste kiss. A proper kiss. But the urgent cry of her body craved more.

How could she tell him that this was not the time for gentlemanly behavior? She melted against him while butterflies in her stomach did a free-form dance.

"I'm fine. I promise," she whispered near his ear. Reaching for his shirt again, she planned to show him just how ready.

"Let me kiss you and hold you." He repositioned himself, then lightly pressed his lips to her forehead. "Don't frown, Branna. We've all the time in the world. Let me just hold you for tonight."

Kisses caressed her jaw, her cheeks, her eyes, and her nose. When his lips found hers, she allowed his kisses to silence her.

For now.

After all, they had all night.

Chapter 30

Early Friday morning, James parked his battered white truck at the rest stop south of Gainesville. Five a.m. and already he was dragging. Coffee did nothing to jumpstart his brain. He grabbed a cooling cup of black liquid and his tote bag, locked his truck, then headed to the other side of the rest stop where Bobby waited in the dual-wheel pickup hooked to a flatbed-semi trailer loaded with bales of hay. Destination—Marathon Key.

"JD, look at you. Holey jeans and old boots. Boy, you're still a damn redneck," Bobby said as he climbed down from his truck. "You know what they say—once a redneck, always a redneck."

"Shows what you know." James pulled open the rear truck door and tossed his tote bag inside. "What 'they' say is, 'You can take the boy out of the country, but you can't take the country out of the boy.'"

"Well, what I want to know, Professor, who the hell is *they* anyway?"

He chuckled. Bobby could twist an argument better than anyone—woman or politician. "Listen up. *They* are the kind of people who pay my salary to teach smart redneck kids so they don't grow up to be smart-asses like you."

"Damn, smart-mouth is what you are." Bobby as he checked the tie-downs on the load. He tugged on each one as he walked around the truck.

"You're a fake, Mr. Parker. Anyone with any sense knows that."

Bobby played his role to the hilt. Bobby's father had demanded that his son get an education and threatened to keep Bobby from working the farm, even inheriting it, if hell-raising Bobby didn't graduate with a four-year degree. Old man Parker was a tough bird. It was his way or the highway.

In the end, Bobby caved. But he made sure it cost the old man a pretty sum. And made sure his education never interfered with people's perception about him. He remained, first and forever, a good ol' boy.

"Come on Professor, let's get go'n. I've been waitin' here for hours. You drive first." Bobby took shotgun.

James slid behind the wheel, cranked the truck, put it in gear, and then rolled down the windows. Country music twanged. Trace Adkins belted out *Chrome* as James eased the truck on to southbound I-75.

He and Bobby had been friends and neighbors forever. Growing up, acres of family farmland separated them. A dusty limestone road and trails through planted pines connected them. Parker property bumped up to land owned by James' grandfather—thirty acres of planted pines created a natural divide.

"Never thought you'd get out of farming, though," Bobby said. He leaned his seat back and closed his eyes. "We had some great times growing up."

"Summers, working from before dawn to noon at Granddaddy's place, then afternoons working for your daddy in hay. Yeah, that's a real party." He'd spent summers in the Parkers' hay fields and took a lot of pride when ol' man Parker trusted him, at fourteen, to

267

let him drive the big John Deere. He cut, fluffed, windrowed, and baled until day faded and it was so dark he couldn't see to get the tractor out of the field. The headlights from the pickup trucks lit his way. Sunday he rested—rising early for church, dinner on the grounds, and "sings" on Sunday night. Sunday was the social day of the week until he had turned sixteen and legally able to drive.

"You beat the odds, man," Bobby said. "A high school dropout with a college degree. And look at you now—fancy professor with a Ph.D."

"Well, I don't recommend it. It's a damn hard way to make it."

The year he turned sixteen he'd quit school. Worked at a hardware store during the day, then worked with the Parkers during hay season. The single thing he'd loved about school was football. But since his family lived so far from town, twenty-five miles one way, participation in after-school activities, like football, got scratched from the schedule. No one to pick him up after practice each night during the season.

"I thought quitting high school was a viable plan. Thought life could happen quicker and sooner. Dropping out made sense since football wasn't an option." He had wanted more than the basic A B C's they taught in small-town USA.

"You were quick enough for college ball, but you'd never make the pros," Bobby said matter-of-factly.

"That wasn't the goal. High school held only one interest for me. Friday night lights."

Getting his GED was easy. The rest of life, not so much. Between the part-time job at the hardware store, morning classes at the community college, afternoons working hay, then cramming all day on Sundays—he lived for Saturday nights.

As though reading his mind Bobby said, "Tipping back a beer or sipping on Wild Turkey 101 was a fine Saturday night ritual."

"We were Dumb and Dumber. Can't say I wish those days back."

Bobby tugged on the bill of his cap until it covered his eyes. In a few moments, James could tell by his friend's breathing that Bobby had slipped off to sleep.

Music from the radio filled in the silence as he drove. Occasionally, he checked the side mirrors for any movement in the load. The triple axle flatbed carried six hundred bales of premium horse hay. Each weighed fifty-five pounds, and baled with custom ordered twine, not wire. He'd learned that horsewomen demanded this particular feed, and wire hurt their hands.

The sun peeked over the horizon. Crowning rays of light fanned across the sky. If the color of the light was a true predictor, the cool dawn would evaporate as the sun climbed higher into the sky. As they drove south, the day would heat up. He drew a deep breath and let it go. He enjoyed the world before it turned crazy. Dawn remained his favorite time of day.

Bobby woke as the truck approached the Sunshine Skyway Bridge. James wasn't fooled when his friend didn't open his eyes. Bobby's lack of snoring was a dead giveaway that he was playing possum.

"At least you kept it between the lines this time," Bobby muttered.

"You're worse than any old woman I know. I drive just fine. Just because one time—"

"You ran us into a ditch and almost rolled the truck."

"We weren't hauling hay. I was fifteen! Besides, I've got the feather from the owl to prove it hit the windshield. I tried to avoid it. Saving it was more important than saving your sorry ass."

Bobby chuckled. "Right again, Professor," he said, then reached into the back seat where they kept a small cooler. Bobby pulled out a bottle of orange juice and biscuits wrapped in waxed paper. "Here. Eat. Your granny made them for us."

James took the food. Laden with ham and smeared with butter, the golden biscuit beckoned. Ham hung over the edges. One bite of the flaky biscuit and honey-cured ham was a reminder of home. His grandmother still made biscuits twice a day, but he hadn't been around much to satisfy his cravings.

"Hey, Sleeping Beauty," he said when Bobby pulled out two more ham biscuits. "You worked up an appetite."

"Man, that was the best four hours of sleep I've had in a while." Bobby took another bite of the biscuit. "Your granny knows how to cook."

"It is one of her finer points," he agreed while holding a biscuit in one hand and steering with the other.

Bobby gobbled up the remaining crumbles in the fold of the napkin.

"So, you slept on the couch after all?" James asked.

"Slept on the couch?" Bobby puffed up like a barnyard rooster. "Man, you don't understand about conjugal rights."

"Really?"

"Oh, yeah. I told Charlene about our little negotiation, 'bout how I would take us all for drinks after dinner, maybe a little dancing." Bobby paused to wipe his mouth. "Maybe we'll go over to the County Line? Live band, cheap drinks, a usual good time."

"Really," James repeated.

"Anyway, she was telling me about who she selected to be your next girlfriend and—"

"My next *what*?"

"You know how women are, they want men to nest. Its hormones or genetic in their DNA. Part of the *X*-chromosome thing." Bobby tuned the radio to a different country station. "Anyway, Char kinda got hot and bothered talking about you and..."

"I already have a date."

"You agreed to this blind date. I'm not going to give you the chance to worm out of it by making shit up."

"I assure you, I have a date. I told you I wouldn't do a blind date again unless I couldn't find one of my own. But for the sake of conversation, what was your woman hot and bothered about?"

Bobby wiggled his eyebrows and a sly lopsided grin spread across his face. "I had her describe to me what moves she thought you might try with this one."

"You're frick'n voyeurs," James said in disgust. "The two of you are detailing my *moves* on someone, someone whom I don't even know, and you're panting about it in bed?"

As if on cue, a singer on the radio crooned about turning the lights down low and doing things soft and slow.

Bobby shrugged. "If you'd get married, you'd

understand what it's like keeping that lusty, brand-new-sex feeling in your life."

"Bobby, I love you like a brother, but you two are not exactly the absolute picture of a wonderful happy marriage. The way the two of you fight."

Bobby laughed and slugged him in the arm, "Son, that's what you don't understand! Make-up sex is the best!" He winked. "Anger makes her burn. It's kind of like a backfire. I come along and put more heat to the problem—and we burn ourselves out together."

"Way too much information." He shook his head. "Way too much."

"The best part is, she thinks I'm being all sensitive and stuff. Yeah, gotta have make-up sex."

"Shut up."

"Wake me in time for lunch," Bobby said, leaning back in his seat.

James turned his attention to the truck's radio. Every song danced with romance and hints of sexual desire—some less subtle than others. His thoughts drifted to Branna. Her vulnerability brought out his protective instincts along with his desire to make love. Leaving her to make this trip left him uneasy. In truth, his rule about no colleague fraternization had evaporated when they walked into the Tin Lizzie. He just didn't know it then. After he'd made love to her, there was no *maybe* about his feelings. She tantalized all his senses.

It had been too long since he'd been in love. So long, it took him a while to recognize it.

One thing for sure—he didn't do anything halfway. He'd learned long ago, with his heart, it was all or nothing.

But how did Branna feel about him? He'd been hesitant to ask in her muscle-relaxer haze. Her touch made him sizzle. His hard-on about killed him. He hurt for hours. If she'd gotten past his shirt...probably any zipper movement would've made him come. Last night, he resolved not to take Branna to bed again, unless she was stone-cold sober. It took all he had to resist her. But he wouldn't risk taking advantage of her condition. She had to have a clear head, clear eyes, and a clear heart.

Had it been any other woman, he'd be a sexually satisfied man. With Branna, the wait would be worth it.

Nearly noon, he exited the interstate at Junction and pulled into a gas station on the southwest corner for diesel fuel. The station could pass for a leftover movie set out in the boonies. The mostly deserted truck stop was straight from the sixties with white fading paint and several old tin advertising signs nailed to the sides. Four overhangs stretched outward from a center building, like marks on a compass showing north, south, east, and west, and shaded fuel pumps.

The spot in the road with cheap eats and girlie magazines on a large magazine rack behind the counter had occupied that corner of Junction since the early forties. No other town around for miles. At night, the place lit up so bright that photos from space identified it. The station's reputation was well known in certain circles. Sometimes vehicles, from the smallest sports car to SUVs to semis required delicate ballet moves to avoid collisions. However, most of the time James had driven this route with Bobby, the place was No-Where's-Land empty.

For the last fifty miles, his stomach had rumbled,

and his mouth watered for the barbeque that waited.

"Where are we?" Bobby yawned, stretching his arms and arching his back.

"Get your arm out of my face," James snarled. "No Where."

Bobby grunted. "We can't be nowhere. We're here, and that's somewhere."

"So you're somewhere. Then why ask?" Hunger made him cranky. Or maybe it was his lack of sleep. It had taken a boatload of energy to resist Branna. Sleep eluded him most of the night. They had plenty of time for sexual exploration once she was well.

"Boy." Bobby slapped him on the arm. "All I can say is, you need to get laid."

"Mind your own business."

They exited the truck at the same time, slamming doors. Bobby went off to the restroom while James slid a credit card quickly through the slot at the pump. He unscrewed the fuel cap, placed the nozzle in the hole, then flipped the lever.

Diesel fuel sloshed into the empty tank, and James scanned the area. He was the only one in the west wing, the other three bays were empty. He glanced over at the other gas lanes and noticed an old Camaro and older Mustang end-to-end fueling up. He admired the rides. During his teenage days he'd considered robbing a bank for the chance to own a low-slung sports car—even if it needed a paint job, the muffler had a hole, and the seats were torn. As long as it had a good stereo and got him from point A to B, that was his dream.

Deep bass rumbled from the speakers in one of the cars, but James couldn't discern which one. A couple of boys hanging out the windows of the old blue Camaro yelled at the kids in the green Mustang. He couldn't hear exactly what they were yelling, but it didn't sound serious.

When his fuel line shut off, he replaced the nozzle. He'd never liked the smell of diesel. He began his walk-around to check the straps on the load, making sure all remained secure. He noticed the top of the load had shifted a bit and using the ropes, he scaled the bales. Thirteen feet off the ground offered a great view from that vantage point.

Tires squealed, and he turned in the direction of the sound. The Camaro burned rubber, shooting out of the station like a blue flash. The teens with the Mustang shouted and gestured at the Camaro as it sped eastward. A second later, the Camaro U-turned, headed back toward the station, squealing tires the whole way. Smoke and the acrid scent of burnt rubber drifted to James' nose.

Movement by the front door of the station grabbed his attention. Bobby sauntered out doing his proud rooster walk carrying a yellow bag of candy. Uneasy, James waved at Bobby to hurry, then gave a loud piercing whistle—their signal to warn the other of possible danger.

The Camaro circled around the station and pulled through an empty bay, barely slowing.

Loud *pops* echoed under the metal roof.

Bobby did a running dive under the trailer while James dropped flat against the top of the hay bales. Screams pounded in his ears. He recognized gunshot when he heard it. A handgun. Thankfully not a rifle or an automatic weapon.

Where was Bobby?

James scrambled to the edge of the load and looked down.

The Camaro circled the west bay and came back again. More shots fired. Screams pierced the air.

Where the hell was Bobby? Grabbing a strap, he rappelled from the top of the load. On the way down, a burning pain seared his arm.

Someone screamed, "I'm hit! I'm hit!"

The Camaro never slowed. It took off westbound. James tried to read the tag number, but was unable to get it.

"Bobby!" he hollered over the screams.

When he made it to the ground, he heard Bobby repeating, "Oh, shit!" Panic grabbed him. He ran to the side of the trailer, dropped to his knees, expecting the worse.

Bobby rolled out from beneath the flatbed trailer, knocking James onto his back.

"Are you hit?" James asked.

Scampering to standing, Bobby grasped James' hand and pulled him up.

Bobby's T-shirt was torn, his hands were scraped from his baseball slide under the trailer, but no blood.

"Damn James! You're shot!"

Surprised, he looked at his right arm. It oozed red. It was more of a burn than pain. A bullet must have grazed him.

Beside the Mustang, a teenage boy lay on the ground shrieking.

James ran to the boy. Bobby followed. One of the station's attendants started administering first aid when another teenaged boy started pointing at the one on the ground and yelling, "Oh God!"

The station's attendant wrapped a bandage on the first kid's arm. He held a blood soaked pad on the kid's shoulder. "Stop squirming. I called 911. Help is on the way."

Three boys hopped into the green Mustang. The engine turned, and they sped away, abandoning the injured kid. The Mustang headed in the same direction as the Camaro.

"Was this crossfire of a gang war?" Bobby asked the injured boy.

"This wound looks superficial, grazed the arm. But that shoulder, that looks serious," the attendant told James.

"What's your name?" James asked, kneeling on the other side of the young teen.

"Yo mama," the boy gritted out.

"I'm gonna get *Yo-mama* some water," Bobby said, then walked back into the store.

A few minutes later, an ambulance arrived and immediately the EMS workers started their triage. One man worked on the kid while another treated James' wound. He refused a transfer to the hospital. "I'll be fine."

When police arrived, they separated him from Bobby for questioning.

"It happened really fast. I don't know if the kids in the Mustang returned fire or not."

"A trip to the hospital won't make you a sissy," the officer said to James.

"I'll be okay. EMS has patched me up."

"You're our only eye witness. If we catch them, you might be called to trial. The kid looks like he'll recover, so at least this won't be a murder case."

The officer took his personal information, snapped some photos, and let him go.

More than an hour after they'd pulled into the station, he and Bobby sat down for barbeque. Adrenaline had erased his earlier hunger pangs, but he ate anyway.

"Damn. Bobby, I thought you'd been shot. The way you were yelling, I expected to see blood everywhere."

"Blood? Me? I took a running dive, and I fell on the chocolate covered peanuts. Squished them flat. That hurt. It was like buckshot in the chest. The nice lady behind the counter replaced my bag for free." Bobby held up the new bag and beamed. "It's all about priorities, man."

"You're right. And this little incident has put mine into perspective." Images of Branna curled beside him in bed filled his mind.

Chapter 31

Branna pulled the Mercedes into a parking spot downtown. The lot was mostly empty, even though noon had barely passed. Did folks flock out of town for the weekend? The trip to the pharmacy was more to burst the bubble of isolation than a need to shop for items. Accustomed to people coming and going on a daily basis, always joined at the hip with someone who shared her same DNA, the solitary quietness of her cozy house made her jittery. Monday couldn't come soon enough. She wanted her routine restored. Though she'd have to deal with the damage to the Volvo, teaching and students would make the days ahead exciting. In the meantime, a milkshake at the old-fashioned soda fountain would do as a boredom buster.

"Be with you in a moment," a man called out when she entered the store. She hitched herself up onto a stool in the middle of the long counter, then turned when she heard a woman behind her.

"You stay here while I finish my shopping. I'll be back in an hour." The tall woman looked like she'd walked out of a fashion spread from *Glamour* magazine. Sundress. Sandals. Bangle bracelet and Coach purse.

"Yes, Momma." With slumped shoulders, a girl took a seat two stools away. She laid a five-dollar bill on the counter and placed an old-fashioned sugar jar on top of it to keep if from floating away as the air swirled from the ceiling fans overhead. She flipped her long, fawn-colored braids over her shoulders.

"Hi. I'm Branna." Branna reached across the space and offered her hand.

Keeping her eyes glued to the counter, the girl mumbled.

"Sorry, I didn't quite catch what you said."

"Don't mind her. She's Ida Walker. I'm her uncle. The usual, Ida?" the clerk behind the counter asked. "And what about you, Miss?"

"What's your usual?" she asked Ida.

"Vanilla ice cream with pecans and caramel sauce on top," Ida's uncle replied.

"I'll have what she's having."

Ida's mouth quirked into a half-grin as her uncle walked away, but she kept her shoulders hunched and eyes glued to the counter, as though pouting was important.

"Well, Ida," Branna said, changing stools to sit next to the girl. "How's your summer going? You're out of school, right?"

"I'm bored," Ida grumbled. "I'm home schooled."

Branna leaned in close and whispered. "I saw you the day you borrowed the nail polish."

"I didn't—"

Branna reached into her purse and pulled out a lace hanky. The blood-red smear couldn't be missed. "Look familiar? So, how about some honesty?"

"I'm honestly bored," Ida said, taking the hanky and stuffing it into her pocket.

"Do you have any brothers or sisters?" Branna tried to sound cheery.

Ida's elbows thumped the counter. She cradled her jaw in her hands, and looked straight ahead, instead of at Branna. "I'm an only child. I don't have anyone to play with me."

Branna's heart pinched. How often had she wished to be an only child? Then she wouldn't have the words, "You must live by example," imprinted on her psyche. There would be time alone and holidays devoid of chaos. She wouldn't have had to worry about anyone but herself.

However, she missed her family so badly she ached. Missed them so much, the silence of her home drove her to town in search of human interaction. A sad thing when the sound of strangers' voices provided comfort.

And she missed James. Was his trip going as planned? Would he call her from the road? What would he think if she suggested something closely resembling phone sex? Her cheeks heated at the thought.

Beside her, Ida grunted, then poured sugar on the five-dollar bill. Teenage mischief that passed for entertainment? Loneliness appeared to be the girl's only friend. Branna's family problems looked different through an only child's eyes.

"How old are you, Ida?"

"Ten, almost eleven, but people think I'm older because I'm so tall."

"Yes, I imagined that you were maybe thirteen. Do you know anything about pulling weeds? Would you be interested in a part-time job helping out with my flower garden?"

Ida straightened. She looked from side to side, then swiveled on the stool to face Branna. "I've got a green thumb. I can make things grow."

The child's enthusiasm made Branna smile.

"Yes, well, I'm trying to *stop* the weeds from growing."

"I can do that, too." Ida nodded. Her braids bounced.

"I live on Townsend Street. Do you live near there?" She was hopeful. She recognized Ida as the child that had darted into the street and caused her to spill tea on Meredith's skirt on her final day of house hunting. She had to remember to contact her realtor. Meredith had never sent her a cleaning bill.

"I live two streets over."

"How about if we sip our shakes and wait for your mother to return? Then, I'll ask her if she'll allow you to help me a few hours a week."

"Okay."

After the shakes arrived, Ida chatted about gardening. Most of her knowledge fell into the category of farming.

"Daddy grows watermelons and corn. Sometimes he stays all night in the country with granddaddy at his farm. Momma works part-time at the bank. So I stay in town with her because I have to practice the piano every day."

The child talked nonstop and made Branna think of the going, going, going Eveready Bunny.

Branna understood Ida's loneliness. Or the opposite of it. Peace and quiet were a rare commodity at Fleur de Lis. Now it made her feel selfish and small. Here this girl wanted a big family, or at least a sibling to play with, while she'd grown up surrounded with playmates and had taken them for granted.

"Wednesdays would work good. What's your name again?" Ida asked.

"Branna Lind."

"Miss Branna, I could come to your house before it gets really hot."

"Sounds like a plan to me."

When Mrs. Walker returned, Ida was grinning from ear to ear.

Branna rose to meet the woman. "Mrs. Walker, I'm Branna Lind."

"I hope Ida wasn't a bother."

"No. Actually, I think she might be a big help to me. I'm an instructor at the community college. Based on what Ida says, I live about three blocks away from you. With your permission, I'd like to hire her to help me in my garden on Wednesday mornings."

Mrs. Walker's face transformed from stern to glowing. "Ida can be a handful. She's very willful. You, a successful teacher, I'll bet you never gave your mother any problems."

"Ah, I think my momma would emphatically disagree."

"A bit of responsibility might be good for my daughter."

"Thank you, Mrs. Walker. My garden thanks you even more than I do."

"We'll give it try. Sometimes her attention span doesn't last. I hope you won't be disappointed."

"See you on Wednesday," she told Ida as the girl left the store with her mother. At the door, Ida turned back and waved. A smile replaced the girl's earlier frown.

Invigorated by her good deed, Branna drove home

and decided on a walk around the lake. She changed into shorts and a T-shirt, then grabbed her sunglasses.

Afternoon temperatures had peaked early. Humidity made the air liquid and walking outside was like strolling in a steam bath with no exit. She wiped sweat from her forehead using the edge of her T-shirt. Sweat dripped from every pore like a block of ice melting in hell. She was thankful for the shade from the trees that protected her skin from burning. The lack of physical activity for the last couple of days made her body ache, more than the discomfort of her injuries.

With purposeful strides, she walked halfway around the lake moving in a quick clip. Tall oaks with long limbs and lush dogwoods provided a partial barrier between the street and the trail. Reaching the halfway point, she stopped and rested on a bench beneath a stately magnolia, it had to be close to a hundred years old. Nearby, a group of men set up chairs around the large white gazebo. She'd seen the posted flyers for the Friday night, outdoor concerts and guessed that night would be the inaugural event of the season. Spring had rolled into summer despite the fact that summer was officially a few weeks away.

Across the lake, above the trees, she caught a glimpse of the yellow Victorian on the hill, the one Meredith had owned. Whoever bought the house had done some sprucing. Maybe she'd continue the walk around and take a closer look. It was stubborn of her to refuse to tour the house when Meredith had offered to show it. But it reminded her too much of Fleur de Lis, then and now. She hated to admit it, but she missed home.

As she cooled down, a black sedan with darkly

tinted windows rolled by on the road that circled the lake. The car stopped and made a U-turn in the street, then pulled into the nearest parking space about a hundred feet away. It looked familiar. Like the one that almost hit Meredith's car. She paused to see if anyone stepped out. Would she at least recognize them? Her wait was in vain. No one appeared.

Maybe the person in the car was waiting for someone else. Maybe a lunch rendezvous. The lake was a pretty spot for a picnic, or even a ten-minute work break with a view.

When she rose, tiredness washed over her. The heat had drained her energy. She began the trek homeward, retracing her steps. The Victorian would have to wait for another day.

Meandering more than walking, she stopped to read the inscription carved into a large stone marker. The black sedan moved into her peripheral view. It headed in her same direction at a slow roll, and then stopped nearby.

A prickly tingle ran down the back of her neck. She quickened her pace, then jogged, cutting through the parking lot and over to the street near her house. Out of breath, she paused, bending at the waist, and rested her hands on her knees.

The sedan rounded the corner.

Breathing deeply, she waited, never taking her eyes off the car. Across the street, an older woman rolled a large garbage can to the curb. Branna waved to the woman and started to cross the street, seeking safety in numbers. If anything was about to happen, at least she'd have a witness. When she reached the middle of the road, the sedan raced by. She jumped back. The darkened windows prevented her from making a visual ID of the driver, and after she'd steadied herself, the car had traveled too far down the street for her to read the tag number.

"Crazy driver!" the woman shouted. "You okay?"

"I'm fine," Branna said, walking toward the woman. "I live on the next street. Moved in recently. By chance, do you recognize the black car? Maybe you know the driver?"

"Never saw it before," the woman said, then headed back toward her house. Over her shoulder she said, "Welcome to the neighborhood."

"Thanks," Branna answered, but the woman disappeared into the house.

"A shower. That's what I need." She trudged the rest of the way home with uneasiness settling into her gut. "Why would anyone follow me?"

Chapter 32

Restless from lying on the couch with nothing to do, Branna tossed a blanket aside and headed for the garden, which had flourished to the edge of overgrown. Despite the sprouting weeds, the garden retained its charm. A few small ornaments from the hardware store would personalize the garden. Adding a statue of a fairy and bird feeder could make the place feel more like home. On Wednesday, she'd have a helper to tame the unruly weeds. Another step in building her own life. The carefree one she'd planned.

So how was it that she had nothing to do on a Friday night? That was as foreign as crossing paths with a Loup Garou, that mythical beast her Cajun relatives threatened would "git her" if she ever did anything wrong. There was no need for parents to threaten children about Santa with his "Naughty or Nice" list with a Loup Garou around.

The silence throughout her house rattled her nerves. She was accustomed to scents wafting from the kitchen. Seafood of some sort or roast beef. Greta was a fine cook, and folks around Bayou Petite vied for dinner invitations.

Her house lacked the background noise of sliding walkers and thumping canes that she'd taken for granted and didn't even know it. There was nothing quiet about G.G. Marie and Great Aunt Grace. The old women would be horrified to know that their hearing aids needed adjustments. They often hollered at one another other so the other was sure to follow a conversation.

Alone on a Friday night. Usually she spent the evening working—planning details of upcoming events or handling last minute must-do's for an already scheduled one. If not working, she played Scrabble or cards with the Old Aunts, or drove to Picayune with Greta to catch a movie. Only once in a while did she see Steven on a Friday night—his night to play poker with his old fraternity brothers.

On the rare occasion when she had time to herself, a good book and a cup of tea provided the purest pleasure.

Yet, after hours spent reading and sipping tea, too much pleasure all at once had overloaded her senses. She wandered the backyard searching for the right spot for stargazing. She plopped into an Adirondack chair, pulled her legs close, and looked up.

The twinkling lights that illuminated the sky made her feel closer to home. If anyone in her family gazed up at the stars right then, they'd see the same night sky and share that moment with her, though miles away. That thought was comforting.

Maybe James was looking at the stars, too. She could hope. And that he was thinking of her.

She hadn't heard from him all day, not that he said he would call, but she'd hoped.

The house seemed empty without him. Her day seemed less bright. She enjoyed his company, even when they were verbally sparring. Something magical had happened between them the day of the storm. It had to be fate that made them cross paths like that at the bookstore. After all, he'd been avoiding her—noticeably absent at each of the organized functions up to that point.

Was their connection growing toward a relationship? That was the last thing she'd wanted when she moved to Lakeview. But now? She didn't want to live without him.

The plan had been—career. Dating. Fun. Her job had to remain a priority. However, coming to Lakeview, she'd hoped to meet a few nice men with whom she had some shared interests. Have fun with no serious commitment.

Balancing a career and a relationship was doable. Momma was the perfect role model for work and love, but for some reason she had always stressed duty and honor with her, more so than with Camilla and Carson. Maybe Momma took falling in love and marriage for granted. She made it all look so simple. Or maybe Momma thought Steven filled that spot in her life, therefore there was no need to focus on it anymore. But of course, Momma didn't know the truth about the man.

Branna looked skyward at a falling star that streaked in the darkness, then disappeared. She stared at the spot in the dark sky where it had last been. She didn't want what happened to the star to happen to her relationship with James. Streak brightly, then burn out.

If the connection they shared continued to grow, would he consider leaving Lakeview for Fleur de Lis? There were jobs in Mississippi. Otherwise, what compromise could she make for her family and James?

But what did James want?

A phone ringing, a faint wail in the distance, sent

her running for the house. She raced across the grass and jerked on the back door before the last ring. Breathless she said, "Hello?"

"Miss Lind, its Sadie. Have you seen the news?"

"No."

"Dr. Newbern was shot. It's on all the channels."

Branna clutched the phone and grabbed the remote. The TV popped on. She flipped through the stations. "What happened?" she asked impatiently. "Crap! What station?"

"It's on the eleven o'clock news. There was a shootout."

Her heart stopped. "Is he alive?"

"Yes, they say he's fine."

"I've got it!" She watched a replay of the video taken by a security camera.

"It happened earlier today," Sadie said.

"He's alive," Branna murmured.

"Yes. He. Is." Sadie sounded amused.

"Ah, thanks for letting me know, Sadie."

"I also called to check on you. Need anything?"

She started to ask if Sadie knew anyone who drove a black sedan with darkly tinted windows *and* who might have a reason to follow her. After all, Sadie did know everyone. But she decided against it. As unnerving as quiet was in the house, if she mentioned the strange car to Sadie, she feared the woman would return with an army for protection.

No need to make a fuss...yet. Maybe she'd never see the car again. "I'm fine. Thanks for letting me know about Dr. Newbern."

"I figured you would want to know."

She hung up after Sadie said good night.

Do I call him or not?

She paced in front of the couch. It didn't matter if he thought her too pushy or that she was sticking her nose in where it didn't belong. If he had wanted her to know, he would have called, right? After all, he wasn't laid up in a hospital hooked up to machines.

The image of James on his deathbed brought wetness to her eyes. Nothing bad could happen to him, she'd just found him. Just found love. Overwhelmed, she let tears fall. They flowed freely.

She'd sworn she would never cry over a man after Steven, but James wasn't just any man. He was the dream of her heart.

No, she wouldn't call. That would make her needy.

She flipped channels and caught the same taped footage on national news. She flinched as a young man fell to the ground after taking a bullet to his shoulder.

No, she wouldn't call James.

But he'd been shot too!

She paced more, but pacing wouldn't solve the problem. She could wear a hole in the floor while wondering about his injury. She needed to talk to him. Could he be out on a date? He'd said he made frequent runs to south Florida to deliver hay. Maybe he had someone he saw down there? A quick stab went straight to her heart. What if he wasn't interested in a committed relationship with her? What if he only wanted casual? This was a man who "typed" everyone. Maybe he had a "like type" and a "not-so-much type."

What if their relationship was exactly like the falling star?

The star's fate had already been determined, but she'd be damned if she would—without a fight—allow her relationship with James to streak and flameout.

Plopping on the couch, she cradled her cell phone. Eleven p.m. What if he did have a date tonight? Then what? She'd deal with it. A phone call would take only a moment of his time. As long as she could know he was okay, she'd handle any feelings about female competition later.

Punching in his number, she waited. He answered in two rings.

"Branna?"

Just hearing his voice allowed her to breathe deeply. "James, I don't mean to disturb you. I won't take but a moment of your time. I'm sure you're—"

"It's good to hear from you." His voice sounded warm, like whisky going down, and smooth like velvet. He also sounded genuinely glad to hear from her.

"I saw the news."

"Ah. TV."

"Yes, the shootout made the news. I had to know that you're okay." Did she sound whiney? Too concerned?

"I'm doing fine, now that I'm talking to you." Was he drinking? Or flirting? Maybe he wasn't out on a date after all. Her imagination had worked overtime.

"I am happy to hear you're fine. I won't keep you."

"I'm just hoisting a few brews with Bobby at our fleabag motel."

"Have a good—"

"I've been thinking about you." His voice was low and sultry. Seductive.

Quivers raced from her head to her toes. She wanted to crawl into bed with the phone and have James whisper to her all night. She clutched a throw pillow to her chest needing to hold on to something to make the moment more real.

"Good thoughts?" Dare she ask for the truth?

"Oh, yeah. You could say that. Miss Lind, would you go out on an official date with me tomorrow night?"

"Official?"

"This is me asking you proper for a Saturday night date."

Her heart pounded. Thudding roared in her ears. Relief flooded her heart. His voice soothed her angst, and the offer of a date made her giddy.

"Branna?"

"Yes, James."

"I'll pick you up at seven. Wear your dancing shoes."

Chapter 33

The next morning, Branna's bedroom showed no bare spot. Skirts and tops and dresses lay strewn across the bed, the dresser, and a chair. A Neiman Marcus dollar sale couldn't have resulted in greater chaos. She wanted nothing more than perfection for her date that night with James; which required trying on every item of clothing she owned.

Why she thought she could put together a jaw-dropping outfit remained a mystery. Always saddled with "reputation" and "family honor" the best she could manage was "conservative" and "tailored." A tired image she wanted to shake.

A black dress with black low heels, a clutch and pearls might work at the country club, but it didn't inspire anyone, most of all her, to dance...*and more*. Bless James for his courage. The man wanted to take her dancing, even after experiencing her total ineptitude. In the future, maybe she could limit the damage to his feet by taking a few dance classes. Surely, she wasn't a hopeless case. She prided herself on being a good student.

But that didn't solve the immediate problem. How to look amazing. She needed that to balance out the number of times she'd be saying "sorry" to his toes.

She remembered seeing several women carrying shopping bags with the logo from the dress shop downtown. Shopping local would be her contribution to the economy. She reached for the phonebook. Flipping through the pages, she found the advertisement she sought, then punched the number into her phone and waited for someone to answer.

"Lovely Ladies. This is Clara."

"I need a dancing dress for tonight. Might you have something that fits that bill?"

"We have a few spring dresses remaining. Our summer collection just came out. Our previews usually run closer to the actual season than stores in big cities. You could take a look online—" A beeping sound blocked out Clara's voice. Branna looked at caller ID. When she didn't recognize the number, she ignored the call.

"—come in now, our seamstress is here to make any needed alterations, especially if you need a dress for tonight."

"I need a dress that says *fun*. I'll be down in a little while. This is a special occasion, and I need a *wow* outfit. Size eight."

She pulled on a T-shirt and jeans and slid into sandals. Fumbling underneath the stack of clothes on her dresser, she tried to find her keys. Her fingers wrapped around a set, not for the Volvo, but the Mercedes. The car made her think of her sister.

She still hadn't reached Camilla. It appeared that the mountains of Wyoming hampered cell service. Did some version of the Pony Express still exist there? Otherwise, how did people communicate? It saddened her that her relationship with her sister had become mostly nonexistent in the last eight months. It was one thing for them to disagree about any given topic, but betrayal? Disloyalty so harsh that it would hurt everyone in the family. Could Camilla be so selfish? When they were younger, they shared with one another after each of their dates. Camilla was always competitive. She had even tried to steal a boyfriend or two when they were in their early teens. Hadn't they outgrown that childishness? But there were good growing-up memories also. Before Steven.

Her cell phone rang as she headed out the door. Same number as before. Whoever called earlier hadn't left a message. Probably a wrong number, or a reporter still looking for a follow-up story. She ignored the call, but couldn't ignore the frequency of the annoying intrusions.

She arrived at the dress shop in mere minutes. A bell tinkled when she opened the door.

"Welcome to Lovely Ladies." The woman who greeted her wore a dress that looked like a colorful Monet painting, and she dripped in ropes of pearls. Branna counted six.

"I'm Branna. I'm looking for Clara. I'm on the hunt for a party dress."

"She's already pulled a few in hopes that you'd come. Please follow me. Clara, you have a customer."

When Branna stepped into a dressing room, it suddenly struck her. She'd never shopped for a special outfit without her mother or sister or cousin, or some female in her extended family. She'd lived joined-at-the-hip for her entire life, which she now understood, had its benefits. There was always someone to share her joy. She thought of Ida and her loneliness.

Clara arrived before she closed the dressing room door.

"Take a look at those hanging there. None of them scream conservative. Try them all on. You never know which one is perfect until it's on your body."

"Ah...the sequined corset with the feather skirt looks like it's waiting for a good time, but...it's just not me. Too over the top. Even if it looked good on, I don't have the confidence to pull it off. It's way out of my comfort zone."

The scooped neck, zebra-print dress made her hips look wide. The hem of the purple ruched keyhole one landed too high on her thigh. A pink sweetheart beaded and fringed dress looked like something a flapper wore in the 1920's. She stared at her reflection in the mirror and huffed out a frustrated sigh. Either the fit or the cut or the fabric of each dress challenged her patience. She was either too short or too hippy or too something. Was there a dress that showed her attributes just enough to be alluring *and* boost her confidence?

"This is a really special night, isn't it?" Clara asked.

"So special. It's an official first date with the man I'm going to marry." She couldn't believe she'd said aloud what her heart had been preaching.

"You think he's really *the* one?"

"My heart does, and that's all I'm listening to right now."

"Well, I have a dress...it was made for someone, and she rejected it when it came in. You said you didn't want black, but this one's special. Beaded cap sleeves with a cowl neckline. Ruched from the waist down. Not too short. If you want to try it on..."

"Bring it to me, sister." Branna laughed. "I've got nothing to lose."

Clara helped her slip the jersey over her head. The fabric floated over her body.

"Before you look in the mirror, slip on these shoes. I think they're your size. They're Manolo Blahnik. Never worn. I got them new at a high-end consignment store when I was last in Miami. The straps will keep your feet in them, no matter the type of dancing. Now come out here to the three-way mirror."

Standing on a dais, Branna stared at her reflection. Her palms smoothed the fabric that hugged her body. "Wow."

"It's perfect on you." Clara beamed as though she'd made the match of the century.

"I will have to thank the woman who didn't want this dress. It's mine now. May I buy the shoes too?"

"I'll wrap it all up for you while you change."

The dress made her feel so good that even if James intended to take her to the Tin Lizzie again, she wouldn't care if she was overdressed. Besides, she had a big surprise for him.

Chapter 34

The clock on the wall clicked to six forty-five. Branna paced in the living room and tried not to pick at the new red polish on her nails. The manicurist had said red, a nail-color neutral, always went with anything. Branna's plan to be ready and waiting when James arrived hadn't taken into account the butterflies in her stomach or the dryness in her mouth.

Buzz. Buzz.

The ringing cell phone sent her diving for her clutch on the kitchen counter. She held her breath. James wouldn't call to cancel their date, would he? Had his return trip delayed him? Was his injury causing a problem?

Caller ID glowed. She wasn't familiar with the phone number, but recognized it as the same one from earlier. The one that had called twice before. "Hello?"

"It's your sister." Camilla sounded somber.

"Has something happened? Are you okay?" Despite their differences, they were sisters. She couldn't hide her worry.

"I need to talk with you. It's really serious stuff—"

"I really want to talk to you, too, but I'm about to go out."

The doorbell rang. "Hang on for a moment. I think that's my date."

Branna walked toward the front door and glanced

at the clock on her way. Six fifty-five. James was always certainly punctual, but would he mind waiting ten minutes for her to talk to Camilla?

She opened the door and nearly dropped the phone. "Steven?"

Framed by the doorway and carrying enough flowers to make three bride's bouquets, Steven stood tall and straight. She blinked. Her jaw dropped.

Steven reached toward her and with his finger, closed her mouth. She continued to stare. His navy blue suit and red stripped tie was one he wore when litigating before a jury, a powersuit. Did he intend to sway her as he often managed to sway a jury?

"Hello?" Camilla's voice screamed from the phone still in her hand.

"Aren't you going to ask me in?" Steven asked.

She fumbled for the phone. "Camilla, Steven's here. I need to go."

"No! Do not hang up on me. Make him wait. I *must* tell you something."

With the cell phone to her ear, Branna held up a finger and signaled to Steven to wait. She closed the front door half way and walked toward the kitchen for privacy. "Seriously Camilla, I know we need to talk, but this is turning out to be an inconvenient—"

"Then don't talk. Just listen. Steven is vile. You cannot go out with him. You absolutely cannot take him back. I don't care what smooth moves he's working on you, promise me you won't go out with him."

"I—" she started, but the doorbell interrupted again. In a huff, she crossed the room to the door and flung it open.

"Really?" Only instead of just Steven on the front

porch, James greeted her. Handsome and relaxed, he didn't resemble a man who'd been shot twenty-four hours ago.

"James!" She hugged him tight around the neck, careful not to touch his arm. She tried to kiss him, but the second before lip contact, he turned his head toward Steven. Her lips met James' smooth cheek.

"Branna!" Camilla hollered. "What's going on?"

Flustered, Branna stepped back inside the house. "We're going to do this civilized," she said to the men. "Won't you both come in?"

"Branna, don't do it!" Camilla ranted. "Don't let him in!"

She gestured toward the couch. Steven took a seat on the end, still holding the large bouquet. A whiff of rose drifted to her nose. She used to love those flowers. Now, the scent reminded her of him and his indiscretions.

James took a seat in a chair at the opposite end of the living room. She didn't blame him.

"My sister is on the phone. I need just a minute. In the meantime, James, this is Steven, my ex-fiancé. Steven, this is James, my lover."

The look on both men's faces made her smile. Let them stew on that for a while.

"Camilla, I'm outside, now. They can't hear me. I'm not going out with Steven. Not now. Not ever. I am going to go dancing with James. You and I need to talk, but tomorrow."

"If you're not going out with Steven, what's he doing there?"

"Little sister, I don't read minds. Rest assured, he was not invited."

"I love you, Branna. I never wanted to hurt you."

"I know."

"You know?"

"Yes, Camilla, I know you slept with my fiancé. I know you weren't the only one."

"Not the only one?"

"Don't be shocked. I love you. You're my sister. We'll work it out. We always do. Let's talk tomorrow. This number is the best way to reach you?"

"Yes, and Branna, I never loved you more than I love you now. You're the best big sister. Tomorrow, I will have to ask about the dancing, though. You really dance now?"

Branna chuckled. "Oh, you don't know the half of it."

After hanging up the phone, Branna took in a slow deep breath and let it out. If anyone had told her a few months ago that she'd have Steven Sterling in her house in Lakeview, she'd have been moved to murder. But there he was.

She marched inside, prepared to do battle. Steven wouldn't know what hit him. She'd let him say what he came to say, then make her position non-negotiable. She would skewer him with words clear enough that even a narcissist like him couldn't misunderstand.

"Seems to me the fish jumped the hook," James was saying to Steven as she entered the room. His tone dripped with sarcasm. Both men rose. Steven held out flowers to her.

"Thank you, but no. I'm allergic." She sat in the other chair that flanked the couch.

"Since when?"

"Since about eight months ago. James, I'm looking

forward to our date. I think Steven will be leaving shortly. May I offer either of you a drink? No? All right, then Steven, why are you here?"

Steven frowned and sat back down. His shoulders slumped. He straightened. His face brightened, and he cocked his head. "Do you like my present?"

"It's protected in the garage."

"Branna, if you and he need to talk, I'll give you some privacy and come back in a while," James offered.

"You won't need to come back at all," Steven said to James.

Steven's smugness made her blood pressure rise. But the old rage that used to make her shake never materialized.

"So, I guess civility is out. Steven, I don't care why you're here." She slapped her palms on her thighs, then stood and walked to the front door. After opening it, she turned back to the men seated in her living room. "Steven, thank you for the gift. I'll send a proper thank-you card. Since you were kind enough to put the title in my name, I believe I'm free to do with it what I wish. Thank you for coming. But don't come back. And if you don't mind, please leave now. My date for the evening is waiting." Had she just said those words? Stood up to him with a calmness she had only hoped for?

"You can't fool me, Branna. I know you're not dating anyone."

"Really? And how do you know so much about me?" She'd murder Sadie if the woman had gossiped about her with Steven.

"The same way I find out information for my

303

cases. I hired a PI."

Forcing her fists to remain at her sides, she asked, "The black car that was following me?"

"He got sloppy, but he's been checking you out almost since you moved here."

"Not only is he sloppy, he's ripping you off. You're paying for bad information. He doesn't know the first thing about my life."

James moved to her side, draped an arm over her shoulder. "Steven, this has been odd, but now I think it's time for you to leave. Like a gentleman."

Steven dropped the flowers on the coffee table and stalked to the door. He leaned in close to her ear and whispered, "Branna, we're not done. You were always smart. You will come to your senses. Your family wants me to be their son as much as mine wants you for a daughter. Have your professorial fling. I'll be waiting to pick up the pieces."

"Not if I tell them about you and Camilla."

"You wouldn't dare." He brushed her cheek with a kiss as though marking old territory.

"The old Branna wouldn't have whispered a word about it, but it's not my shame. It's not Camilla's. It's yours!"

"The gossip will kill your great grandmother."

"Do. Not. Threaten. Me. Get out!"

She slammed the door after he crossed the threshold. That the glass in the small window in the door didn't fall out was a miracle. It felt good to close the door on Mr. Sterling.

James stood in front of her and tucked a strand of hair behind her ear. She smelled the musk of his cologne and wanted to melt into him.

"He's not going to ruin our night," he said, then kissed her nose.

"In case you have any doubt, I'm telling you, I'm over him. My sister and I will work out our problem between us. He won't rip my family apart."

"Is she the reason you never told anyone why you broke off the engagement?" He ran his hands down her arms, taking hold of her hands.

"I will not let him humiliate my family. Not then. Not now. He was the dishonorable one, but people at home gossip. I found out my sister wasn't the only other woman he'd slept with. It's his disgrace to bear, and I will not hang my head at home."

He leaned in close and whispered, "Are you hiding out in Lakeview?"

She started to pull back, but he held tight.

"No," she said adamantly. "I'm living my way, for the first time in my life."

His hands moved and cupped her face. His lips were a breath away from hers. Her heart pounded so hard that the blood rushing in her ears made them ring. Quivers raced through her body. They made her shiver. They made her ache.

"Good," he said, then tasted her mouth. "Now, about dancing."

She kissed him back, pressing her body against his. "Dr. Newbern, I have a different kind of dancing in mind. All you need to do is follow my lead."

Chapter 35

Leading James by the hand, Branna flipped the switch on the CD player, and a soulful saxophone crooned. Candles flickered as she lit each one. Soft shadows danced on the walls. She'd never played seduction and surrender before.

James pulled her close. He kissed her forehead, nose and chin, before pressing his lips to hers. Desire made her flush. Love made her heart pound. Light-headed and giddy, she wrapped her arms around his neck. When she laid her head on his shoulder, they swayed together, their bodies moving as one.

"Lovers?" James whispered near her ear.

"Hmm?" She gazed at him.

"You told Steven we were lovers."

"Yes. Yes, I did. I was going for shock effect, but it has the added benefit of being true."

"I see." His lopsided grin made her want to kiss him.

Not willing to break contact, she ran her hands down his chest and rested them on the sides of his waist. "What do you see?" She continued to sway in time to the music with him.

"Were you trying to shock him or me?"

She giggled. "Maybe both?"

"You have a streak of audaciousness, Miss Lind."

"Now *that,* Dr. Newbern, is certainly a professorial

word. It is the kind of word that someone of your "type" would use." She leaned in and teased the corner of his mouth with her tongue, then sucked on his bottom lip. "I love smart men."

"Not a word that a redneck farmer might use."

"No, probably not."

"I have something to tell you Miss Lind, but before that declaration, I have a confession to make."

"This sounds way too serious. I'm liking the mood just as it is."

"Maybe I can find a way to make you like it better."

Was he turning the tables on her? Fast forwarding her plan? Maybe so. If they delayed, the heat between them might burn them up. If confession was what it took to seduce him to surrender, she'd take that risk.

"Maybe we should move this conversation to a more intimate place?" She wanted him in bed, but visualized her room. That view would not induce romance under any circumstance. It looked like thieves had tossed it. It would take more than one grand sweep of an arm to rid the bed of clothes. Cleaning up was a guaranteed mood killer.

Seduction wasn't going as planned. But desire would not be ignored. She needed a plan B.

When James stepped back, he raised her hand, then gently pushed her away. She twirled, following his lead. When they were pressed body to body again, he placed one warm hand at the back of her neck. His other hand rested on her butt, leaving an imprint of heat.

She ground her pelvis into him and rocked her hips side to side. Tension rose like hot steam building in her body. Soon it would need release. Yet, she wanted to savor every moment of the journey of her seduction of James.

"Are you falling for me because I got shot?"

"You presume much, professor. However, a slight correction. Not falling," she murmured. When she realized her confession, she stumbled over his feet.

Fallen was the correct word. She missed another step and brought the heel of her Manolo Blahnik's down on his toes. Trying to remove the implanted shoe from his foot, she almost lost her balance.

He caught her around the waist, winced, but made no sound.

"I'm so sorry." She couldn't have been more embarrassed. Crushed toes were ice water on seduction.

Without a word, James picked her up and carried her to the couch. He deposited her in the middle, then bent in front of her on one knee.

Her stomach jumped to her throat. What was he doing?

He reached down and liberated her feet from her shoes. She let go of a pent up breath.

His hands created warm friction as he massaged her foot, then he continued the strokes up her calf and rubbed in small circles on the sides of her legs. She relaxed. If death came in that moment, she'd die with delight. The warmth of his hands on her skin made her tingle in all the right places. Her breath caught in her throat when he stroked the inside of her thighs with light feathery touches. She leaned back and closed her eyes, feeling the heat rise. Wetting her lips with her tongue, she anticipated what would come and thought she might die if he didn't make love to her soon.

When the cushions on the couch moved, she opened her eyes to see him rise. He pulled her to standing, and then took the place she had just occupied. His grin was all the invitation she needed to straddle his lap. The hem of her dress rose to her hips as her knees spread, and her thighs settled onto his.

"This is fair warning," James said. "This is your only opportunity to say, no."

"Yes," she purred. Neither propriety nor anything else would keep her from the man she loved. She lifted to her knees and pulled her dress over her head, then tossed it to the floor. Planting her lips on his, she kissed him hard.

She reached for the buttons on his shirt, with trembling fingers released each button from its hole.

"Yes, I want you. Yes, I want to make love. Yes to you, James Newbern." After the last button, she shoved his shirt off him and nipped his shoulder. She wanted to brand him so everyone would know. She. Loved. Him.

In a blink, his hands grasped her butt. He rose, taking her with him. As she wrapped her legs around his waist and her arms around his neck, he tossed the couch pillows onto the floor. Gently he laid her down, then slid out of his pants. His desire was visible, there was no room for doubt.

When he came to her, his weight against her body made her feel safe and desirable. The time for seduction had passed. She moved into total surrender.

His slow removal of her lace panties put her in agony. She lifted her hips to capture his hardness. Tenderly, he touched her.

They connected into a perfect fit.

The heat and fullness of him inside her was

wondrous. They moved rhythmically with the music, in total harmony with each other. Tension curled. Hot and strong. She arched to meet him, grinding against him. She moaned.

"Let go, lover. Let go." His warm breath against her ear produced delightful shivers.

Her pelvis rose. She pressed against him harder.

Harder.

Sensations coursed through her.

She squeezed tight, her body taut, then reached the pinnacle.

Flashes of light and color danced before her eyes. Pleasure flooded in waves. James' body followed her same path. His growling shudder thrilled her. His long, slow moan added delight to her intense satisfaction.

Many minutes passed before the pounding of her heart settled to a regular rhythm.

Later, wrapped in sheets and lounging on pillows on the floor, lying beside James, she traced a line down his jaw. His stubble tickled the pad of her finger. She loved the firmness of his masculine face.

"Branna?" James asked.

"Hmm." The shape of his mouth distracted her.

"I love you."

She blinked. Looked into his eyes. Her mouth formed the words, I love you, too, but she was unable to speak as a flush of warmth crept from her chest to her cheeks. The words she'd waited to hear from a man who said them honestly and with desire, rendered her speechless.

James propped on his elbow beside her. He traced her lips, then ran a line from her chin, down her throat to the middle of her stomach. "Confession time. I know what type you really are."

"A lot of words come to mind—"

"You know the guy in the battered pickup you asked me about at the Westcott's party? The guy you met at the Victorian with Meredith?"

Branna opened her eyes wide. Alarmed, she said, "I never told you anything about meeting that guy."

"The redneck farmer you barely spoke to."

"My not talking had nothing to do with—"

"That was the first time I mistakenly labeled you."

"You? You bought the place? Why didn't you say so?"

"Because I stupidly pigeonholed you the 'beautiful type.'"

"Are you saying I'm no longer beautiful?" she teased.

"Not at all. You're bright, beautiful, and sexy. Brave, too. It took courage to go against your family's wishes and move here, and you did it to protect them."

James' lips met hers with gentle pressure.

She deepened the kiss, holding him close.

"So tell me, Dr. Newbern, in your expert opinion, what type *am* I?" Trepidation fluttered in her heart. Did he love her as much as she loved him? He said she was bright, beautiful, and sexy. Could they lay the "type" issue to rest?

She waited patiently for his response.

"You're totally 'my type,' and I'm going to prove it to you every day. Starting right now."

His kiss was a good first start.

A word about the author...

Linda Joyce is an award-winning writer who loves words. Growing up, she moved frequently courtesy of the U.S. Air Force, and books became her constant friend. Linda was born in Biloxi, Mississippi on Christmas Eve to an Irish/Cajun father from New Orleans and a Japanese mother.

Linda and her husband, Don, a fifth-generation Floridian, now live in Atlanta with their four-legged boys, General Beauregard, Gentleman Jack, and Masterpiece Renoir. Linda shares with Don a love of college football, boiled peanuts, seafood, and grits with eggs.

Please visit her at her website:
www.linda-joyce.com
or her blog:
Linda Joyce Contemplates:
www.lindajoycecontemplates.wordpress.com

Thank you for purchasing
this publication of The Wild Rose Press, Inc.
For other wonderful stories of romance,
please visit our on-line bookstore at
www.thewildrosepress.com.

For questions or more information
contact us at
info@thewildrosepress.com.

The Wild Rose Press, Inc.
www.thewildrosepress.com

To visit with authors of
The Wild Rose Press, Inc.
join our yahoo loop at
http://groups.yahoo.com/group/thewildrosepress/